FOR LOVE,
SHE JOURNEYED
INTO HELL

Valentina stared unseeingly at the landscape flowing past the windows of her carriage—a countryside already filled with the first retreating forces of what once had been the mightiest army on earth.

Behind her, Valentina had left the safety of her ancestral manor in Poland. Ahead of her lay the vast, blizzard-swept plains of Russia, now transformed into a gigantic scene of bloody battle and brutal rapine.

Somewhere amid that awesome carnage was de Chavel, Valentina's lover. Against all advice and all good sense, Valentina had vowed to find and join with him, if only for one more moment of stolen rapture . . .

if he still lived . . .

and if she survived. . . .

VALENTINA

Big Bestsellers from SIGNET

To order these titles,

please use coupon on

the last page of this book.

VALENTINA

by
Evelyn Anthony

A SIGNET BOOK
NEW AMERICAN LIBRARY
TIMES MIRROR

SIGNET TRADEMARK REG. U.S. PAT. OFF. AND FOREIGN COUNTRIES
REGISTERED TRADEMARK—MARCA REGISTRADA
HECHO EN CHICAGO, U.S.A.

SIGNET, SIGNET CLASSICS, MENTOR, PLUME and MERIDIAN BOOKS
are published by The New American Library, Inc.,
1301 Avenue of the Americas, New York, New York 10019

FIRST SIGNET PRINTING, APRIL, 1979

1 2 3 4 5 6 7 8 9

PRINTED IN THE UNITED STATES OF AMERICA

Chapter
ONE

———••◆••———

The month of June in the year 1812 was a perfect month for war; the weather was mild, the roads were dry, the rivers smooth flowing; the rolling countryside was like a garden, bisected by the frontier created between Poland and Russia by the River Niemen. On the Russian side of that river an army of close on half a million men were waiting, the soldiers of the Czar Alexander I, and across, in Poland, the troops of Napoleon Bonaparte, Emperor of the French, ended their long march across Europe and came to rest, waiting for the order to advance. They too numbered half a million men, a hundred thousand of them cavalry. The world had been waiting all through spring, while the Emperor of France brought his great fighting forces into position for his attack upon his old ally the Russian Czar, and the peace moves went on at the same time as the troop movements, but they came from France, and they found no response in the silent, menacing Russians. Russia wanted Napoleon to go to war, and in the last spring month of June, war was inevitable. Only one country with real ties of loyalty to France welcomed the prospect, and that was Poland, dismembered and partitioned three times in twenty-three years. What remained of the ancient Kingdom was now a Duchy of Warsaw with the King of Saxony as its ruler; it existed under the patronage of Napoleon, and Poles followed him and fought in his European wars because they believed he meant to

1

restore independence and unify their country. The city of Danzig was *en fête* that June, because the war was certain, and the Emperor Napoleon himself had just arrived there from holding court at Dresden with his second bride, the Austrian Archduchess Marie Louise.

The Polish nobility gathered in Danzig, which wasn't a fashionable city but was packed with people now because it had become part of the French route to Russia, and they opened their houses and decorated the city in the Emperor's honour. One of the richest and most influential men in Poland was Count Theodore Grunowski; he had made the long journey from his estates in Lvov to present himself before the French and to do any service for his fellow politicians that might be required of him. Early in the evening of June the 8th he sat watching his wife getting ready for a reception in Napoleon's honour.

He liked looking at her because she was very beautiful and it gave him pleasure; he had a keen aesthetic sense. He loved good paintings and fine furniture; he enjoyed music and appreciated good food and rare wines. He had a collection of Chinese jade which was priceless. He was a collector by nature, painstaking, determined and unscrupulous; he had acquired his young wife in much the same spirit as the rest of his possessions, though he had more fondness for his jade, and in the last year or so he had spent more time with his horses than he did with her. He hadn't been in a hurry to marry; a succession of mistresses satisfied his appetites when young and ministered to his vanity as he approached middle age, and they were all women of inferior position who had no redress against him if he chose to treat them badly. He was contented with his own mode of life for many years, and only the need to provide an heir for his name and lands made him decide to cast off the bachelor role and look about him for a suitable wife.

He had first seen Valentina when she was sixteen; he had been staying with her father on his estate at Czartatz, ostensibly to do some hunting, but his real purpose was to inspect Count Prokov's eldest daughter, who was still unmarried. Alexandra Maria was twenty-seven years old, and in an age when girls married in their earliest teens it was not a recommendation to be a spinster in the late twenties. Theodore had made enquiries about her, and was attracted by her enormous wealth, inherited from the Count's first wife, who had been a Russian Princess. He had learnt little more, except that there was a second daughter, the child of Prokov's second wife, a well-born Polish lady, who was not, alas, rich like her predecessor. Both wives had died a few years after marriage and the Count lived alone on his huge estates with his two daughters; he sometimes came to Warsaw and he had issued the invitation to Theodore to visit him. The Count was not impressed by the house at Czartatz; it was too big and gloomy and everything in it was old-fashioned. Being a perfectionist where creature comforts were concerned, the Count was not in the best of humours when he came down to dine and meet his host's two daughters. Neither of them had appeared before, and he thought this odd and inhospitable on the part of the eldest, who should have been waiting at the steps with her father to welcome their guest. The moment he saw her he understood why; the woman who took the place at the opposite end of the table was as arrogant and casual as a man, with a handsome, strong-featured face and slanting eyes betraying Tartar blood. He had been instantly repelled by her; nothing annoyed him more than signs of independence in a woman, and this one was absolute mistress of herself, and no virgin either, if he was any judge. His attention remained fixed for the rest of the evening, and the remainder of his visit, on the exquisitely lovely younger sister, with her pale skin and brilliant blue eyes; the combination of jet black hair with this flower-like colouring was so startling that the Count could scarcely bear to take his eyes off her.

He cultivated her very carefully, and was pleased to find her gentle and quite unsophisticated. Love was not a word in his vocabulary, it was not in his emotional capacity to feel anything for any human being except in the basic terms of tolerance for men or lust for a woman. And his lust for Valentina overcame his desire for a rich wife to add to his own fortune and prestige; he left Czartatz with the understanding that he would marry Count Prokov's younger daughter within a month of her seventeenth birthday, and he extracted from her father a dowry of thirty thousand roubles. In exchange, Prokov received a place on the council of the Grand Duchy, which he had always desired and which was within Theodore's power to obtain for him. Everybody was satisfied with the arrangement, except the bride to be, who wept and pleaded with her father to find someone younger and less forbidding than the Count. His eldest daughter swore at him, and quarrelled fiercely on her sister's behalf. Had Theodore witnessed the extent to which he had judged Alexandra correctly he would have fled the country at the thought of taking such a wife. But it was useless; Valentina's father was obdurate; the bribe of political power was more to him than the sentimental pleadings of a girl without experience or the angry reproaches of a woman with far too much. The marriage took place at the chapel at Czartatz, and the Count had taken his bride away immediately after the ceremony, insisting that they return to his estate at Lvov. They had spent the night at a posting inn on the road, and the Count had observed all the conventions of courtesy, allowing her an unhurried dinner before escorting her up the narrow stairs to the one bedroom in the place. There he had subjected her to an act of callous rape, neither expecting nor caring about arousing her response. He was in a hurry to gratify himself, and his own appetite was all that mattered. Later, when he felt less urgent, he might take trouble with her. He was extremely angry in his cold way to find her crying herself to sleep, and positively furious when she shrank from him the next morning.

The bride who finally arrived at Lvov was wan and spiritless and red-eyed from constant weeping. Her husband gave her into the care of a young widow, the wife of a serf on his estate who had had some training as a maid, and began by ordering her to burn the new Countess's trousseau, which was badly made and out of fashion, and the most experienced dressmaker in Warsaw was summoned to make a suitable wardrobe. The action was typical of the Count's attitude; he made it clear from the beginning that he expected complete obedience from his young wife in every aspect of her life, and that tears or complaints would be punished without mercy. Valentina had learnt a lesson in inhumanity that first year which taught her to discipline her rebellious spirit and force her unwilling flesh to do as she was ordered. There was no alternative, no respite. Her husband had written an irritated letter to her father complaining that she was wilful and unco-operative and he felt he had been cheated in the marriage settlement. He had an even greater cause of complaint when she remained childless after six months of unremitting attention from him. His disappointment was so great that had Count Prokov not died within a year of the marriage he might well have sent her home and asked for an annulment.

Her father's death left Valentina without a hope of redress; she knew it, and she submitted accordingly. The little maid advised her; she was a kindly, simple woman who sympathised from the first with her unhappy mistress, and appreciated her gentleness. Never once had Valentina struck her or threatened to have her whipped, and this was rare in great ladies when dealing with a bonded serf. She grew to love the Countess, and to try to help her. She knew what a bad husband could be like, whether he was a slave or a lord; she had borne the marks of her own marriage to a drunken brute for seven years, until the good God took him, and released her. Jana set about protecting her mistress, warning her of the Count's habits, his humours, his pedantic, irritable insistence on complete protocol in his house. And, slowly, Valentina learnt. Now, after five years of marriage, she was still childless, and he had ceased to trouble her too often; in this respect she found her life much easier to bear. At twenty-two she was in the full flower of her beauty; she was a perfect hostess, a cool, sophisticated wife and a great lady in her own right. He could find no fault with her except her barrenness, and he taunted her with it from time to time when he felt like hurting her a little, and she never replied. He had no idea how she implored God on her knees that she would never, never have a child to carry on his name. She was cold, and that was another pity in his view; but she was virtuous, and he was sure of that. Unlike many women in similar positions, Valentina had never had a lover. She had no interest in men. One husband was enough. She glanced at him now, as Jana combed her black hair into the high curls made fashionable by the French Empress Marie Louise. He was a handsome man in his way, but he was ageing fast, and the selfishness, pride and cruelty were written on his face. She often took comfort from the thought that one day, perhaps in ten years even, he must die. She was no different from many other women. Men ruled the world and made the rules. There was nothing to do but bear it and enjoy the few things God had given freely, like the countryside and fine horses, and moments when visual beauty lifted up the sinking spirits as a great sun set, red and blazing, or the moon turned the gardens at Lvov into an enchanted landscape.

"Jana!" the Count said suddenly. "Put that necklace away. Madame will wear her rubies with that dress." The maid curtsied and hurried away to get the jewels from their leather cases. "Rubies will suit that red dress much better," he said. "You should have thought of that for yourself, Valentina. Tonight's reception is tremendously important. Everyone in Poland will be there. Hurry up, girl, fasten it and then get out. With your permission, my dear?"

"Of course." Valentina looked at him, unable to hide her surprise. "Jana, go, please. Give me my pelisse first."

"I will fasten it for you," the Count said, "but it can wait a moment. I have something to tell you privately, my dear. I was summoned by Potocki today. Napoleon is already in Danzig, and has sent word that he will attend the reception this evening. All the Marshals and members of the General Staff are with him. It's certain now that the Czar Alexander has refused to make peace, and the French will invade Russia within the next few weeks. The whole world is waiting for this invasion and the outcome. But most especially Poland. I'm sure you know this?"

"I know it all," she said. "We are all praying for Napoleon to destroy Russia, so that we can be a free, united Kingdom again."

"Bravo!" the Count said. "That is what we all hope. But we would like a little assurance that His Imperial Majesty Napoleon really intends to re-establish our country. He's promising now, because he needs us to stay firm at his back while he fights the Russians. And he has the use of our troops and supplies. But promises are cheap. The man is only a little Corsican parvenu anyway; one can't rely on anyone who's not a gentleman. If he fails, Valentina, Russia will lay us waste with fire and sword, exactly as she's done before. We must know how far to go in his favour. Now I will stop boring you with all these political details, which I'm sure you don't fully appreciate—Potocki is a great admirer of yours. He mentioned to me that the services of a beautiful woman who kept her ears well open might be more useful to Poland than a dozen regiments. Danzig is crawling with the élite of the Grand Armée. If, for instance, you were to make yourself agreeable to some of them, and repeat everything you heard, you might bring some invaluable piece of news, some real indication of how the Imperial mind is working. Potocki explained all this to me and I had to agree. I have therefore offered him your services as a spy for the Polish government. I want you to tell him tonight how glad you are to do it."

For a moment Valentina didn't answer him. For the past six years, ever since Napoleon's defeat of the Russians at Tilsit, she had been brought up to regard the

French as the champions of Polish liberty and the Emperor Napoleon as the saviour of her divided country. Now her husband had committed her to spying upon the men who were so soon to fight a terrible war from which it was hoped Poland would ultimately benefit.

"If you are hesitating," he said, "may I remind you of the grievous harm a refusal would do my political career in the future? May I also remind you that your half-Russian sister is hardly an advantage at the moment; you might be suspected of treason, instead of mere weakness. You can't afford to disappoint the Count. Or me."

"At least you don't pretend I have a choice," Valentina said. "I shall do as I'm told. But I find it disgusting."

"Think of your country's future," he said coldly, "if you haven't any wifely concern for mine. Regard yourself as yet another martyr in the cause of Poland's freedom."

"Surely," Valentina said, "Madame Walewska knows Napoleon's intentions. What better source of information could you have?"

Six years ago the beautiful Countess Walewska had deliberately thrown herself at Napoleon's feet, primed by the same men who were now recruiting Valentina, and she had become his mistress and Poland's most persuasive advocate. She had left Poland with Napoleon's illegitimate son and lived for some years in Paris. The plan had miscalculated, for the unhappy woman had fallen deeply in love with the Emperor, and her reports were too biased to be trustworthy. At the mention of her name the Count laughed contemptuously.

"I can think of almost any source better than the infatuated babblings of that damned woman; all she does is repeat the politic lies Napoleon tells her for our benefit, and she's stupid enough to believe them herself. It was obvious from the beginning that she was quite unsuitable." He drew out his little dress watch and stood up quickly. "Come, my dear. Let me fasten your pelisse. I told the carriage to be ready half an hour ago." He took up the sable-lined velvet pelisse and wrapped it round his wife's shoulders; his fingers brushed across her bare throat and lingered as they fastened the silk cords across her breast. The caress made her shudder involuntarily; the calculated sexual antics disgusted her, and they alarmed her about his intentions. There had been blessed intervals in the last two years when he hardly troubled her at all, and she supposed he had a mistress. She moved away from him abruptly.

"Come, Theo; we'll be late."

"So we will. Never mind, I shall visit you this evening."

"As you please," she said. She had made excuses once or twice but he had always discovered the deception and now she didn't dare to lie.

He opened the door for her and they went down the wide stone staircase to the front entrance where their carriage and an escort of two outriders with lighted flambeaux waited in the street outside. Twenty minutes later they were announced at the entrance of the Grand Salon in the Kalinovsky Palace where the members of the first families in Poland were giving a reception in honour of Napoleon. A crowd of four hundred had assembled in the three enormous rooms which had been prepared for the reception of the Emperor and his staff. The biggest was almost a hundred feet long. The walls were hung with crimson silk and fine ormolu candelabra stood at intervals down the sides of the room, shedding their yellow light on a scene of glittering uniforms, handsome men, and women resplendent in jewels and magnificent gowns. A buffet had been arranged in two smaller rooms where a sumptuous supper was ready, and finally a part was reserved for the Emperor and any he cared to invite to his private table. The ladies of Danzig society had arranged huge alabaster vases of flowers in the French and Polish colours, and the Marshal Prince Poniatowsky himself had provided gold plate for Napoleon's use. An orchestra played at one end of the huge room, raised up on a gallery; the atmosphere was stifling with dozens of different scents, candle grease and beeswax polish which had made the oak floors as dangerous as glass to walk upon.

Many heads turned when the Count and Countess Grunowski were announced. They paid few visits to the city, but Valentina was well known for her beauty. Certainly the Count had the satisfaction of seeing her cause quite a sensation as she stood in the doorway, greeting Count and Countess Potocki, her red velvet dress contrasting vividly with her jet black hair, and rose white skin; Grunowski's heavy rubies glowed round her neck and shimmered in her ears. Her dress was simple compared with many of the heavily embroidered, colourful creations worn by some of the women, but it had been designed with an artist's eye for the tall, slim figure and beautiful breast and arms of the woman who wore it; the long court train fell straight to the ground from her shoulders and was edged with a band of gold thread embroidery three inches wide.

Potocki himself was a little stirred by her as she stood in front of him that night. She was certainly beautiful enough to turn the head of any man, and probably wise enough to know that her patriotic duty might well entail more than mere eavesdropping, but he had left that part to the discretion of her husband. He would know how to explain it to her, and when the moment was right. At least they were not going to repeat their initial mistake with another lovely victim, and set Valentina at Napoleon himself. A lesser man would do.

"My compliments, Madame," he said. "I have never seen such a vision of beauty, and all the fair blooms of Poland are in flower tonight."

Valentina smiled and thanked him. She decided that this was the moment to do what her husband had ordered. And perhaps it was right; Potocki was a man of honour. He must know that it was vital to spy upon the French, however despicable it seemed in theory. "I am happy to be of service, Highness," she said. "My husband told me of your request and I will do anything I can to help our country. You can rely on me."

"I'm sure I can," he said, and he took her hand and kissed it. "Poland has always been fortunate in her children."

They passed on and began mingling with the crowd. The Count paid her the compliment of staying at her side, but he talked politics to his friends and did not trouble to include her beyond the introduction. Valentina occupied herself with exchanging a few words with some of the ladies she knew and otherwise looked round the room. The Emperor was expected soon, and all his staff were there. If she were supposed to make contact with them, then it was surely wasting time to stay rooted among her fellow Poles, but without the Count's initiative there was nothing she could do. After a time she became aware that she was being watched; the eyes of the watcher seemed to draw her to the left, and when she turned she immediately met the gaze of a French officer who was standing among a group of animated ladies and some senior officers in the Polish Lancers. He was tall and he held himself with an air of arrogance that went with the rank of Colonel in the Imperial Guard and the coveted Legion d'Honneur on his breast. There were touches of grey in his dark hair, and he wore it cut short and without the elaborate sideburns affected by many of the French. The eyes that stared so boldly into hers were a curious colour, a steely grey, and they were set in a hard, aristocratic face, tanned by weather in countries all over the world, and marked by a scar down one cheek. Most men watched Valentina with admiration and this man made no secret of his approval. His glance swept over her from head to foot, and he acknowledged her angry stare with a slight smile. Valentina turned to her husband, anxious to move away, but at that moment the double doors at the end of the Salon were opened wide, and Potocki and his wife, followed by half a dozen nobles, hurried out. "Napoleon has arrived," the Count said. "Come quickly or we will lose our places in the line."

The crowd was dividing rapidly, making a lane for the

Emperor of France, and because of the Count's quickness they found themselves standing in the front rank on the left. The next moment two trumpeters of the Imperial Guard sounded a fanfare, and the French Court Chamberlain appeared, walking backwards through the open doors. He turned and rapped loudly three times with his Staff of Office.

"His Imperial Majesty the Emperor Napoleon. The Countess Walewska."

Valentina had seen his portrait hanging in crude copies in many Polish mansions; she had seen the famous profile, so like a Roman Caesar, on coins and medallions, and she had heard Napoleon described. Nothing prepared her for her first sight of the most formidable soldier in the world, the man the English swore ate babies and who, his soldiers said, was something more than human. He was very small, a few inches above five feet, and he wore a plain dark green coat and white breeches with white stockings and buckled shoes; his only ornament was the Grand Cross of the Legion d'Honneur round his neck, the famous order for gallantry in the field which he had founded himself. Beside him walked one of the loveliest women Valentina had ever seen in her life; she was small and slim, with hair the colour of new minted gold and wide violet blue eyes. There was a look of radiance upon her face which gave it an almost spiritual beauty; her hand was on Napoleon's arm, and the smile on her lips was for him alone. This, then, was the famous Marie Walewska, the virtuous wife of a great nobleman who had agreed to prostitute herself to the Emperor for her country's sake, and fallen victim to a love which was beyond her power to control. It was said that he loved her in return; yet he neglected her for months and he had divorced his first Empress Josephine to marry an Austrian Archduchess who didn't care for him at all. He had a son now too, the little King of Rome, a child he loved as tenderly as any woman. He had seen little or nothing of Marie Walewska's child. And yet she stayed in his shadow, for ever patient, for ever waiting and often forgotten, the woman her own people called the White Rose of Poland, and men like Valentina's husband dismissed as a fool who had let herself be duped by love. As Napoleon came near them, the crowd began dipping in homage; just before she sank to her knee in a deep curtsey, Valentina glanced into the eyes in the olive-skinned Italian face met hers for a brief second. The effect of that glance was like contact with face of Napoleon Bonaparte and the incongruously blue lightning. A current passed out of the man, a magnetism that held and mesmerised even in that fleeting instant, and it was something infinitely greater than the dominance of a man who was supremely male. Greatness was in him, and majesty too, and the unlovely Bourbons, with a thousand years of monarchy behind them, had never possessed it as did this little Corsican General who had conquered all Europe in the span of fourteen years. Marie Walewska was not a fool; the men who had tried to pit a mere woman against such a man were the ones whose wits had given out. It was not until he had passed far beyond them, that Valentina remembered how tired and strained Napoleon had looked. The Emperor made a relatively quick circuit of the room, speaking a word here and there to someone presented by Count Potocki and then disappeared into the smaller supper room. Protocol relaxed immediately and the whisper of conversation became an excited roar while a lot of undignified pushing began round the doorway where the Emperor and his mistress were having supper. Nearly three hours had passed and Valentina had not even had a glass of wine; the big buffet room was impossibly crowded, and as it was obvious that His Imperial Majesty didn't intend to circulate again that night, people struggled for chairs and food and settled wherever they could find a place. "Please, Theo, couldn't we go home? I'm exhausted and quite faint with hunger."

The Count was pale and there were drops of sweat on his forehead; he was as tired and famished as his wife, but he answered curtly: "Not yet. Potocki will be with us soon. We must wait here." They did not have to wait much longer, for soon the Count could be seen making his way towards them. He came up to Valentina and bowed.

"Come with me, Madame. Marshal Murat, King of Naples, has asked to meet you. Will you excuse me, my dear Theodore? I will return Madame to you as soon as she has been presented."

"Make no apology to me," the Count said. "I'm sure my wife will find the Marshal better company than a tired and ageing husband. If I could safely leave her in your care I might commandeer a coach and make my way to bed."

Even as he said it Valentina knew that it was all rehearsed. This introduction had been planned; this was why they had been told to wait.

"Rely upon me," Potocki said. "I will take good care of Madame Grunowska for you. Now, my dear lady, follow me. We must not keep the Marshal waiting!"

Joachim Murat was born in Gascony and he had all the conceit and flamboyance of that stubborn French breed; he had begun his real military career with Napoleon in the Italian campaign of 1796 and having joined the young General and attached himself firmly to his rocketing star of fortune, Murat had risen like a meteor. The Emperor had married him to his sister Caroline and given him the little kingdom of Naples as a reward. As they approached him Valentina identified him easily in the crowd of brilliantly dressed officers. Firstly he was a head taller than most, and he was wearing a uniform of his own design, coated and breeched in scarlet velvet with a profusion of gold lace and so many decorations that he dazzled the eye. His passion for clothes was a joke which no one dared indulge to his face except Napoleon, who complained that when they appeared together the crowds thought that he, and not Bonaparte, was Emperor because of the gaudy way he dressed. But he was quite certainly handsome, with a bold, engaging smile and flashing eyes; he was reputed to be the most

fearless cavalry leader in the world. The bright coloured
uniform was always conspicuous at the head of every
charge in battle, and his troops adored him. His victories
in the boudoir were as well known as those won on the
field and he was said to have been one of Empress Josephine's lovers when Napoleon was away at war. He
moved a step forward to greet the Count and the extremely lovely lady he was bringing with him; the introduction had been suggested to him, with the hint that he
in Danzig, and Murat had agreed with alacrity. He liked
amusement, and at the moment the Emperor was in a bad
would find the Countess Grunowska the prettiest woman
humour and the lull before the invasion of Russia was
tedious and irritating. Nerves were apt to fray at such a
time, and he needed relaxation. As soon as he saw Valentina he was only too hopeful that she was one of the devoted brand of Polish ladies who considered it an act of
patriotism to accommodate French officers.

"Aha! How delightful! How exquisite! Madame, your
devoted servant." He swept Valentina an exaggerated
bow, and immediately offered her his arm. He was not a
man who wasted time, and one look into those beautiful
blue eyes had convinced him that indeed there was no
time to waste. "I'll swear you've had no supper? No? I
thought not—nor have I, dammit. I'm as hungry as the
devil and you must be too. Come and we'll set ourselves
to rights. And you must tell me all about yourself."

Everyone was watching them as they sat down in the
inner room at a table reserved for the King of Naples,
and Valentina flushed as the Emperor himself glanced
up. Murat saw it and laughed. He had a very loud, infec-
tious laugh, and she couldn't help liking him in spite of
his vulgarity. "Dieu—it's an age since I've seen a woman
blush," he confided. "And it's damnably pretty on you.
What's your name, I can't get my tongue round Polish."

"Valentina, Sire," she said. "The Emperor looked at us
as we sat down; I shouldn't be here, my rank isn't suffi-
cient."

"To hell with that," the Marshal said. "Your beauty

entitles you to be over there with *him*, if he hadn't involved himself with that other lady. Isn't it strange how a lovely woman can look so damned miserable? I couldn't endure it myself. I like gaiety. Armand, stop standing there with your mouth open and pour us some wine! And get some food, man, for God's sake. Madame is starving!"

The food was superb: chicken in aspic with fresh cherries, quantities of rich pastries, and out-of-season fruits. Murat drank and ate with uninhibited enjoyment, pressing her to do the same.

"Where's your husband?" he enquired.

Valentina had begun to enjoy herself; it was impossible not to with such a companion; many women had found themselves in his bed while they were still laughing at his jokes; the Empress Josephine herself had been unable to resist his light-hearted, rascally approach to love after the suffocatingly dull passion of her brilliant husband. "My husband has gone home," Valentina said. "He's tired."

It was on the edge of Murat's tongue to add that he was also tactful but he stopped himself in time. Such a lovely, charming creature, and with an engaging air of innocence—she might be frightened away if he were too impetuous. "How fortunate for me; here I am, having supper with the most beautiful woman in the room—yes, Armand, what is it?" He turned to his aide-de-camp, a tall pleasant-looking young officer in a red and green uniform; he bent and whispered something to the Marshal, and passed him a piece of paper. Murat smiled at Valentina and apologised.

"Paper," he said. "The bane of the soldier's life. Permit me one moment, Madame."

The note was short and unsigned. It said simply: *Be careful; this is the one we were warned about. Leave her to me.* Murat read it and grimaced; he put it in his pocket and said lightly: "*Hélas*, duty follows everywhere. The Emperor will be leaving soon and I must attend him. Let me select someone to take care of you till I get back. Armand, fetch Colonel de Chavel."

She knew him at once; the man who had stared at her so deliberately earlier in the evening now bowed and kissed her hand, and for a moment the steel grey eyes met hers again. "I have been admiring you from afar, Madame," he said.

"Make sure you don't shorten the distance, my friend," Murat reminded him. He got up and took leave of Valentina. When he too kissed her hand his lips were hot and they lingered.

"Pay no attention to him," he said. "He's just a dull infantry Colonel. Keep your allegiance for the cavalry. *Au revoir*, Madame."

She sat silently, watching the swaggering figure make its way to Napoleon's table and, after a moment, sit down with him.

"You must forgive me," Colonel de Chavel said, "I have been longing to introduce myself. I'm very grateful to the Marshal."

"He's a charming man," Valentina said defensively. There was something mocking in his voice that made her sure he was laughing at the vulgar Gascon, and at her. "I hadn't eaten a bit or touched a glass of wine," she added. "The crush was abominable; he did me a great service by inviting me to share supper with him."

"But of course," The Colonel said. "The Marshal is always concerned with the comfort of pretty ladies. You don't owe me any explanation, my dear Madame. I'm only too happy to deputise for him for a while. Is there anything I can get for you? A little Polish vodka, perhaps?"

"No thank you. There's nothing I want." She turned away from him angrily. "How long do you suppose the Marshal will be?"

"That's hard to say; I see signs that the Emperor is about to leave. If he takes Murat with him he won't appear again tonight. Unless, of course, you have made an arrangement?" He asked the insulting question in a casual, mocking voice that made her flush to her hair.

"I have no idea what you mean, Colonel. Please escort me back to the main salon where I can find someone to take me home." She had half risen from her chair when the pressure of his hand on her arm stopped her; it was firm enough to make her sit down again.

"Please," he said, "allow me to make amends for having made you angry. I'm only a dull infantryman, as the Marshal said. I've been too long campaigning, I suppose; I've forgotten my manners. Please forgive me."

Slowly he withdrew his hand and she remained in her chair. She didn't want to forgive him; she didn't even believe his apology, but there was something about the man that made it difficult to refuse him. He poured wine for her and for himself and they drank it without speaking; he was watching her intently, studying her with the same arrogant appraisal which had made her so uncomfortable in the reception room, before they had even met.

"Colonel de Chavel," she said suddenly. "Why are you staring at me like this? Is anything wrong with me?"

"I beg your pardon again, Madame," he said coolly. "I was thinking how beautiful you were. Where is your husband, by the way?"

"He left earlier; he was tired." The excuse sounded so lame that Valentina blushed and turned away. "I ought to leave," she said. "I'm sure it's late."

"Unfortunately we must wait until the Emperor goes first," the Colonel remarked. "I'm sorry I'm being such a poor substitute for the Marshal. I was hoping to find favour with you." The hard, shrewd eyes bored into hers, and there was contempt in them as well as mockery.

"Then I'm afraid you've failed," Valentina said. "I do so want to go home; how much longer will he be?"

"Not too long," The Colonel said. "The Emperor doesn't linger at the table; he eats as a necessity. I see Madame Walewska has already finished."

Valentina glanced across at the table where Napoleon

was sitting; Murat was leaning forward saying something to him, and the Countess was clearly in their view.

"She looks so terribly sad," Valentina said suddenly. "Poor woman. I wonder if he cares for her?"

"I doubt it," the Colonel said. "He only loved one woman, and that was Josephine. It's a pity, because Walewska is the only one that's ever been true to him, and God knows, that's a miracle in itself!"

"You have a low opinion of my sex, Colonel," she said coldly. "There are more virtuous women in the world than there are men worthy of them!"

"I assure you," he said, "I adore women, Madame. I think you are all the most delightful creatures. It seems that everything I say annoys you—how can I make amends?"

She shrugged, without answering. She found this man's blend of cynicism and mockery infinitely disturbing; it made her want to cry; it was ridiculous to be affected by a perfect stranger, and she despised herself. With an effort she turned back to him. "Colonel de Chavel, I see the Emperor is about to leave. Will you escort me to Count Potocki, so that he can take me home? I hate to impose myself on you, but I'm not accustomed to being alone in public gatherings, and the Count promised to take care of me. . . ."

"I'm sure he did," the Colonel said. "And we will find him. Have you never been alone before, then? Your husband doesn't usually abandon you?"

"He hasn't," she said quickly, and then stopped because it was useless lying to the man sitting opposite her, and he would mock her if she tried.

"He didn't know that I would be left . . ." she said, and he finished the sentence for her:

"With a boor like me, Madame. I understand. Let me give you some wine; you look quite pale." She drank it quickly, aware that he was still watching her, but that the grey eyes were kinder suddenly. "May I ask you a question, Madame? How old are you?"

"Twenty-two," Valentina said.

"The Emperor's leaving," De Chavel said. He held out his hand to help her rise and unwillingly she put hers into it. It was warm and strong, and it grasped her fingers firmly. As Napoleon left, the company bowed and curtsied, and she saw Murat look over his shoulder at her and make a grimace of apology. "The Marshal won't be coming back," the Colonel said. "I'm afraid you are left with me, Madame." They faced each other across the table; he was a head taller than she was, and in spite of the sabre scar he was one of the best-looking men she had seen in her life. He smiled, and it was the first time he had done so that evening. "Poor lady," he said, "you've had a dismal supper. You've lost your husband, and your handsome Marshal, and been burdened with me instead. Can't we make the best of it? I feel you will never speak to me again."

"I doubt I'll have the chance," Valentina said. "Besides, Colonel, to be fair to you, you were ordered to look after me. You didn't volunteer."

"Madame," he said, "you are mistaken. I have been following you the entire evening, hoping for a chance to meet you. Nothing less than a Marshal and a King to boot would have kept me away. Were you expecting to meet Murat tonight?"

"No, of course not. Count Potocki said he had asked to meet me. I was very flattered, but quite surprised. Why do you ask?"

"I'm curious," he said. "People interest me; how long have you been married?"

"Five years."

He held out his arm and she placed her hand upon it; they moved to the door together. The orchestra had begun playing a waltz in the main reception room. She paused for a moment; the scene was beautiful to watch as the circling couples swept past them, the brilliant dresses of the women and the scarlet, green and blue of the French uniforms making a gorgeous pattern of colour in the candlelight.

"Dance with me," he said. "Just once, before you

leave." He had turned her, and taken her into his arms while she was trying to refuse.

"I should find the Count," Valentina said. "I should go home . . ."

"One dance, Madame," he said quietly, and he began to move with her on to the floor. He held her with the same firmness that had kept her in her chair, and she relaxed and let herself be guided. The Count didn't approve of the waltz; in conservative society it was still regarded as a very daring dance. Valentina found the rhythm irresistible; it swept her on like the strange, commanding man who held her, and she had a sensation of belonging to him at that moment which was quite insane, as if her body had lost its independent power of movement and her will had been stolen from her. They didn't speak; they danced not once but many times, until the couples thinned to a few, and suddenly he led her to a seat near one of the tall windows overlooking the square.

"I'll get you some champagne. You look happier, Madame. I dance better than I make conversation. Wait for me here."

He was back in a moment with two glasses, and he sat beside her. He thought dispassionately that she was the loveliest woman he had seen for many years, lovelier still when she smiled and her face was delicately flushed. And she was not what he had suspected. She was not only a tool of the Polish faction but a dupe. He had danced with her for two reasons: to see if she would try to pump him, and because she attracted him. It was a pity she had this vulnerable quality; it made her very dangerous.

"Good heavens," Valentina said. "Listen, it's chiming two o'clock! Colonel, it's terribly late! I must find the Count at once."

"He left an hour ago," De Chavel said. "I will escort you home."

"Oh no," she said quickly. "No, there's no need. I have my own carriage here—there's no reason to impose on you."

"You are not imposing on me," he said quietly. "And you are not travelling alone through this city at this hour. I am taking you home, Madame. That is decided. Come."

They sat side by side in the jolting carriage; he had refused the rug which was spread over Valentina's knees; he leant back, one soft-booted leg crossed over the other, so still he might have been asleep. In the darkness her scent came to him; he was so acutely aware of her slight movements beside him that he closed his eyes. When he first joined her at Murat's table he had planned a very different ending to the evening. He had expected a sophisticated, *rusée* woman of the world, instead of an inexperienced girl with this damnable quality of being easily hurt. He had actually disliked making the opening moves that evening, goading her with semi-insults. If she had responded differently, indulging in the dubious exchange which was the accepted language between a man with seduction in mind and a woman prepared to be seduced, she would have been in his arms by now, with her soft mouth stopped with kisses, and her beautiful body exposed to his hands. He would have seduced the seductress without mercy, and then laughed in her face. That was his original plan, but the girl herself had defeated him. She may have been five years married, but she might just as well have been a virgin for all her knowledge of the world.

He was sure she was a spy; it only amused him to think how inept she was and the number of opportunities she had missed already. A foolish girl, inspired by patriotism, and undoubtedly used by men as unscrupulous as she was innocent. As Head of the Intelligence Service in Poland, De Chavel had been warned that the Poles would try to plant a spy on Murat, and he had heard that the introduction would be made at the reception that night. It had all gone according to his expectations; the only piece in the puzzle which didn't fit was the Countess Valentina Grunowska.

"I'm home," she said, and he opened his eyes. The

coach pulled up outside a large house in the Kutchinsky Avenue; the footman opened the door and let down the little carriage steps. De Chavel climbed out and helped Valentina down. For a moment they stood close, he holding her arms above the elbow, her face turned up to his. He did something he had never believed he could do, in the circumstances. He tried to warn her.

"Thank you for this evening," he said. "And take my advice. Have nothing to do with Murat. Good night, Madame."

He didn't kiss her hand or wait to see her go inside. He turned away from her abruptly and jumped back into the coach.

"Take me to the Malinovsky Square. Then return here!" She waited by the front door, the sleepy porter yawning and scratching his head. The coach bowled along the cobbled street and turned a corner out of sight. Slowly Valentina went up the marble staircase; she felt tired and yet oddly elated. As she came level with the Count's apartments she paused, remembering what he had said before they left that night. But his lights were out. He had gone to sleep instead. She thanked God, and went on to her own rooms further down the corridor. She couldn't have borne him to touch her, more so tonight than ever before. Jana was dozing on a stool by the dead fire when she went in; she got up and apologised and hurried to help her mistress undress.

"The Count came once tonight, Madame," she said. "I told him you weren't back. He went away again."

"Was he angry?"

"No, Madame. He didn't seem so. It's past three. Did you see the Emperor himself, Madame?"

"I did, Jana," Valentina said. "I saw the Countess Walewska too."

"Ah." Jana's plump face glowed. Even to the peasants, Marie Walewska was a sacred patriot. "God bless her, Madame. She'll save us from the Russians, won't she? Has the Emperor married her yet? Will she be crowned Empress soon?"

"I don't know," Valentina said gently, remembering the sad, devoted mistress with her bastard son and irregular position before the world. Only in legend and the simple minds of humble people did Emperors marry their mistresses and offer them a crown.

"After this great campaign perhaps. We'll see."

She climbed into bed, and Jana drew the covers up and tucked them in. She blew out the chamberstick and drew the heavy curtains round the bed, closing out draughts, and left Valentina alone. She was very tired; sleep should have come at once, but it withdrew immediately and her thoughts flew back to the evening and returned again and again to the man with the scar and the grey eyes. Colonel de Chavel of the Imperial Guards, Chevalier of the Legion d'Honneur. She knew nothing about him, not even his first name. She didn't even know if he were married, and immediately rejected the possibility. He had what she could only describe as an unattached air about him, though he must have been in his late thirties. He didn't belong at any woman's fireside; she was sure of that. He didn't belong to any woman either. Yet he knew how to deal with them; he held them with confidence whether it was in the waltz or at the foot of a carriage while he gave a curt warning which was impossible to understand. She sensed all this about him with an instinct suddenly razor sharp; and she admitted something else. She wouldn't know a moment's contentment until she saw him again. At eight the next morning Jana woke her with her morning chocolate; she drew back the bed curtains and placed the tray with its porcelain cup and silver pot upon her mistress's lap. A bowl of pure white roses was arranged on the tray. Jana looked down and smiled. "These came early this morning, Madame. This note was with them."

It was a white card, with the Imperial Crown and arms of Naples thickly engraved in gold. Valentina was so disappointed that she hardly troubled to read the single line. *From an admirer, desolate at having to leave so early*. It was from Murat, King of Naples, and she didn't care. For one marvellous, mad moment she had thought they came from the man she had been thinking about until she fell asleep, only to find him in her dreams.

"Who is it? May I ask, Madame?"

"Someone I met last night. But no one of importance. Put them over there, Jana. And burn that card."

The maid did as she was told. She had a shrewd instinct, and an incurably romantic streak which longed for something nice to happen to her mistress, for some fine young man to steal her away from the detested Count. Jana believed that the good Lord was very understanding; he wouldn't begrudge a sweet lady her happiness because of a few vows made in church. It was such a shame that she had never had a lover. But someone had sent her white roses, the very flowers of extramarital intrigue, and she was sure of two things: the Countess had been very disappointed that the flowers had come from whoever had a crown upon his head. That meant she was expecting them from someone else. Someone, unlike this unknown with his gold armorials, who was very important to her indeed.

"Never mind, Madame," she said softly. "Don't be disappointed. More flowers may come."

"I'm not expecting any," Valentina said. She shook her head at Jana. "It was just foolishness. I thought someone else had sent them, but why should they—I don't suppose they'll ever think of me again."

Jana paused as she went through the dresses in the clothes closet, choosing a morning wrapper and petticoat for Valentina to wear.

"If they don't, Madame," she said, "and they're a man—I'll be surprised!"

It was late afternoon and Valentina was getting ready to go for a drive when the Count was announced. There had been no word from him throughout the day; he had not joined her for lunch or sent any message, and she had ceased to expect him.

Her head was aching, and she had ordered the light phaeton to take her for a drive through the countryside.

The Count came in on the heels of the footman who announced him; he still wore his cloak and gloves, and he threw both at the servant before he spoke to his wife. He looked at her with the impersonal glance of appraisal which she knew so well. It could turn into a criticism, one of his chilly compliments, or, worst of all, an awakening of desire. It had happened so often before in exactly that way. "You were going out, I see," he said. "May I ask where?"

"Just for a drive," Valentina explained. "I was tired and I have a headache."

"That's understandable. You were very late last night." He sat down on the sofa and stretched out, his legs crossed in front of him. "Send the carriage away. I want to talk to you."

She pulled the bell-cord and gave the footman the message.

"Sit down; you irritate me, walking about like that."

He was very angry about something; his face was pale and the tight mouth was like a steel slit. Valentina sat down opposite to him; her hands were clasped together to hide their trembling.

"What progress did you make with Marshal Murat last night?"

"I had supper with him. He was very pleasant to me. Then he left with the Emperor, that's all. Why are you so angry, Theo? What's the matter?"

"After the Marshal left, how were you occupied until three in the morning?" He wasn't looking directly at her; he was looking at a point somewhere above her head, spitting the questions at her.

"I was with a Colonel de Chavel of the Imperial Guard. He brought me home. Theo, I understood that I was to make myself agreeable to French officers and report anything interesting they said. Isn't that what Count Potocki wanted? Why are you questioning me like this?"

He sat forward and at last his eyes met hers; she was shocked by the dislike in them.

"I've never thought you particularly intelligent, my dear, but I did credit you with a little natural cunning; most women have plenty of it; I can't believe you're an exception. Is it your idea of carrying out the mission I entrusted you by exchanging a Marshal of France who is Napoleon's brother-in-law for a mere Colonel of the Guards? Which of the two would you think the most important to cultivate? Or should I say, which appealed to you the most? Obviously the Colonel! Do you know that I waited up for you until past midnight?"

"Jana told me," Valentina said. "She said you weren't angry."

"Nor was I." His tone had become mocking now, and she dreaded his sarcasm more than his insults. "I imagined you were making use of your time. I imagined that Murat was with you."

"I told you, he left."

"Very unlike him; I presume you didn't show enough enthusiasm. However, you'll have a chance to make amends tomorrow night. He is coming here to dinner. And you'll pay attention to him, my dear. You'll be your most charming to the great man, and I'll see there are no handsome Colonels to distract you. I know all about last night. I could even tell you the number of times you danced with the fellow. I hope you enjoyed yourself. Incidentally you are never to see or speak to him again, whatever the circumstances. Is that clear?"

"Yes," she said slowly. "It's clear. But it's quite unnecessary. You left me alone at the reception; Colonel de Chavel brought me here in my own coach, that's all. If you have any regard for my reputation you ought to object to somebody like Murat!"

"Really," he laughed unpleasantly. "I don't think you derstand, my dear. Your reputation as such is not in question. As for objecting to Murat, have you any idea of the trouble we took to introduce you to him? The plan was laid weeks ago. All you had to do was keep him interested, instead of following your own inclinations with an unimportant soldier whose reputation, incidentally, is even worse than Murat's! Potocki is furious. I had a most unpleasant interview with him this morning. I told him you'd retrieve your mistake; I gave him my word on it!" Again the cold, angry eyes blazed into hers, and she found her courage in spite of him.

"You haven't been honest with me, have you, Theo? What is this plan you laid with Murat? What part am I really expected to play?"

"The part played by better women than you'll ever be," he said. "We need information at the highest level. That damned fool Walewska is no use any more. The next best thing is a woman close to someone like Murat; he talks and boasts, especially when he's drunk. You, my dear Valentina, will gain his confidence. You will be seduced if necessary. You will tell me everything you see and hear during your association. Is that honest enough for you?"

She stood up; her face was as white as the lace at her throat. "God forgive you," she said. "If my father were alive, and he knew this, he'd kill you!"

"Your father sold you to me, for a political appointment," the Count said. "Don't think he wouldn't sell you to Murat too, if the price was right."

"I won't do it." She thought she said it very calmly, but her voice was trembling and she was very near to tears. "I won't prostitute myself with anyone, whatever you say, or Potocki either. He should be ashamed!"

"You have an exaggerated opinion of yourself," the drawling voice said. "A woman only has two purposes in life: to please a man and bear him children. What makes this barren body of yours so precious? Listen to me, Valentina. You are going to do what you are told. You are going to charm this uncouth gentleman and go to his bed and squeeze every scrap of information out of him in the process. This is what you are going to do. Oh, you can cry, yes, and talk about honour, if you like. But you are going to do it."

"I'm not." She said it flatly. "Nothing on earth will make me."

"You are," he said. He got up and they faced each other. "You have a Russian half-sister, my dear. Potocki mentioned her this morning. If you refuse us, she will be arrested and charged as a spy for the Czar. I will personally see that she is hanged and that you stand at the foot of the gallows. I'm not making an idle threat. I anticipated this stupid refusal of yours and Potocki told me to tell you that your sister Alexandra's life won't be worth a kopek unless you do what we want."

"I'll see you damned!" Valentina spat it at him; horror and disgust overcame her fear of him. Five years of repression, bullying and misery welled up in her at the unbelievable threat to her sister. Hang Alexandra. He had said it and he would do it too; and carry out the ultimate bestiality by making her watch. She raised her hand instinctively to strike him, and then paused, sickened by the whole situation.

"That's wise," the Count said. "If you had given way to that particular impulse I would have thrashed you to an inch of your life. Now you're going to your room to calm yourself."

"No!" Valentina backed away from him. "Don't touch me!"

He came to her and caught her arms; she began to struggle fiercely, and he swore. He seized her wrists and twisted them behind her, turning her towards the bedroom door. He was very strong, and his grip was like iron; the pain in her arms made her cry out, and she fought desperately against the force propelling her to the half-open door to her room, but she was helpless to resist him. He thrust her inside, and pushed her so violently that she fell. He was white with anger and for a moment he stood there, looking down at Valentina as she half knelt on the floor, gasping for breath, her dress torn in the struggle. He turned and closed the door and locked it. His voice was flat and cold when he spoke.

"You remind me of a mare I once had. She went well

enough, but every so often she needed a lesson, just to remind her who was master. By God, I'm going to teach you once and for all time!"

An hour later the Count came out of his wife's apartments. The key of her room was in his pocket. He rang for his steward of the household and gave instructions that no one was to go near the Countess or to answer her bell until he gave permission. Any servant who disobeyed this order would be given thirty lashes.

"Aha, my dear De Chavel." Murat half rose from his desk and gave the Colonel his hand. He was in very good spirits; a fresh consignment of horses for his cavalry had arrived from Germany that morning and he had the report on them in front of him. They were fine quality mounts and they numbered fifteen thousand. Nothing appealed more to Murat than a good horse except a pretty woman, and he was looking forward to driving down to see some of the new consignment the next day. "Sit down, my friend," he said. "Look at this—fifteen thousand mounts, first quality, average sixteen-five hands, five- to seven-year-olds, every one. We'll chase the Russians into the Black Sea with these! What can I do for you?"

"Listen to my report on the Polish charmer," De Chavel said. "If, sir, you can bring her back to mind instead of fifteen thousand horses!"

Murat laughed. "I know which I'd rather think about, but you needn't be so damned cutting about it. You're just an infantryman, that's what's wrong with you!"

"I've served in both," De Chavel reminded him. His wife's affair with Murat had made it necessary for De Chavel to transfer from the cavalry to the Imperial Guard.

Murat chose to ignore the reference. He remembered De Chavel's wife only too well; pretty little thing, gay as a lark and as faithless as a stray cat. Such a pity he had taken it to heart; Murat couldn't understand this obsession with female chastity; if all the ladies minded their virtue the world would have been an infernally dull place. He changed the subject.

"You mentioned the Polish charmer. Is she the one?"

"I should say so, definitely," De Chavel said. "I spent the rest of the time with her after you left last night. There's no doubt they're hoping to put her in your way; that introduction was all part of it; so was the husband suddenly absenting himself and leaving her with you."

"Or with you," Murat grinned. "I bet they didn't reckon on your intervention! How did you come out with her? Would you give the little mare a warranty?" He leant back and roared with laughter at his own joke.

"I didn't try her," De Chavel said dryly. "My object was to prevent you sleeping with her, not to sleep with her myself. I'm sure she's been recruited to spy. I'm also sure she doesn't know the full implications as far as you're concerned."

"Really?" Murat raised his bushy brows. "An innocent, eh? How damnably intriguing! You know, you intelligence people amaze me. How the devil did you hear about this business in the first place?"

"We have agents in the Polish government," De Chavel said. "Our particular source here in Danzig said there was a plan to insinuate a woman into the inner circle round the Emperor, and that you, if you'll forgive me, were chosen as being the most susceptible. They had no idea who the woman was, but they had heard the introduction would be made at the reception for the Emperor. And it was, wasn't it? Potocki himself brought the girl up to you."

"He did indeed. Talked about how she had worshipped me from afar," Murat chuckled. "The loveliest lady in Poland, he called her, and I thought to myself: Aha, Joachim, old friend, they're going to make you a present. They know you're bored and lonely, far from your delightful wife"—he gave a mock shudder at the mention of Caroline Bonaparte—"and they've found this Polish blossom to bring the spring back into your wintry life. Instead of which you come in, you damned policeman, and snatch her from under my nose. But not completely, I may say." He gave De Chavel a sly look and waited.

"Why not, completely? I even warned her to have nothing to do with you!"

"Was that for her protection or for mine? Don't tell me you've gone sentimental over a woman, De Chavel—I couldn't believe it."

"You know what I think of women," the Colonel said. "You know there's only one use I have for them, but not when it's part of my duties. I think the girl is prepared to spy as far as reporting scraps of gossip is concerned, but I wouldn't say she'd play the whore. I'm probably wrong, of course. Find me one who won't, sooner or later." He gave the Marshal a shrewd look.

"My official report to you, sir, is don't have anything to do with her. She's a Polish agent."

"Her worthy husband has invited me to dinner tomorrow night," Murat said. "All these dismal Poles will be there, pleading Poland's cause as usual, and boring us to tears. I presume this is part of the plot to ensnare me with Madame? I must say, she was a charmer—didn't you think so, eh?"

"No," the Colonel said coldly. "She made no impression on me at all."

"So you say," Murat shrugged. As a renowned chamberer himself he had a healthy regard for De Chavel's reputation. Once he had been laughed at as the only faithful husband in the regiment, and there had been an undertone of sympathy in the laughter as word of his wife Liliane's repeated infidelities came seeping through. He had discovered her with another officer, long before Murat became her lover for a brief period, and the change in him was quite remarkable. Pain and disappointment had made him a hard and bitter man, and above all a cynic who used women with callous abandon, as the woman he had married continued her useless, shameless philanderings, and then conveniently died. De Chavel never mentioned her; no one mentioned her to him. He lived his solitary life, as the principal intelligence officer in the Imperial Army, and few indeed knew how often he saw Napoleon himself and how many of the Emperor's secrets he knew. He had women, of course, but with the same detachment that a hungry man feels towards the meal he has just ordered. Murat sometimes suspected that he had affairs in order to punish his mistresses for having given in to him. The annoying thing was the number who did. "Will you make a devilish fuss if I decide to accept the Count's invitation?" Murat asked. "It'll seem uncivil to refuse."

"It would be wiser not to go. I can't prevent you from accepting. At least you know what to beware of," De Chavel said.

"It's a problem," Murat said. "What with Russian agents crawling all over the place, trying to find out our strength—one was caught and hanged the other day, I notice—and the Poles spying on their own account, our men are under constant strain. I'll be glad when we get the order to march. The Emperor doesn't really mean to set up Poland as an independent kingdom, do you think?"

"I shouldn't think so," De Chavel said. "Napoleon's idea is to counter-balance the power of Prussia and Austria once he's beaten the Russians, but I doubt whether he will make a third kingdom of Poland even to do that. The Grand Duke doesn't know that, of course. Some of these Poles are very astute. Potocki is no fool. He has hopes, but that's all they are."

"They're good fighters," Murat said. "Brave as lions, all of them. And some lovely women." He gave a sigh, and then winked.

"It breaks my heart to think of that little morsel going to waste," he said. "Eyes like cornflowers. I wonder how she'd look with her hair down . . ."

De Chavel stood up. "I have work to do. Your permission, sir?"

"Of course, of course. About twenty-three, wouldn't you say?"

"Twenty-two," De Chavel said as he reached the door.

"If you insist on going let me know the developments after tomorrow night. I want to finish my report; it'll have to go to Fouché in Paris at the end of the month."

He mounted and rode back to his own quarters in the Kutchinsky Square; it was significant that Murat had not mentioned sending the Countess Grunowska white roses. He might have been warned but the danger was not over; De Chavel had no wish to go to Napoleon with his report unless the Marshal refused to see sense and got himself involved.

Murat couldn't resist women; he doubted very much if he would be able to resist the beautiful girl he had spent the evening with, and been so profoundly attracted by himself. She was a pawn, of course, and he had been surprised by her apparent innocence of the whole affair, but that was only momentary. She would sleep with the Marshal because it was in a woman's nature to betray for the sake of vanity, or to satisfy their greedy senses. He knew a lot about the sensual greed of women; he had seen his own wife's frail, dancing body consumed with heat for love, wherever and with whomever she could find it. He had no illusions about any woman. The beautiful girl he had danced with the night before was no different from the rest. Vanity or lust or both. They were the only genuine emotions that women understood. De Chavel put the thought of Valentina Grunowska out of his mind; he had other things to think about. The troops were moving slowly to a thick concentration on the banks of the River Niemen. Artillery and supplies were moving up with them, and a further consignment of horses, Murat's fifteen thousand, would swell the number of livestock animals to a hundred thousand. There was a lot of stealing of supplies at night, and some incidents of agitating by members of the pro-Russian Polish group led by Prince Adam Czartorisky, the friend of the Czar Alexander.

Poland was divided into two factions: those who placed their trust in the Emperor Napoleon's promises to reunite them and re-establish their old boundaries of

1786 under the hereditary monarchy of the King of Saxony, and those, like Czartorisky, who believed that the Czar was a genuine liberal who would reward Poland's loyalty by granting those same privileges if he won against Napoleon. Neither Emperor was to be trusted, and this too was suspected by their unhappy Polish dependants.

De Chavel had a liking and respect for the Poles which was largely the result of fighting beside them in campaigns all over Europe. Geographically their country was in an untenable position, a land mass without natural borders, encompassed like a fat sheep by the three hungry wolves of Russia, Austria and Prussia. It was miraculous that as a people the Poles had survived and maintained their national characteristics and culture in spite of constant invasions and annexations over the centuries. They had thrown in their lot with France because they hoped that Napoleon would need them as a buffer state against Russia and Prussia; Poland had sent money and men without counting the cost in either to join the French in their long wars against Europe and England, hoping always for the ultimate reward. As De Chavel had said, he didn't think they would get it, but this was not the time to cast a doubt. France needed Poland; France needed all her allies, those who could be trusted, as she had never needed friends before. The Colonel knew his Emperor very well; he had loved him and fought under him from the days of the old army of the Republic, and he knew that Napoleon was facing the final test of his power in the coming war with Russia. England was the primary enemy, and England was unbeaten; his plan to starve her out and ruin her trade had failed because of Russia and Spain and Holland and Sweden to name but a few who had ignored their agreement with Napoleon and opened their ports to British ships and goods. The strategy was simple enough: Napoleon could not hope to concentrate his full attack upon the British with a hostile Russia at his back. If he was victorious, then England would be invaded and con-

quered, and Europe would settle under the domination
of France for a hundred years or more. This was the
Emperor's dream; its price in fulfilment would be paid
by the men massing on the Russian border. The date set
for invasion was early June; De Chavel had petitioned
Napoleon personally to rejoin his regiment in full fighting capacity; he was restless in his present post, and he
had only been appointed because the Emperor didn't
trust his official head of the Secret Police, the unbiquitous
Fouché. He hadn't been in battle for a year, and ever
since his personal life collapsed in ruins he had lived for
war and its excitement. At one time, when he discovered
the kind of woman he had married, De Chavel had tried
to get himself killed; his despair and disgust made living
an intolerable burden, but in the heat of every battle
men fell to right and left, and he, who so desperately
wanted to die, came out unscathed again and again. It
had taken some time for his love to die completely; it
was a painful, bitter process, the first forgiving, the
reconciliation, the second and third and fourth infidelity
for which there was no possible excuse except the appetites of an uncontrollable wanton, who bore his name
and had enjoyed his love. He hated his wife, and part of
his hate was the memory of his love, for love had not
come early or easily to him.

Now, he felt confident that it could never come again.
He had accepted the situation because he had no alternative except the scandal of divorce, and his was an ancient
family with traditions of private pride which forbade
him to parade his marriage in the public gaze. He had
lived in the same house with Liliane when he was in
Paris, but he had never touched her or spoken to her for
two years before she died. And when she died, stricken
by a quick summer sickness that devoured her in a few
weeks, he had covered her dead face and wept. But he
wept for his blighted hopes and lost illusions, and nobody heard him speak her name or show a flicker of regret. He was a hard man; he lived hard and fought hard

and he prided himself on being proof against all sentiment where women were concerned.

He laid down his papers and in spite of himself his thoughts turned again to the woman he and Murat had been discussing. He had lied when he said he was not impressed by her. Her body impressed him with an immediate desire to possess it; he only hoped that the Marshal King of Naples would be able to restrain himself if she were really offered to him, and privately he doubted that he would. But he had been warned of her true function, and God knew it was odious enough. It fitted into De Chavel's opinion of the female sex to imagine them worming confidences out of a lover while they lay in his arms, and their cunning combined with their sensual skill to trick him. The Countess Grunowska had not come to that pass yet, and this alone had saved her from him in the carriage. He had no desire to ravage innocence, if innocence existed. And while he was not in the least concerned with the woman, he believed that the fall from honour had yet to come. His greatest contempt, as in similar cases, was reserved for the husband who would prostitute his wife's honour and his own, for any cause, even pure patriotism, and from what was known of Count Theodore Grunowski other, less admirable, motives were involved. He had a dubious political record; at one point his allegiance to the Grand Duke of Warsaw had wavered to the point where he was suspected of dealing with the pro-Russian Czartorisky faction, but nothing had been proved, and he remained in favour. He was a dangerous man, ruthless enough to use his wife in an unsavoury intrigue, ambitious enough to change sides at any moment for his own advantage. De Chavel took out the folder dealing with the whole affair, and ringed the Count's name in red. This would have him under constant French intelligence surveillance, after the troops had crossed into Russia.

It was daylight, and she had been locked in her room for over twelve hours. She had dragged herself off the bed and wrenched repeatedly at the bell-cord until her arm ached, but no one came. There was no sound outside her door, no passing steps, no voices, nothing. She was faint with hunger and miserably thirsty; as it grew dark the room was cold, and there were no flints for the candles. Valentina had no tears left to cry; her whole body was trembling with hurt and shock. It was the worst experience of her five years of marriage, that savage, brutal assault by a man she now hated with all her soul. It had been done to break her spirit, and it had failed completely. His further cruelty of leaving her without food or water or attention would fail also. She crawled under the bedclothes and slept fitfully.

It was mid-morning when the door opened, and when she saw him standing there she dragged herself up on the pillows, the covers wrapped round her to the chin. He came into the room, close to the bed and stood looking down at her. Her hair was loose and wild round her shoulders; in spite of her extreme pallor and the black shadows under her eyes, he thought dispassionately that distress and disarray became her best of all. "I've come to see you," he said, "because I am very occupied today and I've no time to waste. Will you do as you're told, or shall I send to Potocki word to have that sister of yours arrested and brought here to stand trial? Come, I want an answer!"

Valentina pushed the hair back from her forehead; the movement showed a livid bruise on her upper arm.

She answered him calmly; he was surprised and angered at the lack of fear in her eyes and the contempt in her voice. He had imagined her cowed and weeping.

"After what you did to me yesterday I know you're capable of anything. Even the murder of my sister. I'll go to bed with anyone you choose, so long as you promise never to touch me again as long as I live. Now leave me, please." She turned away from him.

"I'm glad you see sense," the Count said. "I'll send your maid in to you. You must be at your best tonight."

When Jana came in to her, she was already up, brushing her hair. "Madame," the maid said, and her eyes were full of tears. "Madame, forgive me for leaving you . . . the Count gave orders and I didn't dare. . . ."

"Don't cry," Valentina said gently. "I know you'd have helped me if you could. I know what he would have done to you. I'm all right, Jana, don't worry about me now. Help me to bathe and dress."

The maid came up and quickly knelt beside her. She caught Valentina's hand in hers and kissed it; her cheeks were wet with tears.

"He hurt you," she whispered. "I can see he did. Ah, the devil, how I hate him. God forgive me, how I hate him."

"You mustn't," Valentina said quickly. "You mustn't say that, Jana. It doesn't matter. He'll never be able to hurt me again."

"I remember my Eugene," Jana said fiercely. "He got drunk and took a stick to me night after night. Sometimes I starved . . . my child died. I prayed for his death. I prayed and God heard me! He'll hear you too, my poor dear lady; you're sweet and good, and you won't be left to suffer long. Give me that brush, Madame, and let me do it for you. Come now . . ."

She ministered to her as gently as if her mistress were a hurt child, and all the time she muttered under her breath, and sniffed back tears. At last Valentina stopped her.

"If you feel sorry for me, Jana, I shall begin to feel sorry for myself, and that won't do. That way is weakness. I must be strong from now on, and you must be silent and discreet. I may need a lot of help in the next few days. Will you help me, Jana? I have no one else in the world I can trust."

The homely round face grew pink with emotion.

"You can trust me to the death, Madame. What do you want me to do?"

"Nothing yet." Valentina said. "There is a big dinner party tonight. We can do nothing till tomorrow. I've made up my mind, Jana." The lovely white face in the looking glass stared back at her, drawn with resolve and a new courage, born of that last, unbearable outrage.

"After tomorrow we're going to leave this house for ever."

Chapter
TWO

There were thirty guests seated at the table; eighteen of them French officers of the highest rank, including two Marshals, Davoust and Berthier, and the King of Naples himself. The guest of honour sat on the right hand of his hostess, and from the start of the dinner party he had begun to enjoy himself. He had dressed for the occasion in a uniform of purple velvet coat, frogged in gold, white breeches and silk stockings with diamond buckles bashing on his shoes. He wore rings on his fingers and his scented hair was puffed and curled down to his brown cheeks. He had never looked more outrageous or more handsome and he was in the best of spirits. He leant so close to the Countess Grunowska that he presented his back to the lady seated on his other side; she was the extremely pretty wife of a Polish provincial governor, but Murat had failed to notice her existence.

His infatuation was not surprising; every man in the room was watching the Countess Grunowska at the head of the table; only her husband's glance was cold and full of malice. She had dressed deliberately in virgin white. White chiffon covered her shoulders, and he knew the reason for this concealing arrangement. The chiffon parted at the base of her throat, revealing a deep décolletage. The white silk dress was cut so low it exposed her breasts three-quarters naked, and she wore a single diamond on a chain that flashed and glittered like a star between them. She wore no petticoats under the dress, and from the way the material clung to her, he suspected that she had followed the whorish French fashion of a few years ago and damped the cloth. Her hair was dressed very high and there was rouge on her cheeks; her eyes were too bright and her laugh too loud. She wore heavy diamond pendant ear-rings in her ears and bracelets encircled one arm from the wrist almost to the elbow.

She had come down to the Salon late, a few minutes before the guests arrived, and when he told her what she looked like, the shrugged.

"You told me to play the whore; very well, I've got to look the part!"

The Count had been watching her the whole evening. Had anyone told him she was capable of this vulgar flirtation he would never have believed them. He was torn between fury because she was making a fool of him in front of the insufferable French, and gratification that she had bewitched Murat completely. The Marshal gazed at her, and shook his head. The scent of his pomade was so strong that Valentina almost sneezed in his face.

"It's incredible, Madame," he said, grinning from ear to ear. "Unbelievable. I can't get over it!"

"What is so incredible, so unbelievable, Sire?" She asked the question lightly, dropping her voice as he had done.

"The transformation in you," he said. "Last night you were a rose; beautiful and stately, damned prickly too, from what my old friend De Chavel told me—sent him off with a bug in your ear, didn't you? Tonight—by God, Madame, you're magnificent!" His eyes went downwards and stayed there. She felt like dashing her glass of wine into his face. But she smiled, and touched his sleeve with a finger, drawing it along to the edge until she lightly brushed his wrist.

"I lost you the other night," she said. "I was heartbroken. When I received your lovely roses I was overjoyed. Is it true that women find you irresistible?"

He raised his brows, the impudent grin grew wider on his lips; they were thick and over red and his strong white teeth reminded her of some kind of animal.

"I find *women* irresistible, I can tell you that," he said. "And none more so than you. Why are you so adorable? Are you going to torment a poor soldier who may go off to war and never come back? Are you as cruel as you're beautiful?"

She looked into the dark, hungry eyes, burning with drink and sensual expectation, and hoped to God she was playing her part properly. She felt so repelled by him, by the mixture of strong scent and masculine odour, the coarse strong hands and the flushed face, that she felt sick at the thought of being touched by him. But her plan depended on the loathsome charade; she had no alternative and she needed to lull her husband's suspicions. "I could never be cruel to you, Sire, or to any soldier fighting for His Majesty Napoleon. If there is any little favour I can show you . . ."

"There is." He lifted his full glass and drank a silent toast to her. "You've invited me to this excellent dinner. Let me give you supper."

"Tomorrow?" Valentina murmured.

"No." The glass came down empty. "Tonight. It's all arranged."

"I can't." She made a great effort to keep the dismay out of her voice, but she had changed colour.

"Tonight is impossible. Tomorrow I will come. Any time tomorrow evening."

"Why is tonight impossible, Madame?" he asked her gently. "Why do you refuse me, and fob me off with tomorrow when you know I am dying for love of you? There's no difficulty."

"There is," she said desperately. "I have my guests to consider—I can't leave them."

"I can assure you they will leave when I do," he said. "Your husband won't object—he's an understanding fellow—and, besides, I know he's meeting your excellent Count Potocki at midnight. He told me so. There's nothing in the world to stop you having a little supper with a lonely soldier. I insist."

"I'll think about it," Valentina said. "I can't answer you now. Don't press me, please."

Murat had drunk an enormous quantity of wine and brandy but he had a head like teak. He was never drunk and he never missed a point or overlooked a change of nuance. He saw the coquettish mask slip but he gave no sign. He was getting a little tired of the game they had been playing; he decided to put it to one final test before making up his mind about the way to play the final move. He glanced down the table at the husband sitting at the other end, watching his wife being seduced under his nose, and mentally called him an obscene Gascon name. He felt irritated with them all, the damned Poles and their damned women, laying themselves out for the French like virgin martyrs to the Roman swords. They were lucky to have French protection and to fight alongside the best soldiers in the world under the greatest of all soldiers. Lucky to have a French man for a lover, any of them. Who precisely did they think they were going to make a fool of with this stupid intrigue? Murat? Murat, who had risen from the ranks of the Revolutionary Army to being a King and Napoleon's brother-in-law? He felt tempted to rise and tell them what he thought of their impertinence, but his sense of mischief had prompted him to plan an intrigue of his own. She was very lovely, this Countess, and he longed to have her in his bed and teach her not to play tricks with Joachim Murat. He bore her no ill will for trying to catch him. If she passed his final test he would even agree to be caught. For one night and on his own terms.

"Very well, adorable lady. Give me your answer later."

Soon afterwards Valentina gave the signal to rise and the company went through into the withdrawing room. It was a beautifully proportioned room, with formal French furniture and a pianoforte and a harp. It was the custom to have a musician play for the guests after dinner, and the Count had engaged a young pianist to entertain them. He came up to Valentina as she seated herself; Murat had the place of honour beside her but he had lagged behind. Personally he hated music and was prepared to close his eyes and doze till it was over.

"Well?" the Count said. "You've made progress, haven't you?"

"He's invited me to supper." She could hardly bear to look at him.

"Excellent. Tonight, I've no doubt. I've had one or two hints to stay out of the way. You've accepted?"

"Not yet," she said. "Go away, he's coming now."

"You're to go." The Count said it very quietly. "He won't ask you again, and he'll never forgive a refusal. You go tonight or your sister dies. Ah, Sire, let me make way for you. I hope our little entertainment will amuse you."

"How could it fail," Murat answered. He made a gallant bow to Valentina. "The loveliest hostess in the city, the most obliging host"—he saw the Count wince and proceeded blandly on—"magnificent food and beautiful music. I'm overwhelmed, my dear Count. You're too generous to me. But I must crave a favour. May I retire after an hour? I've a dawn appointment tomorrow with His Majesty and he doesn't appreciate yawns. It will kill me to leave you, but in one hour I must." He gave a slow smile full of meaning.

"Have you considered my invitation," Murat whispered, as the recital began. "It is yes, isn't it? You won't reject me?"

"No, I won't," Valentina said. "I'll come to supper with you, Sire. I couldn't refuse the bravest soldier in all France."

He slipped his hand over and squeezed hers. "Not in all France, Madame," he corrected. "In the world."

Five minutes later he was dozing peacefully, while the flood of pianoforte music swept on. At the end of an hour the Count made a sign to end the recital; the Marshal awoke without appearing to have been asleep, and whispered to Valentina that he wished to see the garden before leaving. She excused herself from the company and they made their way to the french windows at the end of the withdrawing room. These opened out on to the gardens, and they were beautiful indeed under a full early summer moon. She stood in the doorway with Murat beside her. She felt his hand on her arm. "Step outside, Madame, so we can see better."

She sensed what he was going to do, and when he touched her she was stiff and tense. His mouth closed over hers and she felt the hot taste of him on her lips, and the pressure of his kiss trying to make them open. Quite suddenly he let her go. He stood back from her in the bright moonlight, and made her a little bow.

"I'll send a coach for you in an hour," he said. "I shall be waiting for you, Madame. We must go back and make our farewells in public. I owe especial thanks to your husband."

Everyone took their leave within a few minutes, and without waiting to see her husband, Valentina ran up the stairs to her own rooms. Jana was waiting for her.

"Let me get you something warm to drink, Madame," she said. "You look so tired; thank God the guests left early." She began laying out her mistress's nightgown and robe, murmuring to herself. In her opinion the Countess was not fit to give a dinner party and force herself to eat and drink and entertain. After her frightful ordeal of the day before she should have been in bed.

"I'm going out," Valentina said. She went to the dressing table and sat down; she looked at her own reflection, and on an impulse wiped off the rouge. It made her look harsh and artificial even in the flattering candlelight.

"Out? But, Madame, you can't! You must rest!"

"It's a royal command. Or semi-royal, if you count Naples as a kingdom. I am having supper with Marshal Murat. You don't know who he is, do you, Jana? No, I know you don't. He's a great man, he's a very important soldier and he's married to the Emperor Napoleon's sister. He sent me those white roses this morning."

Jana didn't answer immediately. She was no simpleton, and she understood the significance of supper invitations to ladies unaccompanied by their husbands. And it was obvious that the gentleman who sent her mistress flowers was unlikely to include the Count.

"Do you like him, Madame? Is he a handsome man?"

"Very," Valentina said wearily. "I only hope he's understanding too. But I doubt it. Get me my blue velvet dress, Jana—with the Mechlin lace fichu. I must change out of this; I hate myself in it."

"If you don't want to go, Madame," the maid said, "I can say you're unwell, if you want to change your mind. Let me do that. Don't fret yourself; I'll see to it."

"You'd see to anything for me, wouldn't you?" Valentina smiled at her. "But you can't help me, Jana. Nobody can help me now, except perhaps this man Murat. At least I can appeal to him. He's powerful enough to do anything."

"What will you ask him, Madame?" Jana was undoing the fastenings at the back of the white dress.

"To protect me and my sister from the Count," Valentina said. "You think this a lovers' meeting, don't you, you foolish girl? You think I'm doing this behind my husband's back? It's at his command! I am to be seduced by this French General so that I can get information for my husband and his friends. When I refused last night was the result. He has threatened to harm my sister, and I know he'd keep his word. I was going to run away, Jana. That's what I meant this morning by a plan, by leaving this house for ever. Now there's no time. I thought the rendezvous with Murat would be in a day or two and we'd have a chance to escape to Czartatz and join Alexandra. Together we might have thought of a way to save ourselves. I had no idea I should have to decide so soon as this. But I must, and I've made my choice. I'll go to Murat tonight and throw myself on his mercy. If there's one spark of pity in him, or honour, he'll help me."

"And if it's at a price, Madame?" Jana said. She had very little faith in the disinterested actions of any man. She had a peasant's practical assessment of such foibles as virginity and honour; there were too many genuine hazards in the life of a bondwoman, like hunger and beatings or being sold to a new master, or having your children taken from you, to worry about trifles.

"If it's at a price, I'll pay it," Valentina said. "Hurry, his coach will be here within the hour."

The wanton dress lay in a heap on the floor; she took off the single diamond on its chain and wound her mother's beautiful pearls round her throat. The dark blue velvet gown was cut high, and her bare shoulders were hidden by the fichu of lace. A long velvet cloak of the same sapphire colour as the dress covered her completely, framing her face in a soft sable collar. She felt exhausted; her limbs ached and her eyes burnt with the tears which were so close to the surface that she feared every word would bring them spilling down. What would he be like, this animalistic, coarse man, who had kissed her in the garden as if she were a tap-room maid? What help and pity could she expect from him, what sympathy, unless she pleased him and satisfied his appetites? And she did not know how to begin. She knew nothing about love; her only feelings had been repulsion and misery, a wretched acceptance of something which brought only pain and humiliation and never manifested itself in any form of tenderness or love. She had hated him when he touched her, hated the roughness and the dominance of the man; it was like being attacked by one of the hefty, hot-smelling peasants who worked on her own estates. And she was going to give herself to him completely, to endure at his hands what she had suffered from her husband, without, she prayed, the perverted quirks which had made their relationship such a nightmare. It was horrible, and for a moment her courage failed her completely; she leant against the bedpost and shivered. But the moment passed. "Go, or your sister dies." Those were Theodore's words and she knew that he meant them. He would have Alexandra killed if she failed to keep that appointment tonight. That much was certain. The unknown lay with Murat and herself, and her own capacity to enlist his sympathy when he heard the truth. He might even be truly chivalrous and not ask anything of her in return. It was her only hope.

"Jana, go down and see if the Marshal's carriage has arrived. It must be time now."

A few minutes later the maid came back. She nodded, and held the door open for her mistress. "It's waiting, Madame. I said you were coming down. And the Count is in the hallway," she added.

"Thank you, Jana. Good night. Don't wait up for me. And gather your clothes together. If all goes well I'll send for you."

"Good night, Madame. God go with you. I'll be ready."

Valentina walked down the sweeping staircase; the hall below was lit by candelabra and the bright burning torches in the walls outside the open entrance. Her husband was waiting; he too was dressed for going out. As he heard her step he looked up.

"Remember," he said, "to pretend to enjoy it. He's a crude fellow, I believe. He may not realise that you're as cold as ice. Tomorrow I want an account of everything he says. You have the whole night to make him talk."

Valentina walked down the last steps and passed him without a word; she hadn't even turned her head when he spoke. He watched her go out and enter the carriage, helped in by a French army postilion. Two mounted soldiers gave the carriage escort as it moved off.

He called out, and the porter shouted for his own coach to come up. He could report to Potocki that the first most difficult part of their plan had succeeded.

"What the devil do you want! I'm busy!" De Chavel was not usually so irritable with younger officers, but he was tired and he had a long report to finish for Paris. He had dined alone and retired to his quarters to work; it was nearly midnight when the ensign came in to disturb him. "Ah," De Chavel said, "Fonécet—I didn't know it was you. I thought it was some imbecile from headquarters. What can I do for you?" Murat's aide-de-camp bowed. He was used to hard words; Murat sometimes flung his boots at his head if he were feeling temperamental.

"His Majesty Marshal Murat presents his compliments and asks you to come to his house at once. He says it is important. He said to tell you it concerns his dinner engagement this evening."

"Does it, indeed?" The Colonel was already buttoning his uniform coat; he paused to pull on his helmet. "I'll come immediately. Have you a coach, Fonécet?"

"No, sir. His Majesty told me to take my horse."

"Damn and blast you," De Chavel said. "Go down and tell those fools in the stable to saddle my bay at once."

"I've already taken that liberty, sir," the young man said. De Chavel nodded approvingly.

"Right enough. I'm ready, come on."

It was a fine clear night and they cantered the short distance to Murat's private quarters in the centre of Danzig itself. He had been allotted a very fine town house where he and his personal staff were quartered. It was the joke of the Imperial Army that one room alone was needed to accommodate the Marshal's uniforms.

The Colonel found Murat in his study, a downstairs room which also served him as an office. He was fully dressed, and smoking a cheroot. There was a decanter of brandy on the table beside him.

"Sit down, my friend. Help yourself to some of this excellent stuff. Polish—compliments of the owner of this charming house." De Chavel knew at once that the Marshal was in a bad temper; the more he bantered on these occasions the more it indicated his rage.

"Thank you; will there be anything left in the cellar by the time we leave for Russia?"

"Nothing, if I can help it. I'm sick to death of these damned Poles!"

"Your message was to come urgently," De Chavel reminded him. He drank some of the brandy and grimaced. "Ugh, good God, Sire, how could you drink this stuff—it's only fit to clean boots!"

"That's the trouble with being an aristocrat," Murat jeered. "You have a fancy palate. The matter is urgent. Sit down. I hope you've dined?"

"I have," the Colonel answered. "So have you, and I presume something's given you indigestion. What is it?"

"You were quite right," Murat said. "The whole thing was a trick; I went to Grunowski's this evening and there was Madame tricked out in a dress cut down to her belly, playing the tethered goat to snare the French tiger. It was obvious that she was set to catch me, and every one of those damned Poles at the party knew it. I made a rendezvous with her for tonight."

"She accepted?" De Chavel showed no surprise.

"Yes, after a hesitation. I tell you, Colonel, I'm sick and tired of having our so-called allies spy on us and sell us out whenever it suits them. They need a lesson. This attempt on me is criminal. It ought to be punished!"

"It's failed," De Chavel said. "That's enough. The Emperor can't afford to make enemies here at the moment. We need the Poles firm at our rear. But we also need to get rid of cliques like the one our friend Grunowski organises. What are you going to do about the woman? Where are you meeting her?"

"Here," Murat said. "In about half an hour. She's expecting to have supper and allow me to seduce her and then the game will begin. You said she was an innocent!" He threw the half-smoked cheroot into the grate. "You should have seen her tonight. You should have seen her with me in the gardens! Bah, if there's one thing I hate it's a dishonest whore pretending to be virtuous."

Nothing would ever make him forget that recoil when he touched her, or the resistance to his kiss. He was mortally affronted, and ready to inflict any punishment on Valentina because she had hurt his vanity.

"I shan't be here tonight," he said. "Now it's my turn to play tricks. You can take my place, my dear De Chavel, and I advise you to take the fullest advantage of her. She'll be expecting it. What you do with her afterwards is your own affair. You might also have a word with her husband."

De Chavel sipped a little more of the brandy before answering. He could have sworn that the Countess was innocent; the picture Murat painted of her as bare-breasted and wanton was impossible to imagine. Yet it was true; women were adept at deceiving; she had undoubtedly played a part for his benefit that night, and revealed herself in her true guise to the man she was hoping to ensnare.

"She certainly made a fool of you," Murat said. "You even warned her against me? Ha, I thought you were beyond being taken in by a *rusée* little slut like that!"

"Wouldn't the lesson come better from you?" De Chavel asked.

"I have other plans," the Marshal answered. "I'm expected by another lady in fifteen minutes, and this one I wouldn't want to miss. Will you take my place, or shall I give her to one of the grooms here? On second thoughts, that might better——"

"No," De Chavel said. He looked up at Murat and smiled; it was not a pleasant smile. He had indeed been made to look a fool. It was not a role he enjoyed; he had filled it for too long during his marriage. "No, I have nothing to do this evening. I'll entertain the lady in your absence. For purposes of interrogation, of course."

"Of course," Murat laughed. He felt better; he would have given a month's income to see her face when she found herself alone with the Colonel, her shabby scheme discovered. To be raped by the wrong man—it was what the cold-hearted, calculating bitch deserved. That would teach her to shut her mouth and shiver when he, Murat, held her in his arms. He rang the bell and his valet came

in, carrying the Marshal's fur-lined jacket and his enormous plumed helmet.

"I bid you adieu," he said. "You will find everything
prepared upstairs. First floor; champagne and food and
anything else you may require. Enjoy yourself!"

"Thank you," De Chavel said. "I will."

"This way, Madame." The Marshal's aide-de-camp
made Valentina a bow. His smooth young face was expressionless; he had personally escorted Murat to his carriage ten minutes before. The servants had gone to bed;
except for himself the house was empty. He had orders
to show the lady upstairs to the supper room and then
retire. It was none of his business what happened after
that. Valentina mounted the wide stairs after him; she
felt numb and beyond shame.

"If Madame will come with me." The young man
opened the double doors of a room on the first floor and
stepped back for her to enter. It was a small room, comfortably furnished in the early Directoire style, with a
round supper table in the centre, covered with a white
cloth; silver dishes and fine porcelain and crystal were
arranged in two covers, and a bottle of champagne
cooled in a large silver epergne. There was a fire burning
and the only flowers in the room were white roses.

"If Madame will wait a moment," the aide said, and
bowing slightly he closed the door and she heard his
steps going down the corridor. Valentina went to the
sofa and laid her velvet cloak down; there was not a
sound anywhere. She moved over to the fire and warmed
her hands. She faced the door, waiting for Murat to
come in. In the carriage she had rehearsed over and over
again what she was going to say and do. Throw herself
on her knees, tell him how she had been coerced and
threatened, implore him to help her and save her sister. It
sounded easy enough when she said it all to herself; it
seemed far less credible now when she had only a moment or two before she was face to face with the Marshal.

"Good evening, Countess. May I get you some champagne?"

She swung round; the voice came from behind, and it was not Murat standing in the doorway of another room leading off this one. The man came nearer into the light, and she recognised the mocking, arrogant face with the sinister scar on one cheek.

"Colonel De Chavel!"

"At your service, Countess." He bowed, and stepped close to her. "You look surprised. Weren't you expecting me?"

"Why no . . . I thought . . . Marshal Murat invited me . . ." She stammered helplessly, and there was something in the cold grey eyes that made her shrink away.

"Alas," the Colonel said, "His Majesty was called away. Won't you make do with me instead? I'm a French officer and I know a deal more secrets than he does." He looked into the lovely face and the blue eyes, widening with fear and bewilderment, and he could have struck her for lying to him that first night. She had a marvellous acting talent, but he was not the man to be deceived a second time.

"I don't know what you mean, Colonel. I came to supper with Marshal Murat. What are you doing here?" She made a move towards the door.

He stepped in her way, one arm stretched out across the fireplace.

"What's wrong with me, Madame? You seemed to like me well enough the other evening. I can be as charming a supper companion as the Marshal, I assure you. Calm yourself; you don't have to play-act with me. Will you sup first, or shall we wait till after?"

"I don't know what this means," she said desperately. "I want to leave. Please step aside."

"Don't play-act," he repeated. "You want some secrets—try and worm them out of me!" He came close to her and caught her round the waist. She hadn't a chance of resisting; he was strong and he had kissed a multitude of women, some of them initially against their will. He bent her back, and kissed her on the mouth. Desperately she wrenched her head away, thrusting against him.

"Don't, don't," she begged. "You don't understand, you don't know the real reason——"

"Oh but I do," he said; his face was in her hair, his lips burnt her throat with kisses; his grip on her had tightened so that she couldn't move. "You came to take a lover. Now you're going to take me."

She gave a scream, but he only laughed and half lifted her in his arms, taking her to the inner room.

"No one will hear you, and if they did, they wouldn't come. Stop struggling, Madame. Pretend I'm Murat."

She was crying as he laid her on the bed; she struck at him with her fists, and her resistance made him furiously angry; it seemed so real, when he had Murat's word for what she really was. And what had begun as a trick to play upon the trickster had become a blind and angry passion to possess her. He held her unwilling body in his arms and forced his kisses on her and at last he felt the slackening which he knew presaged response. There was a moment's respite when he raised his head and looked at her; her eyes were closed, and her face was wet with tears. He had a moment of doubt, but he wanted her so much that he banished it. She was ready to make love to Murat. She must learn to accept him instead. He undid the blue ribbons fastening the lace fichu at her breast and uncovered her shoulders to kiss them. For a moment he didn't move. Valentina opened her eyes; she was exhausted, unable to fight him or protest.

"Who did this to you?" His voice was a whisper; he raised his head and looked at her. "Who made these marks?"

"My husband." She turned her head away and the tears began to flow again.

"My God!" De Chavel said. He touched her and she winced.

"When did this happen?"

"Yesterday. When I refused to go to bed with Murat."

"Good God in heaven!" De Chavel's voice shook. "Why didn't you tell me?"

"What difference would it have made?" she asked him bitterly. "Why have you stopped, Colonel? How different are you from him?"

"I've never hurt a woman in my life," he said slowly. "I'd like to kill him for this. Wait, let me help you." He lifted her very gently up on to the pillows, and she relaxed and let him hold her. She had a wild impulse to throw her arms round his neck and weep and weep; he took the crumpled lace and covered her with it. "Forgive me," he said. "I must have hurt you abominably."

"It doesn't matter." Valentina wiped her eyes. "I've known nothing else. I came to tell Marshal Murat the truth. I thought he might help me."

De Chavel had taken her hand in his; he held it and stroked it as if she were a child. "I doubt he would have listened to you. He said you led him on, he said you were willing. That's why I treated you as I did. I'm sorry. I'm sorry with all my heart. Will you give me a chance to help you? Tell me exactly what happened."

"My husband told me I must spy on your officers," Valentina said. "He said it was my duty."

De Chavel nodded. "I guessed as much. Go on."

"When he saw me the night after the reception he was very angry. He accused me of letting Murat slip through my fingers because I preferred you." A little colour crept into her face and she looked away from him.

"And did you?" he asked.

"Well, yes. . . . I mean I didn't think it mattered . . . it was harmless."

"Yes," he agreed gently. "Of course it was. Quite harmless."

"He forbade me to see or speak to you again," she said. "When I asked him what he really expected me to do, he told me. I was to be seduced by Murat; it was all arranged, all planned by him and Potocki. I refused. I'm not a whore, Colonel, no matter what you think."

"No, I'm a fool. A blind, unforgivable fool, that's all."

"If it had been only myself I would have held out," Valentina said. "But I'm not alone. I have a sister—a half-sister, who lives in Czartatz. Our father's dead. Her mother was a Russian. Theodore—my husband—said he would denounce her as a Russian spy and have her hanged unless I did as I was told. He would have made me watch. I know him. He doesn't threaten without meaning it. I thought I would have time to run away—I thought if I could reach Alexandra we might save ourselves. She's older and she's not afraid of anything . . . but it all happened at once. The dinner party—the Marshal's invitation. I had no choice. I would have done anything to protect my sister."

"I see," De Chavel said. "I knew about the plan. I even knew you were the woman. But I was sure you didn't know how far it went. And I was right, thank God. Don't worry about asking Murat's help. As it happens, I can be more useful to you than he could. Much more useful."

He lifted her hand and kissed it. It had taken all the self-control which he possessed not to bend down and kiss her beautiful quivering mouth.

"Come, let me help you up. We've got to plan what must be done." He lifted her up and she stood against him; for a moment the temptation was too strong for him and he held her close, but as gently as he had been harsh before, and she felt his lips brush against her face. It was her first experience of joy in an embrace; warmth and sweetness swept over her; she longed for his mouth to move and find her lips. But he released her; he put her away from him very gently but with a firmness which was for his own benefit. He felt shaken and shamed by what he had done and how close he had come to committing the final outrage. He was aware that, worst of all, the combination of force and skill had brought the unhappy girl to the point of total surrender. It was unforgivable; he detested himself for the advantage he had obviously gained over her. He detested the whole ugly, pitiless situation, in which she was a tool for the ambitions of others.

"Come and sit down, and let me give you something to drink." He took her hand and led her back to the outer room and made her sit before the fire. A moment later he handed her a glass of Murat's champagne.

"Drink that," he said. "And don't try to talk till you're completely calm." He had always hated women's tears; they embarrassed him and aroused his suspicions. Liliane used to cry, and she always looked pretty and unruffled when she did it. Her sobs meant nothing, she could dry her eyes and burst out laughing seconds later. But Valentina's tears were silent, and they were flowing freely. The emotional strain had been far greater than she realised. The kindness of the man who had so nearly violated her was worse than any cruelty; she wept and shivered until he wrapped her in her cloak, and the gentleness unnerved her. She felt like a child, desperate for comfort, and there was something so strong about him and so safe that she gave way for a few moments and clung to him.

"Poor little one," De Chavel said. "Stay quiet now; it's all over. You're safe, I promise you. I'll take care of everything." He held the glass to her lips and made her finish it; he wiped her face and smoothed back her hair, and put cushions behind her, as if she were indeed a child.

"What am I going to do?" Valentina whispered. She looked up at him standing before the fire. "I can't go back. Theodore will find out what happened tonight."

"You're not going back to him," the Colonel said. "He'll never be allowed to touch you again. I give you my word on that. If it wasn't for the situation here, I'd call him out tomorrow morning and put a bullet through him. I've been thinking if I could risk it. But I can't, Valentina. The Emperor would never forgive me. Your husband is a powerful man; it might seriously affect Polish opinion if a Frenchman were to kill him and then run off with his wife." He went to the table and poured himself a glass of champagne. He had indeed been thinking of killing the Count, and the thought gave him such pleasure that he had almost succumbed to the temptation. But not quite. He couldn't touch him yet. Later, when the war was won, and he returned, he would remind the Count that gentlemen do not ill-treat their wives.

"The first thing is to get you to a place where you'll be safe. How far is your sister from here?"

"About two hundred miles; Czartatz is very near the Russian border."

"We can get there in two days, or three days at the most, if we travel fast. But the first thing I have to do is put you under official French protection. And your sister."

"How?" Valentina said. "I tried to spy on you. Why should the Emperor protect me?"

"The French Secret Police will protect you," he said. "And it's easier to defy the Emperor himself than to meddle with us." He smiled a little. "Yes, I am a policeman of a kind. At least while the Army is in Poland. I told you, I am more use to you than any Marshal."

"So you knew all the time?" Valentina said. "Did Murat know what I was doing?"

"Of course," De Chavel said. "He made me a present of you. As things turned out, I can only thank God. Now, I suggest you eat some supper while I write a letter to His Majesty explaining the position and send a word to my personal staff that your name and your sister's are to go on our special list."

"She's Princess Alexandra Suvaroff."

"I know that name," De Chavel said.

"Her ancestor was a famous General under the Czarina Catherine," Valentina said. "She has always used her mother's name. It made Father very angry."

"She must be an unusual woman, this sister," he said. "How long since you've seen her?"

"Five years; since I married. Theodore hated her. He wouldn't let us meet. He told me once he had intended marrying her until he saw me. She's very, very rich. I love her dearly."

"Good," he smiled. "Now eat, while I do what must be done. I shall send a messenger to the house for your clothes."

"Oh, and my maid," Valentina begged. "You must let her come with me."

"If you wish it. I shall bring her back myself."

"Bring her back? You mean you're going to my house yourself?"

"I am," he said. "I am going to say a word or two to your husband. In case he thinks he can try and get you back. Then I shall return and we will be on the road to Czartatz at dawn."

"I can't believe it," Valentina said. "I can't believe I'm getting away from him." She came up to him and held out her hand.

"How can I ever thank you for all this?"

He stood still, determined not to touch her. If he did, and she responded, they were lost. "You can forgive me for what happened this evening," he said.

"With all my heart." Valentina flushed and turned away. Something had happened to her while she was in his arms, something had broken and melted away like ice in the sunshine. No matter how it had begun, she knew she would have consented to his love-making. She would consent to it now, if he asked her.

"I'll write what has to be written," he said. "You rest and I'll be back for you in an hour. I'll put a guard on your door, so you have nothing to fear from anyone. Not even the Marshal," he added. "Until one hour, Madame."

"May I ask what brings you here at three o'clock in the morning?" The Count had been in bed when the Colonel's summons came; he had been asleep and very inclined to tell the intruder to go to the devil at that hour. But he recognised the name De Chavel. This was the gallant who had paid such marked attention to his wife that first evening. He got up, and went down to see what he wanted. He had gone to bed in an excellent humour; Potocki had been very gratified, full of praise for him. The Grand Duke himself would hear of the service both Grunowskis had done their country. He had assured himself that Valentina had not returned and gone to bed without a qualm. He was not disturbed by the thought of her sleeping with Joachim Murat. He despised Murat as a common, low-born soldier of fortune and he felt sure his wife would find the affair a detestable ordeal. He could only hope that Murat wouldn't be bored with her after one night.

He glared at the tall, good-looking man in the greatcoat and helmet of the Imperial Guard, and took an instant personal dislike to him. De Chavel regarded him with an insolent stare that sent the blood flushing angrily into the Count's face.

"I asked you, Sir," he repeated, "what the devil you wanted? Either you tell me or my servants will throw you out!"

"I wanted to see you, for one thing," De Chavel answered. "I wondered what sort of a man it was who would thrash his wife because she declined to go to bed with someone else. Now that I have seen you I consider you exactly what I thought. A miserable, cowardly cur. That's one thing I came for—to tell you that. And also to say that I shall repeat it, at a later date, with the appropriate action. Unfortunately I can't kill you at the moment, Count; that will have to be delayed. Secondly, your wife is safe and under my protection. I'm sure you will be glad to know that."

"If my wife has run off with you, Sir," the Count said, "believe me I shall get her back. After I've killed you. And if she objected to my little lesson of the other evening I don't think she'll like the one I teach an unfaithful wife!"

"But only if she's unfaithful with the wrong man," the Colonel said softly. "Let me correct you. Madame has not become Marshal Murat's mistress. She is at this moment in his house, under the protection of the Imperial Secret Police, of which I have the honour to be in charge. Madame, and her sister, will be under our protection in the future. There is a signed order to that effect, and any attempt by you, or anyone else, to molest or disturb these ladies will be punished by the authority of the Emperor. They are State persons, my dear Count. Not even Count Potocki will try to interfere with either of them now. As for the unsavoury practice of using women to spy on your allies—your party did it very clumsily. We have been aware of your intrigue for a long time. Be good enough to have Madame's maid collect her clothes and bring them outside. I have transport waiting."

"I'll see you damned first," the Count shouted. "She'll take nothing with her—as for that maid, she's my serf and I'll have her flogged to death! Tell my wife that!"

"The Emperor abolished serfdom—she's a free woman. Also I have a detachment of a dozen men outside your entrance," De Chavel said. "No one in this house will lay a hand on Madame's maid or stop her packing Madam's clothes."

Within a minute there were two soldiers of the Guard standing on either side of the Count; when he protested they crossed their bayonets before his face. Soldiers moved quietly through the upper floors; in a little while one came downstairs carrying a trunk on his back, followed by Jana in a thick wool travelling cloak, her few possessions in a bundle.

De Chavel came back after he had put her into the coach. He dismissed his soldiers and the Count faced him alone.

"You'll be sorry for this," he spat at the Colonel. "You've covered your adultery with my wife very cleverly, haven't you? She's not in Murat's bed, but by God I wager she's been in yours tonight!"

De Chavel moved so fast that the Count never saw the blow; his open hand crashed across the furious older man's face, splitting his lip and sending him reeling back against the wall.

"That's on Madame's behalf," he said quietly. "My answer will be a bullet through the heart when I get back from Russia. If you go within twenty miles of Czartatz the local police will have orders to arrest you."

At dawn that morning a large travelling coach started off from the Marshal's house in Kutchinsky Square. Murat himself had come to the supper room where Valentina and her maid were waiting to leave.

He had bowed to her and wished her luck; some of his pique still remained, but it was mollified by De Chavel's story. He didn't like the idea of the girl being bullied and ill-treated. It explained some of her reluctance to succumb to his charm. He forgave her, and kept a straight face when De Chavel said he was going to Czartatz himself.

"You haven't, by any chance, a little personal interest in the lady?" he inquired. He had believed the Colonel when he said that nothing had taken place between them. Very surprising, but he believed him.

"None whatever," De Chavel told him. "I feel I owe it to her after what happened. I shall take her to her sister and see her safe, and then return here. I threatened to kill her husband, and I shall certainly do so. But not, I assure you, because I am in love with his wife."

"If you say so," Murat shrugged. "It's no concern of mine. She's devilishly pretty, though."

"And devilishly vulnerable," De Chavel countered. "I haven't many scruples, but this is one woman I refuse to take advantage of; the poor child's been hurt enough already. Adieu, Sire. Enjoy yourself; but beware of pretty Polish ladies! I can't rescue them all!"

For the first two hours they travelled at good speed, and then the roads were little better than cart tracks, uneven and full of pot-holes after the recent spring rains. At midday they stopped at a posting inn for food, while the horses were watered and fed. She and the Colonel had hardly spoken on the journey; Jana dozed most of the time. He was very attentive to her, but somehow withdrawn, and almost too polite. After the meal they started off again, and as the darkness came, their pace slowed down and the lurching stopped. They sat side by side, wrapped in bearskin travelling rugs, and, thinking him asleep, Valentina leant against his shoulder and drowsed. She awoke at the final stop for the night to find his arm around her and his scarred cheek resting against hers.

Chapter
THREE

Valentina woke after an uneasy sleep on the third day of their journey. They had spent the nights at posting inns along the way, but these grew more and more primitive as they proceeded. At the last place the beds were too dirty to sleep in, and she had spent the night on the floor wrapped in her cloak while De Chavel slept outside the door. Now they were on her own lands, and she leant forward to look out of the window. He was asleep beside her, and Jana snored opposite; they were all dishevelled and exhausted. It had been a tiring and dangerous journey, and without De Chavel's protection the two women travelling alone would have been robbed and molested before they had gone halfway. Valentina moved very carefully so that he shouldn't wake, and pulled the fur-lined rug over him; in the early-morning light his face was lined with fatigue. He had kept vigil most of last night while she and Jana slept. For the first time in five years Valentina knew what it meant to be protected and cherished, to have her needs anticipated so that she never had to ask for anything. It was extraordinary to her that a man could be so gentle; it was painful and disturbing to be in such close physical contact with someone who had held her in her arms and kissed her till her mouth ached, and never be touched by him except to sleep with her head against his shoulder. He had cared for her on the journey as if she were a child; he had never again given a sign that he was aware of her as a woman. Looking at him as he slept, Valentina surrendered to the pain and yearning of her new-found love, for she knew that love had come to her at last. It hurt her to study that face, so stern and distant in repose, with the scar of an old wound riven into his cheek; it hurt unbearably because she longed to lean across and wake him with a kiss, to put out her hand and stroke his face until he opened his eyes and took her in his arms. And yet there was happiness in her disquiet, joy because the emptiness of life was gone, and he was still beside her. She would not allow herself to think for how long or to what end.

The rough road branched into a narrow track; the coach bumped and lurched, so that the two sleepers woke. When De Chavel opened his eyes Valentina was gazing out of the window.

"There's Czartatz! There, up on that rise!"

De Chavel pulled on the cord attached to the coachman's arm and thrust his head out of the window. "Whip them up, we're there!"

The house at Czartatz was first built as a fortress, part of the scattered fortifications designed to repulse Russian invasion and the occasional raid for cattle and women made by isolated Russian marauding bands.

It was not beautiful; the stone towers were square and grey and the front façade was flat and built of the same forbidding stone. Valentina's ancestors had lived there for three hundred years, and only in the last century had her grandparents made improvements and given the old castle a few civilised amenities. Czartatz itself was built on a steep rise, almost a hill, and surrounded by woods and parklands; the estate numbered fifty thousand acres, and by the standards of the big landowners it was a modest holding.

When the coach stopped in the paved courtyard liveried servants came running up to hold the horses and help them down; at the sight of Valentina the senior footman dropped on his knees, kissing her hand and stammering with delight. "Madame, Madame . . . after so long. Ladislaw! Go and fetch Her Highness! Hurry!"

She was so stiff that she could hardly walk up the flight of steep stone steps to the entrance, for a moment she paused, looking round her at the familiar countryside and the faces of servants she had known since she was a child; there were tears of happiness in her eyes. They were in the dark, stone hall when Valentina's sister came to meet them.

"Sandra!"

"Valentina!"

They ran into each other's arms and embraced for a long moment without saying anything; De Chavel stood waiting until at last the elder sister raised her head and looked at him. She put Valentina gently away from her.

"Who have you brought with you?" she said.

She had a rather deep voice; De Chavel stepped up to her and bowed. "I am Colonel de Chavel, of the Emperor's Imperial Guard, Princess. I have accompanied your sister from Danzig."

She was tall for a woman; she was dressed in a black serge riding habit and she carried a crop in one hand. She was not beautiful; her pitch black eyes were slanted in an arrogant Tartar face, framed in black hair. Not beautiful but certainly arresting.

She had her arm round her sister and looking down at her she smiled; a tenderness that was almost maternal transformed her face and made it soft.

"You've both had a long journey," she said. "And a damned uncomfortable one. I'm not going to ask a single question until you've bathed and changed and you've eaten breakfast, little one. And you too, Colonel. My house is at your disposal. Ladislaw! Janos! Attend to this gentleman! Come upstairs with me, Valentina. And someone unsaddle my horse—I shan't be riding this morning."

Still with her arm round her shoulders, Alexandra went upstairs with her sister. De Chavel followed them and at the landing they paused and he saw Valentina turn and look back at him.

"If there's anything you want," she said, "just ask; Ladislaw will get it for you."

"Thank you," De Chavel nodded. He was so weary he could hardly speak; all he wanted was a bath and to sleep through the day.

Half an hour later he was in a deep feather bed, some of the ache and strain gone out of his body after a hot hip bath, and within seconds he was fast asleep. His mission was accomplished; she was safe and with her sister; from the little he had seen of Alexandra Suvaroff, she would be well able to take care of Valentina. He could leave with an easy conscience; he could forget about the whole affair and sleep in peace.

"I had given you up," Alexandra said. "Not a letter from you for two years. I thought you were amusing yourself and had forgotten me." She leaned forward and squeezed Valentina's hand. They were in Alexandra's private sitting room; it was a very feminine room for such a commanding woman, full of flowers and pictures, and the Russian furniture which Irina, Countess Prokov, had brought with her as a bride. Valentina lay on the sofa, her sister beside her; she had no wish to sleep; she was too happy and excited and she had already told the whole story to Alexandra. Only her sister's insistence had made her eat breakfast but when the eggs and sour bread and chocolate came, she discovered that she was famished with hunger.

"He wouldn't let me write," she said. "I tried once but he found the letter, and the poor soul who took it was whipped. I didn't try again."

"I always hated him," Sandra said. "I told our father he was a brute and would make you miserable. What a pity he didn't choose me!"

"You wouldn't have stood against him," Valentina said. "My darling sister, even you would have been cowed after a time. You saw my shoulders——"

"I did." The black eyes gleamed with hatred. "If he'd

done that to me I'd have poisoned him. Poor little one!"
She smiled again, and her voice was gentle. "How he
must have enjoyed bullying you! And then to try and
push you into this Frenchman's bed as if you were some
bondgirl—you Poles have a strange sense of honour!"

"You're half Polish," Valentina reminded her. "You
can't deny that." This was the only point on which they
had ever disagreed.

"I'm nothing," Sandra said. "I belong to no country. I
live here and mind my own business. That's all I ask."

"Even when the war begins?" Valentina said. "When
we're helping the French fight your mother's people?
Won't you take sides then?"

"No," Sandra said. "What is a war to me? Czartatz is
far away from all of it. Let them kill each other; I've
better things to do. And so have you, now that you've
escaped that monster. Tell me," she asked the question
very casually but her glance was shrewd, "what is this
Colonel's real interest in you?"

"Why nothing." Valentina coloured. "I told you the
story. That's all there is." She had omitted that scene in
Murat's private room, because nothing would convince
Alexandra that he had let her go. And being Alexandra,
she wouldn't think any the more of him if he had.

"Very well, if you don't want to tell me, you needn't.
I'm not prying, little one. You have a lover if you want
to; it's about time you learnt that all men aren't swine
and some of them can be quite agreeable, shall we say."
She laughed, and stood up.

"He's not my lover, Sandra," Valentina said. "You
don't know him. He's not like other men."

"Bah! What do you know about men to compare him
with? I may not know him, Valentina, but by God I
know the type! It's not one that takes a woman two
hundred miles in three days for nothing. And puts her
under Imperial protection. I believe you've stolen his
heart, you minx! Incidentally, I'm very grateful to him
for taking me under his policeman's wing. I have a
feeling that our odious Theodore will try and pay you

back—the Poles would dearly love to hang a Suvaroff—even a woman!"

"We're safe," Valentina said. "Nobody will dare touch either of us now. Oh, Sandra, you don't know how happy I am! I can't believe that I'm home with you, and free at last. I can't believe that I'll never see him again! And all this time I've done nothing but talk about myself. How are you—you look so well, and just the same. You never change, Sandra!"

"Nor you," her sister said. "Except that you're prettier than ever. Now you've told me everything, or nearly everything," she mocked, about the Colonel, I mean, you're going to go to bed and sleep. I have some state business to see to, and sooner or later I shall have to ride my new stallion today. None of these clumsy imbeciles can manage him. I'll show him to you tomorrow."

"Perhaps I can ride him, Sandra——"

"Certainly not!" her sister said. "He eats Poles for breakfast, this one. Tadeus broke his arm trying to ride him, and he knows how to deal with horses better than anyone on the estate. You'll have plenty of time to amuse yourself. Now you're going to sleep. We will celebrate tonight, you and I and your Colonel!"

As Valentina explained to De Chavel, the dining hall was too big and gloomy for three people, and unfortunately they had no near neighbours to invite to meet him. Alexandra had prepared their father's old study for the dinner. It was a warm room by the medieval standards of Czartatz; there were fine tapestries on the walls and rugs from Persia on the stone floors. A huge fire of logs burnt in the open fireplace, and three tall eight-branched silver candelabra gave them light. There was a beautiful Russian-embroidered tablecloth on the table and some superb silver, which De Chavel guessed was also Russian, like the silver goblets with the Suvaroff crest engraved on them. He came in dressed in a plain green coat and white breeches, and even Alexandra admitted that he was extraordinarily handsome. He was not the type of man who appealed to her; he was too dominant, not in the sinister way of her brother-in-law Grunowski, but with an unconscious arrogance that challenged her, rousing her own aggressive spirit. He came to her and bowed, kissing the hand she held out to him. She was wearing one of the largest cabuchon rubies on her finger that he had ever seen, and it was matched by a massive necklace that glowed round her neck; her dress was the same rich colour, slashed low across her breasts, and in spite of her height and the way she carried herself, she was surprisingly voluptuous. He looked into the black eyes and they were full of challenge. Some man might overcome this woman, but he would be as rare a specimen as she was. He could hardly believe that she and Valentina were even half-sisters.

"Are you more rested now?" Valentina came in, and he turned to her and took her hand. When he kissed it he noticed that her fingers trembled slightly. She wore a dress of pale yellow silk with a gauze scarf embroidered with gold thread. Her only jewel was the collar of pearls she had been wearing the night she came to Murat's house. She was so beautiful and as he looked at her she flushed.

"I feel extremely well, Madame," he said.

"I only wonder how you've survived the journey." He turned to Alexandra. "It was very uncomfortable, Princess. I've never known anything so welcome as your marvellous bed this morning!"

"Let's hope the dinner will please you as much, Colonel," she said. "We live simply here, but at least my late father kept a good cellar, and he took the trouble to teach me something about wines. Shall we sit down?"

It was a very gay meal; they ate venison cooked in wine with herbs, and De Chavel could truthfully say he had never tasted anything better from the best chefs in Paris. There was a wide selection of delicious Russian and Polish sweetmeats and wines of memorable quality. He noticed that the Princess drank as much as he did and had a head like rock. She was a brilliant conversationalist; she was amusing and stimulating, with a wry and ribald sense of humour, yet he knew that she was watching him and her sister like a mountain lioness with one cub. De Chavel sensed her purpose quite clearly: she wished him to enjoy himself because it would make Valentina happy, and in her fierce way she was showing her own gratitude for what he had done to help her sister. But had she suspected him of one dishonourable act towards Valentina she would have told her servants to cut his throat. They sat on after the food was cleared away; he and Alexandra drank cognac in paper-thin glasses shaped like tulips which marvellously conserved the bouquet, and Valentina sipped champagne.

"If you wish to smoke, Colonel," Alexandra said, "I can offer you some of my dear father's cheroots. It's a pity he had such a poor character; his taste in other things was really quite remarkable. I suppose my lamented mother's fortune helped him develop it." She leant back and laughed, and her white teeth gleamed.

"You'll shock the Colonel, Sandra," Valentina said. "He's not accustomed to hearing parents described like this. But I assure you, it's true. I can remember the day my father told me he had arranged my marriage to Theodore; I always imagined he was fond of me till then. He was delighted, simply delighted. 'It's an excellent match for you,' he kept saying, 'and I shall have a seat on the Diet Council.' He didn't even listen to me when I said I didn't want to marry him."

"He was always trying to make a nice suitable match for me," her sister remarked. "But by God, none of the gentlemen stayed long enough to make the offer! I saw to that!"

"You'd make the most wonderful wife in the world—for anyone who could cope with you," Valentina laughed. "But I can't think of anyone off-hand, can you, Colonel?"

"No." De Chavel shook his head and smiled. "I can't; but no doubt this Prince among men exists, and if you'll forgive me, Princess, I doubt if any ordinary man would do!"

"Marriage," Alexandra said. "what's marriage! Just a life contract with all the advantages to the man! Every time I saw one of those little creatures coming here, all tricked out to catch the rich girl's fancy, I felt like spitting in their faces! 'You'll be a miserable old maid,' my father used to say—mind you," she raised her glass to De Chavel, "he was a little afraid of me too. He could never have done to me what he did to Valentina. I'd have stabbed Theodore on the wedding night, and Father knew it. In the end he left me alone to go my own way. And I like my way very much, thank you. I can do without marriage."

"You know . . ." De Chavel looked up at her; the wine and brandy had affected him more than he knew; he didn't want to look at Valentina; he wanted to talk to the woman on his right who had this refreshing masculine approach to life. She didn't attract him in the least, and all this talk of marriage had opened the old wounds a little.

"You know," he said, "you're the first woman I've ever met who has the same view on that damnable institution as I have! Only I don't think you have the perspective quite right. It's the woman who gets the advantages, Princess; the woman who gets the better of the poor booby of a husband—not all women, of course," he made a gesture towards Valentina. "There are scoundrels like Grunowski, but by God they're few and far between compared to the women who cheat and lie and fool their husbands. Marriage is for idiots, Princess. You and I have better sense! Let's drink to that!"

"To ourselves, Colonel. To the wise ones!" Alexandra drained the glass; she had seen her sister turn white as he spoke. "You should drink with us," she said, and she was suddenly gentle. "Freedom is better, little sister, and you have yours now. We owe you thanks, Colonel, and I would like to express it to you personally. You have brought my sister back to me. God bless you for it."

"I'm happy," he said. "Happy that she's safe. No one will trouble either of you here. I can promise you that."

"So long as the eagles of France fly over Poland, we won't be harmed," Alexandra said. She leant across and patted Valentina's hand. "We will both have to pray for the success of French arms, in spite of what I said this morning about being neutral."

"I shall pray for them every moment," Valentina said.

He didn't mean to look at her; he had turned away because the effect of the wine and the atmosphere was too insidious and she was very near. But he was drawn in spite of himself, and when he met her glance he saw her eyes were full of tears.

"I shall pray for you," Valentina said quietly. "That you will come back safely from this war." She raised her glass and drank to him. "To the victory of France, Colonel!"

They drank the toast, and after a moment Alexandra said, "How long can you stay with us here?"

"No longer than tonight," De Chavel answered. "I have only leave of absence to deliver Madame to her home and then I must return immediately. The order to advance into Russia will come at any moment. I must go back tomorrow; the Emperor himself is on his way to Truro to join the main body of the army."

"Tomorrow?" Valentina said. "You've got to go tomorrow? Can't you wait even one day?"

"Not even one hour," he said quietly. "Believe me, I should like nothing better than to spend some time here. But I am a soldier, Madame, and I can't please myself."

"I didn't know," Valentina said, "I didn't realise it would be so soon. . . ."

"What time will you go?" Alexandra stood up. "We will say goodbye."

"As soon as it's light," he said.

"Sandra," Valentina said suddenly, "Sandra, I would like a few moments alone with the Colonel. I want to thank him and say goodbye in private. Would you leave us, please?"

To his surprise her elder sister smiled; the dark pointed face had a slightly wicked look. She shrugged.

"Of course, little sister. Make your private farewells. I will see you at dawn tomorrow, Colonel. Good night."

At the door she paused. "My sister is still tired," she said. "I know I can rely on you not to keep her up too long."

She closed the door, and De Chavel said abruptly, "May I help myself to some more of this excellent brandy?"

"Of course." Valentina walked away from him to the fire; suddenly she turned and faced him.

"You think I'm very immodest, don't you, asking to speak to you like this?"

"No." He said it deliberately. "I think you're very foolish. Have you forgotten what happened the last time we were in a supper room alone?"

She shook her head. Tomorrow he was leaving. Tomorrow. "I wish I could forget it," she said. "I wish I could say goodbye to you with Sandra tomorrow and never think of you again. But I can't. Something has happened between us.

"That's where you're wrong," he said. "Nothing has happened between us and nothing is going to; I'm going to finish my brandy and you, my foolish little sentimentalist, are going up to join your sister!"

She came to him and faced him. She was strangely calm. Tomorrow he would be gone. She might never see him again.

"I love you," she said. "I don't even know your Christian name. I loved you that first night at the reception. Even afterwards, when you nearly took me by force, I wanted you. I want you now, my love, if you will have me."

He had never meant to touch her; he had no idea how she came to be in his arms, whether he reached out or she came to him first, but the next moment she was pressed against him, and her mouth was covered by his, and he felt her tremble as he drew her down to the sofa, blindly with his eyes closed. There was no force needed now; her passion met his with fierce abandonment. She freed her lips to whisper again and again, "I love you, I love you with all my heart."

And that was what stopped him before it was too late and she had made the complete surrender. "I love you." It was the lying catch-phrase which every woman whimpered in the extremes of pleasure and it meant no more than any of their cries. "I love you, my adored." Liliane used to murmur that with her lips to his ear when she had left another lover a few hours before and he knew nothing of it. Women he couldn't remember had said it to him when they made love, and now this girl, inflamed with passion, whispered it against his lips. Of them all, she was the only one he had ever believed.

She opened her eyes and looked at him; her head was swimming and her heart felt as if it would burst.

"Why," she whispered, "why . . ."

"I don't love you." The words choked in his throat. "I won't make use of you. You ought to thank me for it. Tomorrow I'll be gone. We'll never meet again. Now for the love of Christ go upstairs!"

"I thought I meant something to you." The tears were running down her face but she was unaware of it.

"I thought perhaps you felt a little for me of what I feel for you. I can't believe you don't . . ."

"I want you," he said. "I can't deny that." He put her away from him almost roughly. He couldn't bear her tears; that much weakness still remained in him. That and the sense of honour which had baulked at her seduction. "You're beautiful and I want to make love to you. But that's not love, Valentina. And love is what you need. I can't give it to you. I can't feel it any more for anyone. I had a wife once; I loved her and she betrayed me, with my own officers, my friends, everyone she could get hold of—even Murat. I'm finished with love. But I'm not low enough to take advantage of a foolish girl, however much she thinks she wants me to; go to bed now, for God's sake, child. Forget all this nonsense about love."

"I can't," Valentina said, and she was sobbing. "I can't

forget you and I never will. If you've been hurt, I understand—I'll say goodbye now, and God bless you and bring you safely back, my love."

He felt her tears on his cheek as she kissed him, and then she had gone. He got up and went back to the table; his glass of brandy was still there untouched. He drank it in one swallow, and then, for no reason he could explain, he threw the glass with all his strength into the fireplace.

"I hope you slept well, Colonel."

Alexandra stood unannounced in the doorway of his room; she was dressed in the black riding habit with an old-fashioned tricorn hat under her arm. The dawn was breaking; in half an hour the sun would be up.

"Very well, thank you, Princess. I didn't expect you to be up so early."

"I spent a spent a sleepless night, listening to my sister cry," she said quietly. "What have you done to her, Colonel de Chavel? Hasn't she suffered enough?"

He closed the door. "Sit down; we must discuss this properly. And let me assure you, before we begin, that I have done nothing to Valentina. Thank God."

"Then why is she unhappy?" Alexandra crossed one booted leg over the other; her skirt was divided so that she could ride astride like a man. "She wouldn't tell me anything; she just lay there weeping as if her heart would break. Have you made love to her?"

"Yes. But not in the way that you mean. Your sister is very beautiful, Princess. When we first met I had entirely the wrong opinion of her and I behaved in a way that makes me bitterly ashamed. Luckily I discovered my mistake in time. I tried to make amends by bringing her home to you. Last night she told me she loved me."

"Any fool could see that!" she interrupted curtly. "May I ask what you said to that?"

"I told her the truth," he said. "For her own sake. Believe me, that was my only motive. I told her I didn't love her. Lust is one thing, but not love. I told her to forget the whole affair."

"You surprise me," Alexandra said after a moment. "I have detected some tenderness in you towards her—or am I imagining even that?"

"You are certainly imagining it if you think it means anything more than pity and respect," he said sharply. "I will make myself clear, Princess. I am not Valentina's lover and I am not in love with her. I haven't the slightest desire to become entangled with an inexperienced girl who is dying for a love affair. Your sister is a child in these things. She has been married to a brute, and that's all she knows about men. I think nothing of women; my only concern is not to turn Valentina into one of the sisterhood by spoiling her innocence or destroying her faith. I should certainly have done both if I hadn't told her the truth last night. She's better to cry a few tears and then forget about it. And she will."

"You're very certain, aren't you?" Alexandra said. "You know all about us, don't you, Colonel? You said so last night. Cheats and liars, fooling their poor booby husbands. I am sure you speak from experience. But my sister is a woman as well as a child. She loves you. This is her very first love; I am only afraid it may be her last. There are women for whom there is only one man. If it turns out to be the case with Valentina, then she'll never be happy again. For a man who's got such insight into the female mind, you seem to have made a remarkable mess of the whole business. I hope the first Russian that takes aim at you blows your head off, my dear Colonel."

"Thank you." He made her a bow and she laughed and stood up.

"I like you," she said. "It's a pity the poor little one isn't like me; she's never learnt to take pleasure as it comes and not rely on love." The bright black eyes grew narrow suddenly. "I understand we won't be seeing you again?"

"I think not, Princess," De Chavel said. "Especially if your wish comes true."

"And is my sister really safe from Theodore?" she said. "I know enough about him to be sure he'll try and get her back, certainly when your armies have gone into Russia. He's a vindictive swine, and he won't let Valentina escape without a fight."

"I have made all the arrangements necessary," De Chavel said. "You and Valentina are on the police protection list. So long as she stays here, on the estate, the Count will be powerless to touch her. The same applies to you. Whatever you do, keep Valentina here till the campaign is over."

"And what then?" she said. "Supposing you're victorious, of course."

"We will be," he said shortly. "I give it six months before we return in triumph. If I'm one of those lucky enough to get back, then I shall kill the gentleman. It's the least I owe him for what he did to your sister, and you have no man in the family to do it for you. If I don't come back, I will see that someone else does it for me."

"And if your Emperor loses?" she asked quietly.

"Then you must fend for yourselves," he retorted. "I have the greatest confidence in your ability to take on any man, Princess. Even Count Grunowski. I must go now; the sun is well up."

"I'll ride part of the way with you," Alexandra said. "My sister is sleeping; I shan't wake her."

"Better not," De Chavel said. "You can make my farewells. Take care of her. And tell her to forget me."

"I shall," she said. "I'll do my damnedest."

"I'll be very grateful," he said gravely. "She deserves to be happy."

The carriage was waiting outside, and he climbed in; a big black stallion was brought up. It fretted and reared, and it took two men to hold it. De Chavel leaned out of the window and watched while the Princess sprang up on it; she held it in like a drawn bow, waiting for him to move. As the coach and the rider gathered speed out of the courtyard and down the long road away from Czartatz, Valentina watched them from her window. She stood there until the flying horse and the coach itself dwindled to specks in the distance and then disappeared; while she watched she prayed that in spite of war and her husband, and the agonising fact that he was not in love with her, one day he would come back to Czartatz.

"I appreciate your point of view, Count. I have every sympathy with you." Potocki shook his head at the furious man sitting opposite him; "I'm very sorry but there is nothing we can do."

Grunowski leaned forward in his chair; he had spent twenty-five minutes waiting in the ante-room for his interview with the Count and he was livid with temper. He was angrier still to see the cause of the delay walk out of the Count's room, and recognise the young Major as a member of Murat's staff.

"Do you mean to say, Count, that a French officer can seduce my wife and run off with her, and I have no redress? I can't get her back, I can't make a complaint? It's intolerable."

"I received a call from Major Montesant this morning—you were here when he left, I think—and the version of this incident he gave me is not the same as yours. Colonel de Chavel took your wife to her sister at Czartatz and left her there. He also informed me that both ladies were under French police protection. Our plan, my dear Count, has seriously miscarried. If you have lost your wife in the process, I'm sorry. We have lost an opportunity which will never come our way again. And I hate to think what effect it would have if the matter came to Napoleon's attention. The Major assured me it hadn't, so far. It's been very badly bungled." His eyes were very cold. "You should have told me your wife was capable of betraying the whole plot. I would never have trusted her."

"I believed in her patriotism. And her attachment to her sister. I had no idea she would turn traitor. And for that," the Count said, "she should be punished. You can ignore the affront to my honour, the fact that her lover threatened me in my own house and removed a servant and my wife's possessions under guard—you can accept these outrages, and tell me to do the same—but what of her treason? Her betrayal of Poland? Is she to hide under French patronage for ever?"

Potocki opened a little gold and enamel snuff-box and took two strong pinches; he waited and after a moment sneezed into his handkerchief.

"Forever is a long time," he said. "We can be patient. In a week or so Napoleon's army will march into Russia. We can keep the Countess and her sister in our minds."

Grunowski stood up. "Officially we can do nothing. But unofficially, Count—if I were to take some men to Czartatz and ask to see my wife——"

"You would be arrested when you returned, and I should completely disown you!" Potocki snapped at him. He was not concerned with private vengeance; he was bitterly disappointed at the collapse of their plan to seduce Murat and the unpleasant way in which it had rebounded on his head. The young Major had been polite but very firm. He had explained the intrigue with great courtesy and the assumption that, of course, Count Potocki knew nothing about it, while conveying that French Intelligence held him wholly responsible, and made it very clear that the lady concerned was protected by one of the most powerful men in France, with ready access to the Emperor. Potocki's own impulse was to punish the traitoress at once, but he could afford to counsel patience to the angry husband whose own motives were purely personal. He could wait; he would have to wait. More than likely the Colonel would be killed or wounded in the next few months; most probably official vigilance would relax in Poland during the campaign and it would then be possible to deal with two women on a lonely estate. But not if the vindictive Grunowski made a premature attempt. That would ruin everything.

"You are to do absolutely nothing!" Potocki said. "All

you'd accomplish by any action at the moment is to have the two of them sent to France where we would never be able to lay hands on them. You are partly responsible for this failure, Count. You totally misjudged your wife, and I was bound to rely on you for that. You further misjudged her by letting her go to meet Murat that night and so escape. And I'm not blaming you as much as others will, believe me! Now you must keep quiet. Let the scandal die. Lose your wife before the world, and wait until you hear from me."

"One thing," Grunowski said. "Promise me that when the time comes to take her you will give that task to me. And to me alone, to do it as I see fit. It's my due, as a husband."

"I promise that you will be the one," Potocki said. "When it's safe to punish the Countess's treason I will send for you myself. For the time being, you must be content with that."

Grunowski stood up and bowed. "As you command, I shall do nothing till I hear from you."

"Good." The Count held out his hand. "Be patient," he said quietly, "and we will have our revenge."

Chapter
FOUR

━━━━◆◆━━━◆━━━◆◆━━━━

Three pontoon bridges straddled the width of the River Niemen: sappers of the French Army had been sinking the supports and erecting the framework to bear the weight of the heavy wooden flooring. They had taken some weeks to complete the work, and after the pontoons were finished they spent a few days fishing or swimming in the river, and amusing themselves with the local Polish women who came swarming down to their camp. The bridges were magnificently constructed to bear the weight of half a million men, their horses, artillery and supplies over the week-long period it would need to transfer them all to Russia. They waited under the hot June sun on the morning of the twenty-fourth, untried and untrodden, like three dark virgins for their soldier bridegrooms. It was a superstition of the sappers that, before an invasion, nobody crossed the bridges before the advance guard. For weeks the countryside around the river where the bridges were had been filling up with soldiers. The camps spread over the fields like a mushroom crop; canvas, wagons, bivouacks, stockaded horses, artillery and mountains of supplies. There were soldiers and quartermasters and artillery men and cooks and orderlies and army surgeons, and the staff officers had been arriving in their carriages and taking the best accommodation in the neighbourhood. Which is the way of staff officers, and why, next to their generals who seldom see the front, the Army hates them. Women and

children were part of that enormous confusion of men
and materials, thousands of army whores and common
soldiers' wives and families, camped out in the fields with
their men, and at night there were fights and singing
around the fires, and some deserted with Polish women
and were mostly brought back and immediately shot.
The Cuirassiers, the Chasseurs, the Polish Lancers, the
Imperial Grenadiers, the Seventh, Ten and Fourteenth
Artillery regiments, the Ordinance and Stores, the corps
of field surgeons; these were only a few of the regiments
of the greatest army of invasion that the world had ever
seen. There were men from the south, from the east and
west and north and from central France; men whose pa-
tois made them impossible to understand, men of all
types and ethnic variations within the borders of French
domination. There were Italians and Poles and Serbs, ex-
iled Scots and Irish and a few renegade English, and
these were joined by twenty thousand hostile Prussians
and thirty thousand unreliable Austrians, part of the human levy Napoleon had forced out of his allies. On the
morning of the 24th, two hours after dawn, three
columns moved in formation towards the bank of the
Niemen and drew up before each of the three bridges. A
regiment of cavalry, comprising Marshal Gouchy's
Cuirassiers, and two infantry regiments from the Corps
of Marshal Ney. At a signal from the central column, led
by a magnificently mounted officer in the bright breast-
plate and red plumed helmet of the Cuirassiers, the first
horses and men began to cross the pontoons. The army
behind them began to cheer. The cheers were uneven
and spasmodic at first but as the trickle became a stream
they found impetus and co-ordination. The cheers rolled
over the advance guard like thunder; the sun rose higher
and the men began to sweat in their thick uniforms; the
bridges creaked beneath their ever-moving burden and
the river flowed on underneath. By the time it was dark
twenty thousand men and a thousand horses had crossed
into Russia. The invasion had begun.

De Chavel had been travelling with Napoleon's entourage for the past three days; the Emperor had received him coldly on his return from Czartatz. He was fully informed of the reason for his Intelligence Chief's absence, and the knowledge that his supposed allies in the Grand Duchy were spying on him, combined with the details of a stupid intrigue involving Murat with yet another woman, had put him in a bad temper which he vented on De Chavel. "You are not, I trust, meddling with this Countess Grunowska yourself," he said; his eyes were as flat as stones, with the dull glint in them which meant he was about to lose his temper. De Chavel had countered quickly and cooly.

"I was not the man the lady was set to catch, Sire. I merely prevented the liaison and then gave the unhappy person our protection. Which, I assure you, she needs very badly."

"Everybody needs something from us," the Emperor said curtly. "We are called upon to give, and give again and again, and when we ask something in return—ah, that's a different tale!" The Austrians were being as difficult as they dared over his demand for more troops and more money to help in the Russian campaign, and considering that he had beaten them into the ground at Wagram, and then married their Archduchess and bolstered the Austrian Emperor because he was his father-in-law, Napoleon was furious at their ingratitude. Everyone hated and envied him and snapped at his heels like furtive curs when his back was turned, however much they cringed before his face. He had married into the Hapsburgs, and he knew he couldn't even trust them. Or his wife; she was stupid and superficial—it was his grief to be able to see her so clearly, but he felt the need of support from someone close to him, beside his soldiers. In the last few months he had spent more time playing with his little son, in his search for affection, than he wasted on seeking it from his wife. Only Marie Walewska welcomed him with warmth and never asked for anything, or uttered a reproach. He loved her for that in his own way, but it was not enough. Sexually she had always been timid and haunted by scruples; in the end when she pleaded to withdraw from that aspect of their relationship, so that she could make peace with her conscience, Napoleon had agreed without much regret. She could not be beside him now, when he needed not a former mistress but a wife, an Empress, to support him and guard France till he returned. Even Josephine, whom he had adored with such public, foolish passion, had intrigued against him and taken lovers while he was away at the wars. He was not disposed to listen to the story of the Countess Grunowska with any sympathy.

"Very well," he said. "The affair is finished. You have made arrangements to have this Grunowski watched? And his associates? Including Potocki—one can't trust anyone, it seems!"

"It has been done, Sire," De Chavel said. "And now I have a request to make."

"I am busy," the Emperor said coldly. "If it's a personal request, I advise you to ask another time."

"It is personal, Sire," De Chavel said. "But now is the time to ask you, and not later. I want to return to my regiment."

Napoleon looked up. "You are asking to go back into the field? You want to go back under Ney's command?"

"Yes, Sire. My work here is finished; I shall be wasted on the intelligence staff in Russia. I've served you in that capacity for a year; now I beg you to let me fight again."

"Eh," the Emperor said, half to himself. "It's a change to hear someone wanting to get into the battle instead of out of it. Tell me something, De Chavel! The truth, no lies—the plain truth!"

"Yes, Sire, the truth, I promise you. What is it?"

"In your heart, do you think we'll win?"

The question shocked him; it shocked him even more to see the Emperor's sallow face with the dark eyes sunken into it with anxiety, watching him and waiting to hear his fears allayed. Do you think we'll win? It was incredible.

"I surprise you," the Emperor said suddenly. "I can see it in your face, Colonel. I surprised myself. *I* am confident—make no mistake about it! *I* believe in victory. But all around me people are whispering, doubting. . . . I want to know what my soldiers think—*they* are the important ones. Answer me. Do you see victory?"

"Yes, Sire." De Chavel didn't hesitate. "I have served under you for nearly fourteen years. I have fought with you from Egypt to Italy right through Europe. I have never seen you lose a battle. You will defeat the Czar, just as you've defeated all your enemies. Your army knows this. As you said, Sire, it's the soldiers who count. And they will follow you over the edge of the world."

Napoleon stood up; there was a slight flush in his face, and like all Italians he was easily moved to tears; they were in his eyes as he held out his hand to De Chavel.

"You are relieved of your duties, Colonel. I personally attach you to myself, under the command of Marshal Ney. And I thank you. When the Army speaks with that voice there can only be victory ahead."

Three days after the advance guard crossed the Niemen into Russia the Emperor and his staff arrived. He came attended by Murat and his favourite, Marshal Junot, who had served under him as aide-de-camp from the Italian campaigns in 1789. Napoleon rode his grey horse; the veteran of many campaigns, it had carried him across Europe, and many thousands had seen it in the smoke of battle standing sentinel well within enemy fire, the little Emperor motionless on its back, directing the attack. Now the famous grey approached the central pontoon at the head of a long and brilliant cavalcade of Marshals and staff officers, their splendid uniforms and richly accoutred horses contrasting with the small man in his dark field grey coat and black hat with the cockade of Imperial France on its brim, riding his plainly saddled horse up to the bridge. There was absolute silence for the first few moments; the hot sun beat down upon an incredible scene that June day, setting flashes of light off the massed bayonets and lances and the glittering breastplates of the great host of men waiting for their Emperor to join them on the opposite bank of the river, dancing like fire amongst the bright caterpillar stretched out behind him, moving so very slowly forward. De Chavel was with the advance party of the Imperial staff. He was mounted on a fine chestnut and he kept it standing, tossing its head with impatience, as Napoleon advanced to the pontoon. There was not a sound beyond the irregular jingling of bridles among the escorts as the grey horse walked forward on to the bridge; there was no sound except that of the hoof-beats of Napoleon's horse crossing the wooden bridge into Russia. It was a moment of extraordinary simplicity and indescribable emotion. It only lasted a few minutes, and then the head of the column began to move forward after the Emperor and they crossed the pontoon three abreast. As Napoleon reached the opposite bank there was a cheer from his waiting armies which shook the ground and rolled over their heads like thunder. De Chavel was directly behind Marshal Davoust; as they too stepped on to Russian soil, Davoust turned and looked at him. He was a small man with a precise manner and he was staid and unemotional except when he was fighting.

"I don't suppose there's another man in the world who knows how to win his troops like the Emperor," he said. "Listen to them; you'd think we'd won already!"

"He has something," De Chavel said. "Men who fight with him, love him. That's all it is. I'd follow him to hell."

"Yes, well," the Marshal said, "that's what you're doing, my friend. And we're all doing it with you. God help us!"

The nearest town was Kovno, and it was said to be garrisoned by a small Russian force; it was a few days' march away, and beyond it was Wilna, where the Czar Alexander and his staff were quartered. At Wilna the French Army would meet the Russians in what they expected to be the first major engagement of the war.

Very slowly the enormous mass of men, animals and

transports began their journey, and the character of the countryside began to change with every mile. De Chavel rode with his own detachment of the Imperial Guard; there were now fifty thousand of the élite of the Imperial Army, men of such fighting calibre that there were no troops in the world to equal them, and they were commanded by men like Marshal Ney, by Murat, by Davoust and by Lannes.

For the first few days of that long march De Chavel felt a renewal of his old happiness at the idea of combat; he had grown cynical and stale in his intelligence duties; now, with a good horse under him and men of the first fighting quality behind him, he was expectant and alive again. War did not frighten him, he felt no shrinking at the prospect of death or wounds; he meant what he said to Davoust as they crossed the Niemen. He would have followed his Emperor to hell and fought the devil himself. One of the Majors in his platoon was a graduate of St. Cyr Academy with the improbable name of Marie Jean Macdonald; he was a kinsman of the famous Marshal and a descendant of the fugitive Catholic sects who had taken refuge in France after their ill-fated rebellion against the English nearly seventy years before. De Chavel liked the younger man; he was brave but well disciplined and he had seen action in many of the major campaigns, including the disastrous Peninsula War where he had served under Marshal Soult.

He spurred his horse to come up with the Colonel and they fell into a slow jogging trot. The sun was blazing down and the clouds of dust they raised met that which drifted backwards from the advance guard; it was fine yellow dust and it settled in the eyelids and nostrils, and wedged itself under the collars of tight uniforms. The horses disliked it and were restless and all along the lines men were coughing and spitting.

"It's damned hot," De Chavel said. He wiped his face with a handkerchief, easing it under the line of his helmet where the sweat had gathered. "I'll be glad to see

Wilna. We should have some word from the advance at Kovno."

"We should," Major Macdonald said. "Tell me, Colonel, how much of the terrain is like this? It's very barren."

"I don't know," De Chavel said. "It should improve as we go further in."

"I hope so," the Major said. "There's hardly a tree or a bush in sight and there's no grazing for the horses—nothing at all. It reminds me of Spain in some ways."

"I notice what an impression that country made on you," the Colonel said; he was becoming irritated by his junior officer's constant references to the one campaign in which he had not taken part. "I'd advise you to forget it. The Emperor's sensitive about that war—you ought to know that!"

"I know it only too well, sir," Major Macdonald said stonily. "Everyone who fought in the cursed place hates the sound of its name. Those of us who came back, at least. But I'm sorry to say it again. This country reminds me of it. There's the same barrenness, the same lack of natural supplies. I hope to God we have taken that into account."

De Chavel didn't answer him at once. The discordant note in all the fanfares of glory jarred on him and he was more sensitive to any appearance of doubt because it had come first from Napoleon himself. Then Davoust, making that remark at the Niemen; God help us. And comparisons in a defeatist attitude. "I should go back with your men, Major," De Chavel said, and the Major saluted and, turning his horse's head, rode back to his place in the column.

On July 1st the Emperor entered the ancient city of Wilna, where his enemy the Czar had stayed only a few days before. Heat, thirst and lack of provisions in the arid countryside had cost his army the astonishing total of twenty thousand horses and two thousand men in the space of the few days since they had crossed the Niemen.

And the Russians had not waited to give battle to Ney at Kovno or to Napoleon himself at Wilna. They had simply taken everything in the way of food and fodder and set fire to what they had to leave behind, and withdrawn deeper into their own country.

"Alexandra! Has the messenger come?" Valentina called out as she ran up the stairs; she had been out riding for the past two hours. They had been waiting for news for three days and the suspense was more than Valentina could bear. It was also trying the patience of her sister, who declared that if she were asked the same question about the messenger one more time she would scream. As she dismounted Valentina saw one of the grooms leading away a horse that was covered in dust, its head hanging wearily.

"Alexandra! Alexandra! Where are you?"

She stopped for a moment at the head of the stairs, and her sister came out of her study. "He's here," she said. "Come and read it for yourself."

She gave Valentina a stained and creased copy of a Polish news sheet; the man who had brought it had ridden for a week from Warsaw; he was down in the servants' quarters being given something to eat.

" 'The Imperial Army has advanced to within fifty kilometers of Moscow, where it is reported that the main Russian forces under General Kututzov are waiting to do battle with them. The forces of His Imperial Majesty the Emperor of the French have suffered heavy casualties in the advance since the battle of Smolensk where the numbers of Russian dead exceeded fifty thousand and thirty thousand French perished on the field. . . .' " Valentina threw the paper down, and covered her face with her hand. "Oh my God, my God! Thirty thousand. He's dead, Sandra—I know he is!" She sat down and began to weep.

"Don't be ridiculous," Alexandra said quickly. She picked up the sheet and read it. Then she went and knelt beside her sister. Gently she put her arm round her. For the past three months Valentina had spent her time waiting for news of the war in Russia, and lying sleepless with anxiety for the man she loved. Morning after morning Alexandra found her drawn and hollow-eyed after a vigil spent in tears and prayers; time had done nothing to alleviate this hopeless passion for someone who had told her plainly that it was not returned. Alexandra had begun by laughing at her and then reproaching her angrily for lack of pride and common sense. Now she admitted that what her sister was suffering was beyond taunts or reason. There was nothing to be done but comfort her. Her own words of prophecy to the Colonel had come true. For some women there is only one man. One love. And this had happened to Valentina. She had fallen in love in a way that Alexandra could not begin to understand; she understood passion, but even so the depth and power of Valentina's longing for De Chavel was a revelation to her. But the aching pain of loving, of needing to give and give again to another human being, was something alien to her own spirit. Except in respect of her own sister. But not for a man. She could never suffer for any man as Valentina was doing. Privately she wished him dead and damned to hell a thousand times before he had come into her sister's life to utterly destroy her happiness.

"Listen to me," she said. "I don't believe your Colonel's dead. He's not even wounded. I know it."

"How can you know?" Valentina asked her. "No, Sandra. This time I'm right. My instinct tells me something has happened to him at last. I'm sure of it. This battle for Moscow—what's the date of that paper?"

"September 20th. Don't you see that news is weeks out of date—the battle is fought and over long ago! Valentina, there were half a million men fighting for France—why should your Colonel be one of thirty thousand?"

"I don't know," Valentina said. She folded the paper and dropped it to the floor. "I don't know where or how it happened. Until now I was afraid for him, but not sure. Now I'm sure. Leave me alone, Sandra. Please."

"Very well." Her sister got up. She stood looking down at Valentina. "I think you're being foolish, my poor little one. I've said all this to you before. I won't say it to you now. If he's dead, it may be months, a year or more even, before you will be able to find out. Meanwhile you sit here grieving, wasting your life! I can't do anything with you. God help me, I can't do anything *for* you, either. I'll leave you alone, if that's what you want."

Valentina sat on until it grew dark, the news sheet lying on the floor at her feet. She didn't cry or move; the certainty that De Chavel was dead or mortally wounded was too strong to allow her the relief of tears. For the past three months the reports had been the same; Napoleon's army was advancing further and further into Russia without ever forcing the issue of a major battle. Disease and constant harrying by Cossacks along their route had cost the French enormous casualties. The Russians were setting fire to their own towns and villages, poisoning the water and destroying the crops so that not one grain of corn or blade of grass or cut of fresh meat was left for the invaders.

Even with the sparse information available, most of it presented in terms favourable to France, it was obvious that Napoleon's campaign was not going in the way he had expected. Valentina was not concerned with the outcome of the war; every skirmish was a threat to the man she loved, every rumour of dysentery and typhoid outbreaks among the French troops brought her the mental image of De Chavel lying sick and dying of the disease. The inactivity of her life at Czartatz was a torture to her; the days passed so slowly that their tranquillity drove her mad; all the pursuits she once loved, the long walks and rides, needlework and reading, and the stimulus of her sister's company, meant nothing to her now. She lived in a useless vacuum while the world beyond was blazing and De Chavel was fighting, perhaps falling under Russian bullets while she sat safe and idle. At least there had been no major battle until now; but thirty thousand had fallen at a place called Smolensk and when that report was written, the French and Russian armies were facing each other for the decisive battle before Moscow itself. And it was all over. The dead were mouldering unburied on the battlefield, victory or defeat had been decided weeks ago, and she knew nothing of the outcome. She had no guide but instinct, and for the first time that intuitive sense told Valentina that De Chavel had fallen, and she knew the premonition was true. When Jana came into the room she didn't look up or speak; the maid glanced at her anxiously and lit the candles, drawing the window curtains, and putting wood on the dying fire.

"It's nearly supper time, Madame," she said. "Her Highness says won't you come down?"

"No, Jana." Valentina shook her head. "I've no appetite tonight. I'll see my sister in the morning."

"I hear there's been a battle," Jana said; she watched her mistress anxiously.

"Yes, two battles by now. With heavy losses."

"And the Colonel, Madame . . . ?" She hardly dared to ask the question.

"There's no way of knowing," Valentina said slowly. "And as long as I hide here I shall never know. I've made up my mind, Jana. I can't stay here like this. I'm going back to Warsaw."

On September the 7th, very early in the morning, the battle of Borodino, which was to decide the fate of Moscow, began with the opening French bombardment from six hundred guns. The weather had deteriorated in the last few weeks; rain had turned the countryside into a blackened sea of mud where nothing grew and the miserable starving horses floundered, the wagons sinking to their axles. For the last part of the advance the artillery had to be hauled by teams of exhausted men; morale was low and tempers, even among the Marshals, were dangerously short.

Davoust and Murat had quarrelled violently; they had

never liked each other and the contrast in personalities
between the dour, brave professional soldier and the
flamboyant Gascon King irritated both into childish dis-
plays of spleen and futile arguments. The Emperor himself was gloomy and suffering from lack of sleep. On
that September morning he had a heavy cold and a low
fever. The terrain was marshy with low hillocks and the
ribbon of the Moscova River ran to the left. Borodino itself was a village, and the Russian forces were estimated
at one hundred and twenty thousand with more artillery
of heavier calibre than the French. They had entrenched
themselves in a series of redoubts along the right of the
land where the road to Moscow lay; their positions were
protected by scattered woodlands and the hummocks of
ground and treacherous marshes. For hours the two artil-
leries bombarded each other; the noise was intolerable
and there were not many in the French ranks with
enough left to enjoy the overture to the play in which
they were soon going to be the principals. The French
had been advancing through one of the worst countries
in the experience of any veteran among them. Major
Macdonald's comparison with Spain was more than justified; the men had been bedevilled by scorching heat before the drenching rains, by flies and the accompanying
diseases where water was in short supply and the horses
perished in thousands. There was no food or shelter; the
Russian peasants fled, or were driven away by their own
troops; the villages were set on fire, and everywhere
they marched the sky was dark with the smoke of burning crops. There was no livestock; what couldn't be
evacuated was slaughtered on the spot and left to pu-
trefy; often the carcasses were thrown into the streams
so that man or beast who drank from them was poisoned. And at night when they were tired and hungry
the mounted Cossacks struck, harrying and raiding, so
that the exhausted men got little sleep. Stragglers were
found with their throats cut; sentries mounted guard in
twos and threes for fear of the lightning attacks by

bands of Russians, who struck and then galloped off before a shot could be fired at them.

There had been no pitched battle, at which the French excelled, no opportunity to vent their frustration and their misery upon the ever-retreating enemy, and the lack of fighting affected discipline. Of the half a million men who had crossed the Niemen that hot day two months ago, only one hundred and eighty thousand were left fit to do battle. The rest had died of disease, had been cut down at the rear, or killed at Smolensk where the hopes of forcing a decision had been lost when the Russians once again withdrew after a bloody engagement and huge casualties, before Napoleon could beat them decisively.

Countless thousands had deserted, only to be hunted down and killed by the Russians.

And yet the heart of the French army, the élite fifty thousand of the Old Guard, was untouched. The Emperor had kept them in reserve at Smolensk.

At dawn the French bugles could be clearly heard in the Russian redoubts blowing the "advance" and across the uneven ground the first lines of French troops made their attack against the smaller redoubts; the major forces were concentrated against the great redoubt in the centre. A wind of gale force blew over the battlefield.

De Chavel took his troops against the great redoubt that morning; the attack on it was led by Marshal Ney, one of the best soldiers De Chavel had ever served under, and a man of complex and emotional character. He was the son of a cooper from Alsace Lorraine, and there was a peasant's thickness in the sturdy build, the square face and stubby features of the great Marshal in his brilliant uniform. Essentially he was a man of action, a man with Teutonic qualities always at variance with his French temperament; happy to carry out a direct order no matter how impossible the odds, completely without personal fear in combat, a General whose men would follow him anywhere. Sensitive to a pathological degree about his origins, Ney was irritable, always suspecting slights, and, in peacetime, apt to make the wrong decisions.

De Chavel admired and understood him; he preferred the touchy lion-hearted soldier to someone equally brave like Murat. Only last night Murat had called him over during an inspection and asked him whether he didn't wish himself back with his little Countess in Danzig and then passed on, laughing. De Chavel had scarcely thought of Valentina except when he was restless for a woman, and it was always her face and body that came to mind, and the memories of holding her that haunted him. He would have given his soul for the chance to take her in his arms during the last few weeks; but this was lust for her and not love; love had no place in his emotions any more. He had resented Murat's jibe with unreasonable bitterness. It reminded him suddenly of his wife Liliane, and how the night before a battle he used to write her long letters full of tenderness and passion, as if she were a kind of talisman against death. Murat had been her lover; perhaps in his heart he had never forgiven him, more than any of the others who had enjoyed his wife.

Perhaps that was why he resented the remark about Valentina, and why on this particular day he was glad that Ney was his commander and not the Marshal King of Naples. He had a strong presentiment that he would never fight another battle, and he felt very calm. He was not afraid to die; he no longer actually sought death as he used to do, now he could merely meet it and feel indifference. It was the best frame of mind for any soldier, this placid acceptance that the day would be his last. He had made ready during the bombardment, inspected his men and had a bottle of wine with Major Macdonald. The two had become friends. He was in his place with his troops when the order to advance against the great redoubt was given.

Again and again the troops rushed the entrenchment, only to be driven back down the slopes by blinding fire from the Russians, and then counter-attacked by the enemy. The fiercest hand-to-hand fighting with bayonet and sword took place that morning and on into the afternoon, until at last the French had overwhelmed the first line of entrenchments, and then the second and third were taken and the redoubt fell. It was within the last twenty minutes of that final assault that a Captain Nickoliev leapt down from the third escarpment and threw himself on the French officer who was leading his men up from the second line. For a moment they came face to face, and De Chavel brought his arm down in a sweep of steel that met bone and sinew and was torn out of his hand as it wedged in the Russian's body. In the moment before he fell and died, Nickoliev fired his pistol at point-blank range and De Chavel met the red flash and the excruciating pain for a second of consciousness before he pitched down on top of his enemy. The troops fought round them and over them and then passed on. By mid-afternoon the left-hand redoubt had been taken by the French and the redoubt on the right was evacuated, its Russian forces fleeing back. A savage counter-attack gave the central redoubt back to the Russians, and towards late afternoon the final French assault was launched upon it, led in person by Marshal Ney. Bodies lay thick upon the scarred and blackened ground. Bodies sank in the stinking marshes and lay in the woods and the scorched ruins of Borodino itself, shattered cannon and dead horses shared the battlefield with mounds of dead and wounded, and it was thickest on the slopes leading to the great redoubt, where at last the French flag was flying in what was to be the costliest victory of the whole campaign. In his tent the Emperor sat with bowed head, counting the appalling total of his losses, and the dusk came, covering the frightful sight of war all round the countryside while searchers began moving over the field looking for wounded, and often mercifully killing those too badly hurt to be moved. Major Macdonald himself and an orderly found De Chavel's body, half covered by a dead infantryman, with the corpse of a

Russian Captain underneath him. The ground was sodden with blood, and nobody moved or groaned.

"He's dead, Sir," the orderly said. He bent down to the Colonel and placed a hand on the other side of his shattered chest and arm. He had been shot at a range of a foot or less, and someone had sabred him afterwards, probably when he made a movement.

"Is there no heart-beat? Nothing?" Macdonald demanded.

"So slight it's hardly worth the trouble of bringing him in," the orderly said. "He's as good as dead already. Leave him, Sir. I can hear a man groaning over there—may I go to him?"

"Yes, go," the Major said. He bent down and tried to feel some murmur of life in the still body of his Colonel. It was growing darker, and it would soon be too late to pick his way among the bloody debris on the field.

On an impulse he heaved De Chavel up and lifted him upon his back. If he was dead when they got back to the encampment it would hardly matter. Nothing mattered to Macdonald after that frightful day in which he had lost so many friends and a full three-quarters of his men, except that the man he had come to love and admire during the whole hellish campaign shouldn't be left to rot like a dead dog upon that filthy field.

The surgeons had set up improvised field hospitals, and these were full of wounded and dying men; they were rough tents pitched on the bare ground, and the doctors worked by the light of pitch torches. The sounds and smells were indescribable; Macdonald himself carried De Chavel to the nearest centre, and though he was a hardened veteran of war and not much moved by the bloody aftermath of battle, he almost vomited at the scene inside the tent flaps. Men lay on the earth, groaning and screaming; the smell of blood was so overpowering it was like an abattoir; orderlies moved among the wounded, stepping over them, stumbling over bodies, trying to bandage gaping wounds. At the far end of the tent two army surgeons in crimson aprons operated on

tables by the flickering torch lights. Arms and legs and
several hands and feet lay underneath like offal at the
butchers. An orderly came up to the Major.

"We've no room here, Sir," he said. "As fast as we
throw out the dead, the quicker more wounded come in.
He looks gone to me—"

"Fetch me a surgeon," Macdonald snapped. "Hurry,
damn you," he shouted as the man began to speak again.
"Don't argue with me or I'll break your neck! Get a surgeon here!"

Carefully he eased the Colonel's body down in a space
near the flap; a dead trooper of Cuirassiers lay nearby,
and Macdonald dragged him feet first to the entrance
and left him outside. Burial parties were collecting the
corpses and bundling them into shallow trenches. It was
the best they could do; there was no hope of burying
the thousands out on the fields and in the woods.

He moved De Chavel into the dead trooper's place,
and knelt beside him; a moment later an army surgeon
came up wiping his hands on the red apron. "Major—I
have twenty men waiting for operations—"

"Examine this officer," Macdonald said angrily. "I
think there's a heart-beat left. He's a favourite of the
Emperor's. He must be saved!"

"Very well, in that case. But he looks dead to me."
The surgeon cut away the tattered uniform coat, and exposed a hideous blackened wound encrusted with hard
blood. He grimaced, and bent to the left side of the
chest, listening to the heart. After a moment he
straightened up, and lifted one closed eyelid in the ashen
face.

"Well?" Macdonald demanded.

"He's still alive," the surgeon said. "It's incredible
what the human body can endure. There's a bullet in his
chest—that right arm looks bad—nasty sabre slash—can't
tell if it's cut into the bone. I'll have to take the bullet
out and clean that wound. Orderly! Bandages and a
chest dressing here!" He turned to Macdonald. "I don't

think for a moment he'll live to get on the table," he said. "He's lost too much blood and the ball must be a few inches from the heart. But when I've finished with the next case I'll see what I can do for him. His name, please, and rank; if he's so important I must make a note for the casualty lists."

"Colonel De Chavel, Imperial Guard," the Major said. "I'll come back in an hour."

"Two hours would be better. We'll do what we can for him."

It was more than two hours before the surgeon sent an orderly to see if the Colonel was still alive, and to his surprise the man said that he was, and was showing signs of consciousness. They brought him to the plain wooden table which was black and slippery with blood, and strapped him by the arms and legs; there was no laudanum left to deaden pain, and the surgeon kept his meagre supply of brandy for those who were fully conscious. De Chavel lay motionless, a leather thong between his teeth to prevent him biting through his tongue, his face and body the colour of clay, except where the blood seeped through the bandages.

The surgeon extracted Captain Nickoliev's bullet, and muttered to himself; it was indeed a bare four inches from the sluggishly beating heart. A quick examination of the damaged right arm and shoulder joint showed bone splintering and jagged edges. He had seen too much gangrene in wounded men to leave anything to chance. If the Colonel survived that hole in his chest he would be dead of the arm in a few days.

The surgeon took it off at the shoulder. When the Major returned in the small hours he had an order signed by Ney himself to remove Colonel de Chavel from the hospital tent to the stag quarters, if he were still alive. When Macdonald saw what had been done to him, he wished with all his heart that he had left his friend to die.

"You are perfectly certain she is coming to Warsaw?"

the Count demanded. The messenger who had brought the newspaper to Czartatz nodded. The Count had been paying him for some weeks to report everything he saw and heard at Czartatz and he seemed very interested in his latest report.

"I heard the Countess arguing with her sister," the man insisted. "She said: 'I'm going to Warsaw to find out what's happening—if he's dead I want to know. I shall die if I stay here any longer!'"

"Ah," the Count said, "and what did the Princess say to this?"

"She was very angry," the man said. "She said the Countess would be lost if she left the estate. They had a quarrel in the end, and I heard the Countess say: 'I'm going, I don't care what happens to me. I'm going to Warsaw, I'll go to Russia to find him if I have to!'"

"Very good," the Count said. "You've done well. Here." He counted out four silver coins and gave them to the man. "What you must do is go back to Czartatz, find some place where you can lodge, and the moment you see or hear that the Countess is leaving, send word to me. Then keep a watch for her sister."

"I'll go to Russia to find him." So they were lovers after all, this French Colonel and his wife. Theodore had never been jealous in his life before; what he experienced then was a sense of impotent fury at the fact of anything belonging to him being stolen by someone else. And of his wife loving the man enough to risk her life by leaving her safe refuge and venturing out in search of him. Even to Russia. It was hysterical, of course, and quite unlike Valentina. She had been so calm and level always; even after he had thrashed her she had kept her self-control. It convulsed him with rage to think of her losing it in this fashion over the Frenchman; what had he done to awaken in her the response, the passion which had always eluded the Count? It was an unbearable humiliation, and only the extraordinary news his spy had brought gave him hope of revenging himself.

She was leaving Czartatz. In spite of her sister, in spite of what her lover must have made her promise, Valentina was coming back to Warsaw. He smiled to himself and set out immediately for Count Potocki's house.

"I told you to be patient," Potocki said. "I told you we would deal with her in time. I'll confess I didn't expect it would be so soon. The moment she leaves her own boundaries, she's ours!"

"I propose to take a small force of men, say a dozen, and make the arrest myself," Theodore said. "I can then remove her to my house at Lvov, where sentence can be executed. No one will ever know."

Potocki hesitated. He knew that if the Count were allowed to spirit his wife away to the isolated fortress house at Lvov he would exact a punishment far in excess of what any Diet Court would pronounce. He waited, weighing the advantage of having her disappear without trace against the danger of French reprisals when it was known that she had been given over to her husband. The fortunes of France were in the balance at that time; the news from Russia was slow and unreliable. There were constant reports of battles and huge casualties, and these were followed by rumours that the Czar has been assassinated, or had sued for peace. The latest news was of a French victory at Borodino, but at frightful cost. It was impossible to say whether the final outcome would be worth all that the campaign had cost Napoleon in men and war materials. Potocki decided to take a middle course in the Grunowski affair. It might still be necessary to explain to the French military authorities what had happened to the mistress and protégée of Colonel de Chavel.

"I will authorise you to make the arrest," he said. "I promised you that, and I shan't break my word. But you are to bring her to Warsaw to stand trial. A secret tribunal will consider her case and she can be kept in the Lubinski prison. Your wife is a traitress, Count, and if she's to be punished, then it must be done according to the law. She cannot be put to death by you, or it will be said that her real crime was adultery. You must appreciate this."

The Count didn't answer. He stood up, facing the impassive statesmen, and knew that if he argued he would not be allowed any part in the affair. "You are afraid of French enquiries," he said at last.

"I must bear them in mind," the Count Potocki said. He didn't add that he intended keeping Valentina Grunowska alive until he knew whether to expect what remained of the Grand Armée as victors or fleeing in defeat. She could rot in the Lubinski for a few months, and be quietly put to death when he felt sure she was no longer protected or remembered. "It's a pity we shan't catch her sister in the same trap," he remarked. He had hated the Russians all his life, and the existence of the wealthy Princess Suvaroff at Czartatz had been an irritation to him and other members of the Diet for some time.

Grunowski smiled. "Oh, but we will," he said. "I assure you; the moment she finds out that her sister has been taken, she will come looking for her. We will have them both!"

"Excellent." Potocki smiled his wan, cold smile, and stood to end the interview. "*Au revoir*, my dear Count. I shall wait till I hear from you again."

"That will be when I bring my wife to Warsaw," Theodore said quietly.

"Madame, I beg of you—don't go!" Jana had done as her mistress ordered and packed a few clothes in a valise, and ordered the coach which hadn't been used since their father's death. Now she implored Valentina, with tears running down her cheeks, to wait until the Princess returned from hunting before she set out.

"No," Valentina said. "You know perfectly well that she would stop me. I'm leaving in half an hour; she won't return until the light goes."

Every time she mentioned going to Warsaw there was a violent quarrel with Alexandra, and she had finally threatened to detain Valentina at Czartatz by force if she persisted with her plan to leave. To placate her and gain time, Valentina had pretended to be convinced; she no longer spoke of going in search of De Chavel, or read the reports of the campaign a dozen times a day. She kept her fears under control and played her part so well for the last two weeks that even Alexandra began to think she had come to her senses and was trying to forget the Colonel. But only Jana, who saw her weeping every night in her own room, and listened to her restless pacing when the household was asleep, knew that she had lost nothing of her determination to find the man she loved. Now, dressed in a plain travelling cloak and bonnet, Valentina waited for the coach to be brought round. She had refused to allow Jana to come with her, and this increased the maid's anxiety.

"How can you travel alone?" she wailed. "How can a lady make a journey like that with only that fool Kador on the box and a coachman? It's not right, Madame, it's not proper! Let me come with you!"

"No, Jana," Valentina said. "I am travelling as simply as possible. If anyone is looking for the Countess Grunowska they will expect to find her with maids and servants; no one will connect her with a woman travelling alone. You are to stay here and give my letter to my sister."

"She will kill me," Jana said. "She will have me flogged—"

"No, she won't," Valentina said. "I've explained that you are not to blame. She won't hurt you, Jana. Go and see if the coach is ready."

She was not afraid; for the first time in weeks of miserable inactivity Valentina felt alive again. The strain of acting a part with her sister had worn her nerves threadbare, and the unvarying routine of life at Czartatz was killing her with frustration. She had accepted her intuition that De Chavel was seriously wounded or even dead; the only purpose which sustained her was the determination to find out what had happened to him, and to that determination she had added a more impossible objective still, which made Alexandra smash and swear when she discussed it with her. She was going to Russia. Warsaw was only the first step in a journey of incredible peril and difficulty, a means of gaining all possible information about the position of the French army and the names of casualties available, and if De Chavel was not among them, to set out along the path of Napoleon into Russia. If he were alive she would join him; wounded, she would nurse him; dead, she would kill herself on his grave. It was as simple and terrible as only the decision of a desperate women can be, and nothing Alexandra had threatened or pleaded or argued could change her mind.

She went to the door and called out, impatient to be gone. Jana came running upstairs to tell her that the coach was ready. The journey would take the best part of a week or more; Kador the postilion was only seventeen, but she had given him and the old coachman a pistol each to protect them from being robbed at the wretched inns on the road, and she carried no money, only her jewels sewn inside the lining of her valise. Kador was entrusted with the few kroner needed on the journey to pay for food and lodging and the care of their horses.

"Goodbye, Jana. You have the letter I gave you? Good. Give it to my sister as soon as she gets back. And don't be frightened; she won't hurt you."

"Madame, Madame," Jana cried out after her, "supposing the Count finds you!"

"He won't," Valentina said. "I'll try and send word from Warsaw." A few minutes later the coach started out on the same road taken by De Chavel more than four months before, when she had watched him from her window and asked God to send him back to her. She had changed radically since that morning; the cruellest anxiety had matured her. She had learnt the meaning of a sexual desire so strong that it made sleep impossible, and of a tenderness so deep that it caused physical pain. She had learnt what it meant to love, and she had become a woman in the process. When she assured Jana that the Count would never capture her, Valentina meant it. She also had a pistol and she would shoot him if he tried.

Chapter
FIVE

The Count had been riding for three days since he left Warsaw; a dozen armed servants were with him. He had started off as soon as he received his spy's message from Czartatz, and they had searched two of the dirty posting inns without finding Valentina. She must have travelled slowly; he was confident that the frightened innkeepers told the truth when they assured him that no travellers had passed that way. She must be ahead, and they would coincide within the next day or two. They had food and provisions with them. The message had said she was alone, with only two menservants. Her sister had not succumbed to the temptation to follow her yet, or he would have received another message. It was a pity. He would have enjoyed confronting Alexandra with her sister as a prisoner. Theodore and his men had slept under some trees that night, disdaining the shelter of the last posting inn; he had sent a man ahead to see if his wife had arrived on the further stage of the journey, and an hour after dawn the man came back, his horse lathered from the pace he had forced out of it. He threw himself down and came running to the Count. He was a powerfully built ex-soldier of the Polish Lancers who had been dismissed for stealing, and the Count had specially selected him and the others for this mission.

He knelt and pulled off his cap.

"There's a woman at the inn ahead, Lord," he said. "I saw a coach there and I went in and bought something to eat while my horse was watered. The keeper is an old Jew—filthy—" He turned aside and spat contemptuously. "I asked who the coach belonged to, and he said a lady was travelling to Warsaw. They'd just arrived."

"It must be the one," the Count said. "How far ahead is it?"

"About an hour's ride at a good pace, Lord. It took me longer because of the light, but we should get there in an hour. They'll be sleeping still."

"You've done well," the Count said. "I only hope for your own sake you haven't asked too many questions and alerted them. If I find them gone, I'll have you hanged. Get the horses saddled up!"

The inn was a two-story wooden building, with sprawling roofed stables, and as they came close to it, the Count could see the coach standing in front of it; there were no horses in the traces, but a little smoke twisted upwards from the chimney, so that someone must be about inside the inn. He signalled his servants to dismount and they approached the inn on foot. He opened the door himself and stepped inside; it was dark and the atmosphere was sickening with the smell of stale wine and unwashed human bodies, and old food; he grimaced and swore under his breath. A man knelt by the emormous communal stove, pushing sticks into its belly; there were a few benches and a rickety table, with a stained top; the mud floor was covered with a few wisps of straw. The Count moved so quietly that the man heard nothing; he fed the fire in the stove and muttered to himself in Yiddish. The Count put his pistol to the man's ear.

"Make no sound," he said quietly, "or I will blow your head off. Get up and turn round."

The innkeeper was an old man; his grey hair hung down beneath the round black cap and mingled with the strands of grey beard. He gazed up at the stranger in terror. Centuries of persecution had taught him and all his unhappy race to fear the unexpected. For them it usually meant violence and death. He and his wife had kept the desolate, poverty-stricken inn for twenty years; they had been robbed and threatened and cheated of their money more often than they were paid, but at least they lived and had enough to eat. He recognised the man as a noble by his dress; he thanked God it wasn't a visit from some band of roaming thieves. He fell to his knees and bent till his head almost touched the ground.

"Lord, what is it? What have we done?"

"You have a woman staying here," the Count said.

"Yes, yes," the old man said. "A lady; she came yesterday." His eyes widened in fear as he saw more armed men coming into the room. The leader was a big man, carrying a Russian knout, and the innkeeper recognised him as the visitor of the night before.

"Where is she?" the Count asked. He aimed a kick at the old man to focus his attention.

"Upstairs, Lord. We have only one room. Her two servants are in the back there."

Theodore addressed the ex-Lancer. "Kill them," he said. "Bury their bodies and take that coach and burn it."

The old man doubled up, moaning. "My Lord I have a wife," he whimpered. "A harmless old woman; she sleeps near these men. I beg of you don't do her any hurt—she'll make no sound, no trouble—let me wake her first. Lord, Lord, I beg you—" He embraced the Count's feet and tried to kiss them. He received a kick in the face that sent him sprawling backwards. The Count was overcome with irritation and disgust. "Someone silence that miserable old dog." He started up the narrow steps to Valentina's room.

The journey had been a nightmare since she left Czartatz. One of the wheels had split the first day, and it had taken four hours to repair it while the coach leant drunkenly on one side and she paced the dusty road; they hadn't reached shelter that night, and she had slept inside the coach and woken so stiff with cramp and cold that she could hardly move. At the first inn she had been afraid to sleep, remembering that here De Chavel had spent the night outside her door because he felt the innkeeper and his son were so ruffianly. At this inn she had fought the impulse to throw off her clothes and fall on the dirty bed and sleep and sleep. Instead Valentina wrapped her cloak round her, hid the pistol under her mattress, and lay down. She didn't hear the door creak as it opened. She slept with her head turned to the tiny window and the early light streamed in on her. Her husband moved like a cat across the bare wooden floor; he had his pistol in his right hand, and the impulse to shoot her as she slept was so strong that he almost gave in to it. He had never imagined that he could hate a woman as he realised he hated his wife. Her beauty shone in the murk of the squalid room, luminous and different to what he remembered. She had changed, and her love for the Frenchman was the cause, her love had driven her from a safe refuge into danger and the hands of her most implacable enemy. Himself.

He had imagined what he would say when he found her; now his tongue was thick with anger, it couldn't find words to wake her. He couldn't bring himself to speak to her at all. He bent down and struck her hard on the jaw. She went from sleep to unconsciousness without making a sound.

She came to her senses with a pain that ran from her wrists to her elbows; when she opened her eyes she was looking at the floor, her head hung down over the edge of the bed, and she tried to move her arms to ease the shooting cramp in them. They were bound to her sides and her hands were tied behind her back. She was pulled round and into a sitting position, and she was face to face with her husband. She cried out, but the cry was wordless.

"Yes," he said; his voice was thick with rage, and his hands trembled. As he bound her hands while she lay dazed and helpless, he had longed to take the cords and knot them round her neck. "Yes," he said, "you're not mistaken. It's your husband, come to claim you back."

"Kill me," Valentina said. "I swear that the moment I'm free I'll kill myself before I let you touch me!"

He leant forward and hit her across the face.

"You whore and traitress." he said. "Open your mouth again and I'll put a gag across that lying tongue which won't come out until we get to Warsaw!"

He dragged her to her feet and threw her cloak over her; he forced her down the stairs and out into the road. His servants were waiting; one had a riderless horse on a rein. There was no sound from inside the inn; the coachman and Kador had been clubbed to death while they slept, and the innkeeper's wife had been stripped and lay motionless where they had left her, her head wrapped in her own petticoat. Her husband hung from a low tree branch, his shirt in bloody tatters from the flogging the Lancer had given him as an expression of his dislike for Jews, and as a punishment for trying to interfere while they raped his wife. He held the lead rein of the waiting horse, the bloodstained knout tucked into his belt. Nobody spoke as the Count led his prisoner up to them. She was young and very beautiful, and the rumour that she was his wife and had run off with a lover was probably true. The ex-Lancer dismounted and helped his master lift her on to the horse; she sat astride, and the servant tied her feet to the stirrups, and knotted the loose reins round the animal's neck; the Count refused to have her hands tied in front of her so that she could ride more comfortably. The man himself had made the request, fearing that she would lose her balance if she were forced to ride in that fashion; the woman said nothing; she looked ahead of her and sat straightback in her bonds.

"Take her horse," the Count said. "She is not to speak to you, you understand? If she utters one word, or gives any trouble, bind her face down across the saddle. Mount up—we'll be in Warsaw before the week is out!"

The return to Warsaw took three days; the Count insisted on a maximum pace, and by the end of the day, Valentina was so stiff and weary that she could hardly stand. They slept out, making a rough camp where any shelter could be found, and then her hands were loosed and she was given food and drink under the eye of the ex-Lancer. He had been watching her closely during the nightmare ride across country so rough that every man was exhausted by it, and she had neither faltered nor complained. She asked for nothing; when food was given to her she ate it, she submitted while her raw and swollen wrists were fastened again before the company settled for the night, and she maintained a contemptuous silence. The big peasant couldn't equate his opinion of women with this courage and endurance. Service in the Army had taught him a respect for bravery which was a substitute for the other human feelings he had lost through discipline and natural brutishness.

On the second night, when the Count was asleep and the others lay without moving, Valentina woke with a violent start to find him bending over her. He covered her mouth with his hand and whispered.

"Don't scream, lady. I'm not meaning any harm to you. You can't sleep like that."

To her astonishment, she felt him loosening her hands, and then he moved away from her. "I'll have to fasten you before morning," he said.

"If your master finds out that you've done this, you know what he'll do to you," she said.

"I see what he's doing to you, lady," the man muttered. "I'll wake before he does, don't fear. You'll lose the power of your arms if you go on too long in bonds. I saw some of our men in Spain after those dirty Spaniards had kept them tied for days on end, and they were crippled." He spat into the darkness at the memory. "Sleep now; there's a hard day ahead tomorrow." There was nothing incongruous in his mind in the rape of an elderly Jewess and his flogging of an old man, and his act of gallantry towards a courageous Polish lady. He hated his master and admired the woman, whatever she had done. It was as simple as that. Every night he crawled near to Valentina and made her free so that she slept in comfort; he pretended to fasten her hands each morning, but just before they mounted he eased them so that there was no friction and she didn't suffer pain. On the last night of the journey, Valentina reached out and touched him.

"You've helped me," she said. "Why? You've taken a great risk for me. How can I reward you unless you help me more?"

He half raised himself and then lay down again.

"I can't do more than I've done," he said. "And I want nothing for it. He had me given twenty lashes the first week for something I didn't do. I'm glad to make it easy for you, lady, that's why. But that's all."

"If you help me to get away," Valentina said, "we can scatter their horses and be back on the road to my home. We'll be safe there; no one can touch us. I'll give you a hundred pieces of gold." It was a hopeless chance, but the only one she had of escaping even at this last moment. The man had shown kindness and a willingness to disobey his master. Though she shuddered at the risk of putting herself in the hands of such a brute, it was better than being at Theodore's mercy. He hesitated. A hundred pieces of gold. It was a fortune; he could buy land, build himself a house. All he had to do was run the horses loose so that they couldn't be followed, and then ride off with the lady. It was simple. And possible, so long as they were quiet and no one woke.

"Will you do it?" Valentina urged. "One hundred gold pieces. My sister may even give you more. Think— we can do it easily!"

"Stay still, then," he muttered. "Don't make a sound. I'll make our mounts ready—no, by God, I'll take the master's horse, it's the best! Then when I signal you creep away and come to me; when we're both mounted I'll fire my pistols and stampede the other horses. Not a movement now, until I give the sign!"

It was a brilliant moonlit night and she could see him clearly as he got up and began moving between the sleeping men, bent almost double. The horses were tethered fifty yards away by some deep trees; he had got clear of the camp, and was creeping up on them, when one of the mounts raised its head and whinnied. Valentina sank back and shut her eyes, not daring to look. There was no other sound, and after a moment she raised her head enough to see the big's man's figure moving in among the horses. He had made no noise, and now he was out of the revealing moonlight. In a few minutes she would be riding for her life back to Czartatz; a lot would depend on how quickly the Count realised what had happened. They would make perfect targets in that light for the first hundred and fifty yards. She shut her eyes again for a second and prayed. Oh God, let him do it. Please, please let me get away.

"Who's there! Come out, or I'll put a bullet through you!"

The Count's voice barked out, and she stiffened and then went slack as if she had been struck a paralysing blow. The ex-Lancer shouted in answer.

"It's me, Lord. I thought I saw something moving near the horses!"

"Nothing's moving," the Count snapped. "Where's your prisoner—by God if you've let her move . . ." He came towards her, and she saw the pistol barrel gleaming in his hands. She lay still, her eyes open, but not looking at him. She had never once glanced near him since they set out. "By tomorrow you'll be in Warsaw," he said. "If it weren't that Potocki wants a trial, I'd leave you staked out here. In a month or so some traveller might find you. You whore." He said it deliberately, and he stirred her with his foot. She saw the man come up behind him and for a moment she thought there was something rigid about him that meant he was going to strike the Count down, but the impression passed as quickly as it came, and instead he bowed low, and said: "Everything is in order, Lord. My pardon for disturbing you."

"It's light enough to ride," Theodore said suddenly. "We've slept long enough. Get yourselves together; we'll start off now. And she will ride with me," he added. "Make her ready."

The man bent over Valentina as the Count moved

away. By the moonlight he saw that she was weeping. "The devil's own luck," he whispered. "We haven't a chance now."

He bound her securely and carried her towards her horse. "Don't cry, lady," he muttered. "It'll make him worse to you. He loves to see suffering. There's naught I can do for you now."

"Now," Alexandra said. "What has happened to my sister?" She was sitting in the small study where she had entertained De Chavel the night before he left, and she was leaning back in her chair, her fingers pressed together, watching the man before her with half-closed eyes. She had last seen him when he brought the newspaper more than a month before; Janos and Ladislaw her two senior footmen were on either side of him, holding his arms.

He had been seen lurking near the house, and they had brought him in and challenged him. Ladislaw didn't think his explanation satisfactory and he had informed the Princess. So far she had extracted a confession from him that he had been living on the estate and had in fact paid a local family to lodge him, and had sent one of them off with a message the very day after her sister had left Czartatz.

"You've been spying on us, haven't you?" Alexandra said gently.

The man shook his head; he was grey with fear. "No, Highness, I swear it!"

"Yes, Highness," she mocked him, "who paid you to spy on this house? Who sent you to spy on my sister? If you don't answer I'll have your eyes put out." she added. "With that!" There was a poker in the heart of the blazing log fire; the man's eyes went to it and almost rolled up in his head with terror.

"The Count Grunowski, Highness. I didn't want to do it, but he forced me—he threatened—"

"I can imagine how difficult it was for you," she sneered. "What did he want you to do? Answer me, or you'll suffer. And by God I'll put that iron to you myself!"

He fell on his knees, grovelling. "He told me to report anything I saw or heard when I came here. I told him the Countess was going to leave and go to Warsaw. He sent me back to watch and send word the moment she set out. That's what I did, Highness, I swear that's all. I was too frightened to refuse him!"

"So you sent him word when she left here," Alexandra said. She leant forward, her slanting eyes glittered in her face like jet.

"Yes, Highness," he whimpered. "I sent the message. I think he was going to take her by force."

"Exactly," she said, She dropped her hands suddenly. "She is in his hands by now. Why are you still here, Judas? Didn't you want your reward?"

"I was to spy on you," he said. "You were to be seized too, if you tried to follow her. Oh God, Highness, have pity on me! I had no choice but to obey him!"

"Enough," Alexandra snapped. "Janos, take that miserable dog outside and cut his throat!"

She got up and went to pour herself some wine, impervious to the screams of the spy who was dragged out of the room. Theodore had caught Valentina; she was sure of it, and she was only too thankful that her instincts had prevented her from giving immediate chase to her sister. She too would have been taken prisoner. Now she could begin the search for her, while he waited for the report from his spy which would never be sent. She had cursed herself again and again for going hunting that day and leaving Valentina, and as often she cursed the Frenchman who was responsible for her sister's reckless action. She drank the wine in one swallow and filled up the glass again. Her sister had been gone for four days. If she was in the Count's hands then he would probably take her to Lvov, if indeed he hadn't murdered her on the road. It would depend on where he had caught up with her; if he found her at one of the inns on the way, then someone must have seen the abduction. She might gain information in that way which would indicate the route they had taken. Alexandra made up her mind. She wrenched the bell-rope, and shouted at the footman who came in answer; he was a handsome, strapping man in his late twenties and a few months ago she had intended taking him as a lover before Valentina came. Out of respect for her sister's feelings, she had postponed the plan. She didn't even remember his name at that moment.

"Tell my maids to pack some clothes for me, and have my horse saddled. I shall need Janos and Ladislaw to come with me. Tell them to dispose of that wretch's body, and make ready. I want enough food and water to last a week, and tell them to come armed. Hurry!"

Two hours later she set out, her big black horse leading the others in a powerful sustained gallop that ate up the miles. It took Alexandra only two days to reach the inn where the Count had found Valentina. It was very silent; they saw the charred skeleton of a burned-out coach and Alexandra sprang down from her horse and ran inside the open door. There was no sign of anyone; the central stove was out, and when she touched it, it was cold. In the outer kitchen they saw bloodstains which had dried on the floor, and a moment later there was a shout from Janos, who had been searching outside. He had found two shallow graves, and they were newly dug. Alexandra ordered him to open them; she didn't believe that Valentina was dead. It wouldn't be Theodore's way to kill her quickly and bury her. She had taken two men with her; Janos confirmed that their bodies were in the bits.

"Where is the innkeeper?" she demanded. "Where the devil is everyone? They can't have murdered them too!"

"It's possible, Highness," Janos said. "If they wanted no witnesses."

"Then search till you find the bodies," she ordered. "I'll look upstairs."

In the little room she found her sister's gloves; for the first time in many years, Alexandra's eyes filled with tears; quickly she wiped them away and swore angrily at her own weakness. She ran down the stairs and shouted to Ladislaw.

"Have you found anything? Where are you?"

"Here, Highness. I've found the innkeeper and his wife. They were hiding in the stables."

The old man lay on a heap of straw, his wife crouching beside him. Both were dumb with terror; the woman's hands picked at her clothes and her mouth worked in soundless weeping. Alexandra stood over them; she saw that the straw where the man lay was stained with blood and that his chest was bare under a ragged blanket. She knelt quickly beside them and they shrank back, the woman making a wild movement to cover her husband.

"Don't be afraid," Alexandra said. "We're not going to hurt you. Tell me what happened here." She addressed herself to the woman. "He's hurt," she said. "Who did it?"

"Some men came," the woman quavered. "They attacked me and they beat Ruben. That's all we know, lady. We've done no wrong, leave us in peace! I beg you, my poor man can't walk yet, he's so weak. . . ."

"There was a woman here," Alexandra persisted. "I've seen the coach. I've seen the bodies of her servants. What happened to her?"

"I don't know, lady." The woman shook her head; she was rocking backwards and forwards in distress. "They tied my head up so I saw nothing. I don't know what happened after that. When I came to myself they were gone and I found Ruben hanging from a tree—" She began to cry. The old man raised his head and looked at Alexandra. His eyes were sunken in his head with pain, but hatred gleamed in them. Hate had given him the strength to live after his wife had cut him down. "They took her away," he whispered. "I heard the man say something as they came out of the house. They had whipped me hard—but I heard something."

"What was it?" Alexandra said. "Think well. That woman was my sister. She's been abducted. What did this man say?" She felt tempted to take him and shake him violently.

"He told them to mount up. I heard him say something about Warsaw. That's all I can remember."

"It's enough." Alexandra got up.

"If they come back," the woman wailed, "if they know we've told you anything—what will become of us?"

"They won't return again," she said. "You've nothing to fear now. My servants will put your man to bed in the house. Janos! Take him inside, see what you can do for him. And you take this."

She emptied her purse and poured the gold and silver into the woman's hand. "When I find the man who took my sister," Alexandra said quietly, "I'll remember what he did to you."

By night they had covered a good distance; they camped out, and started off again as soon as the first light came into the sky. Warsaw. All the way Alexandra had been thanking God that they had found the innkeeper alive. He hadn't taken her to Lvov; this must mean that he was acting with the authority of the Diet, or some of its members. Valentina was going to Warsaw as a prisoner of her own government. That meant there was still a chance of appealing to the French authorities before any harm could be done to her.

It would depend on what the latest news was from Russia; it couldn't be encouraging or the Polish government would never have dared authorise the kidnapping. If France was declining, then French protection for her sister could be safely ignored by her enemies. It was one thing to claim the immunity of the French Secret Police list while that force was operating in the country and its power was backed by the might of Napoleon himself; it was another matter when the occupying armies had gone and the only reports of them were rumours of defeat and crushing casualties. The protégée of Colonel de Chavel had little hope of escaping her countrymen's revenge under these circumstances.

During that long journey, covered in dust from endless fast riding across the rough countryside, hungry and thirsty and stiff with nights spent sleeping on the ground, Alexandra planned what she must do. And the most important part of that plan was to get to whatever French authority she could find before Count Grunowski or the Diet's agents got to her.

September 18th had been a fine warm day; the Emperor Napoleon and his armies had been quartered in Russia's ancient capital city for five days, and the relief of capturing Moscow had only been tempered by finding it abandoned. Not a shot had been fired at the French after Borodino. The Russian General Kututzov had withdrawn his sadly depleted forces from that dreadful battlefield, leaving the road to Moscow open for Napoleon, and they had entered the city itself in deathly quiet a week after the battle of Borodino had begun. The wounded came on after the army, travelling slowly in wagons and those who could walk dragged themselves on foot in straggling columns. In one of the leading wagons some senior staff officers were brought in the van of the main forces, and De Chavel's first sight of the famous golden domes of Moscow was when he was lifted out on a litter and carried to an improvised hospital on the outskirts of the main city. The French had taken over one of the noblest fine stone-built palaces as their main hospital; it was more suitable than the large rambling wooden buildings which were of much earlier date. The Colonel lay as still as possible while he was being moved holding to the wooden sides of the litter with his left arm. The amputated right arm ached and twitched and tried to clutch with phantom fingers. The pain in his cut nerve ends had been unbearable at first; he had been unconscious for most of the second and third day after the battle; now he suffered agonies from his lost arm.

His friend Major Macdonald had told him that he was crippled; he rode part of the way with him in the wagon

as they made the lurching journey away from Borodino
towards Moscow, and tried to explain to him that there
had been no hope except to take his right arm off. De
Chavel hadn't answered immediately; he hadn't really
understood. He was so weak from loss of blood that he
fainted at the least exertion; his chest throbbed with every breath, though the wound was healing well and had
stayed clean. His right arm had a demonic life of its
own, this arm which Macdonald said had been cut off.
He couldn't believe it, when he could raise it high above
his head and every finger moved at his command. Only
when he tried to look at it for confirmation did he see
the bloody shoulder bandage and the useless knotted
sleeve of his shirt. He had turned his head away and said
quite distinctly, "God damn you, Major, why didn't you
let me die?" and then lost consciousness again.

He was used to it now; he knew he was crippled, his
career finished, condemned to a civilian life if he survived at all. And out of his despair he found the will to
live, to conquer his pain and his wound and rise to fight
again before it was too late. He lived for this hope; he
swallowed the weak soup they gave him when his stomach revolted at food; he bore the agonies of having his
dressings changed, and fought the impulse to give way
to weakness and sleep until the sleep became a death
coma. He refused to die, and while others in the wagon
with him faltered, and their bodies were taken out and
buried by the roadside, De Chavel hung on in spite of
everything. Out of thirty officers who started out from
Borodino in the wagon, he was one of the eight remain-
ing to be quartered in the empty Russian palace.

Food was short, and the Russians had poisoned most of
the water supply; there was no stores or fodder left, and
crowds of troops roamed the deserted city, getting
drunk on looted cellars, carrying away furs and jewels
and gold. It was almost as if the treasures and the wines
and brandy had been left behind deliberately to under-
mine what was left of the army's discipline. The effects
were so serious that the Emperor issued orders that the

looting was to stop, and further offenders would be shot. It was useless to try to make the men disgorge what was already stolen, and soldiers added their loot to their packs, many of them throwing away equipment or ammunition to make room for women's silk dresses and sable cloaks. The ballroom in the house had been turned into a general officers' ward, and all through the four days it was filled and emptied as more wounded were admitted, died and were replaced. The journey from Borodino had accounted for half the subsequent fatalities. The surgeons were doing their best under impossible conditions; the doctor who had performed the operation on De Chavel had gone down with dysentery and was a patient in the ward. Clean water was one of the army's worst problems; men had died in thousands from the effects of drinking from polluted streams, and the loss of cavalry and pack horses had been catastrophic. One hundred thousand men were all that were left out of the half a million who had crossed the River Niemen three months before, and contrary to everyone's hope, the Russians had given no indication that they wanted peace. De Chavel knew little or nothing of their situation; he was too weak to think of anything except in the narrowest terms of his own hospital environment, and that was distressing enough. Ney had been to see him after the battle; it was a signal honour for the Marshal to visit him, but he was delirious and didn't recognise him. Macdonald had spent as much time with him as he could, and hounded the orderlies to take care of him with the dogged spirit of his Scottish ancestors. Murat had sent him a bottle of fine burgundy, which he was too sick to drink and which was stolen by one of the orderlies, but the Marshal stayed away; he hated suffering and army hospitals. The Emperor himself had enquired after him, and then forgotten what he had been told. There were so many casualties, and he had lost forty Generals at Borodino, among them men he could ill afford.

There were no beds for the wounded; De Chavel lay on his litter on the floor, and he was better off than some who had only a blanket between them and the bare boards; a crude kitchen provided the food, and this was in the main hall, near the ballroom. Stoves were set up and fires burnt, priceless furniture was chopped up for fuel, and gilded walls grew black with smoke. The sewage systems in the most splendid Russian establishments were of the most primitive kind, hopelessly inadequate for the needs of a hundred and fifty men, and three hundred more who could not walk. The chief medical officer, tormented by fear of typhoid outbreaks and further attacks of dysentery, demanded men to prepare proper latrines, and was told there were more important things for the troops to do than dig cesspits because he objected to a stench. Near to the Colonel, a young Lieutenant of Grenadiers was slowly dying of internal injuries; he had been horribly trampled by Russian cavalry, and since there was nothing visible which the surgeons could stitch up or cut off, they were uncertain of the extent of his injuries, and he was given a place on the wagon when the battle area was evacuated. Many hundreds who were dying were left behind.

It was late afternoon, and the army surgeons had finished their inspection for the day, and there was only the final change of dressing for those whose bandages were soaked through. The vast linen closets in the house had provided a God-sent supply of material for dressings. De Chavel closed his eyes and withdrew from the pain as they began rebandaging his wounds; he forced his muscles to relax and sent his mind as far from his surroundings as possible till the ordeal was over. The effort exhausted him; men were groaning and calling out, and when he opened his eyes he saw three bodies being carried from the room. The boy beside him started coughing; he spewed blood and moaned. De Chavel tried to raise himself and call for help. "Orderly! Orderly, here!" The voice was cracked and weak and no one heard him. He fell back and for the first time tears ran down his sunken face, and they were tears of helpless pity for the boy in his twenties who was going through the final paroxysm of violent hemorrhage, and of rage with himself because he was too weak to help him. He called again, and this time someone heard and a harassed orderly came running. De Chavel fainted, and when he came to his senses the enormous room was in semi-darkness, a few candles burned at either end where there were medical officers on duty. He had forgotten what had happened earlier; his senses swam and his lost arm throbbed. With an effort he turned to his left, instinctively looking for the boy who had been his travelling companion since Borodino. The space on the floor was empty, and a soldier knelt wearily wiping away the traces of death with a dirty rag.

The Colonel shut his eyes and drifted into sleep, and while he slept he cried, but no one heard him, and he didn't wake again until the small hours. The ballroom was as light as if it were the middle of the day, and there was a continuous crackling noise with an occasional muffled bang. The tall windows were suffused with brilliant yellow light. Men were muttering and raising themselves, and the medical staff were clustered by the windows.

"What is it? What s happened?" De Chavel asked the question again and again in a whisper, and at last someone passing paused and answered him.

"The city's on fire! That's not the dawn you're seeing, Sir. That's Moscow!"

A few Russian patriots had stayed behind on the orders of the city Governor Rostopchine, and they had started fires at selected points throughout the city. Within minutes the flames were raging through the wooden buildings, fanned by a high wind which carried millions of blazing sparks from roof to roof.

The lack of water supplies made it impossible to control the fires, and fresh outbreaks occurred all over the area. French patrols caught and shot the fleeing Russian arsonists, but they were helpless to stop the inferno from spreading. The sounds De Chavel had heard were hasty dynamiting of adjacent buildings in the attempt to create a gap the fires could not bridge, but the fierce winds carried sparks and flames in a whirling, glittering cascade that spouted fresh fires wherever it touched. Twenty-four hours later, the order came to evacuate the hospital.

The Emperor himself had been driven from the Kremlin; the army, which had looked forward to shelter and time to regroup, was now forced to evacuate the blazing city and camp on the outskirts while their only hope of winter protection burned for five days and nights. The French emissary General Lauriston set out for St. Petersburg to try and persuade the Czar Alexander to negotiate; the former Ambassador Coulaincourt refused to undertake the mission. He knew from experience of the Czar that it was hopeless. He dared not make peace with France even if he wished; his family and Court were prepared to assassinate him if he tried. Any hope of peace Napoleon still held was abandoned when the Russian General Kututzov surprised Murat and his troops at Winkovo and soundly defeated them. Orders were given to march away from the smouldering ruins of Moscow and take the road back to Smolensk where it was proposed to shelter the army for the winter. No one near the Emperor dared to speak of the manœuvre as a retreat, though everyone knew that it was nothing less. His rage and desperation expressed itself in an order to Mortier to blow up the historic Kremlin buildings as they left.

The slow backward procession began on October 19th with the wagons full of sick and wounded bumping their way in the rear of the army and its artillery. De Chavel had insisted on sitting up; his first halting steps ended in a humiliating fall, when he lay gasping on the ground, and the wound in his chest seeped blood again. Now he rode with his back to the wagon's side, holding to the seat for support; a dozen wounded men ranged on either side of him, and men desperately sick, or too weak to sit up, lay bundled on the floor at their feet.

A certain Major Beaufois, who had fought with Ney's division at Borodino, and lost an eye from a dreadful sabre cut on the head, turned to the one-armed Colonel beside him and said: "Back the way we came, eh? This is the first retreat I've known in twenty years' service under the Emperor. Do you know where we're going, Colonel?"

"I've heard rumours, nothing more," De Chavel said. "It must be the Emperor's plan to winter somewhere and then mount another attack in the spring."

"What with?" the Major said. "Dead men? I tell you, Colonel, none of us will survive this winter—I was talking to a Prussian Lieutenant the other day—before we moved out again—and he said the winter here was the worst in Europe. That's why they burnt Moscow, he said, to force us out, to make us turn back. I have a wife and children in Nantes; I doubt I'll ever see them again. In a way it's just as well; my wife wouldn't welcome me with this face. Are you married, Colonel?"

"No," De Chavel said. "My wife is dead. I have no children."

"It's better so," the Major said. "Then one can fight with a free mind."

Through his delirium and pain De Chavel hadn't thought of any woman or seen any face; now Valentina was clearly in front of him as she had looked that last night at Czartatz when she told him she loved him. He had no wife, no sons or daughters, no one but friends who were soldiers like himself, and they were all probably doomed as the Major said. He had forgotten the girl until that moment, and he couldn't understand why the thought of her moved him. He remembered her sister's words before he left. "For some women there is only one man. If this is true of Valentina, she'll never be happy again." It could not be true, of course. He had dismissed the idea as ridiculous as soon as she said it, and only weakness made him consider it seriously now. She had forgotten all about him; three and a half months was a lifetime to a woman when the man was out of sight. Liliane had been unfaithful to him within a fortnight of his departure of Egypt. It was strange that it no longer hurt him to think of that betrayal; his wife was a fading memory, her face so indistinct that he couldn't recall it. The other face intruded, haunting in its beauty; the blue eyes followed him, bright with love he had dismissed as a romantic fancy, and he felt suddenly angry that the Major should think him completely alone in the world, that when he died no one would mourn.

"I have a mistress," the Major went on. "A nice girl; she was at Danzig when we were there. She wouldn't like this face either. You must have a woman, Colonel—sometimes a mistress is more fond than a wife." The Major put his hand to the bandage swathed round his head and the right half of his face. When the scars healed and began to pucker he would be grotesque.

"There is someone," De Chavel said. "In Poland. But what she or anyone else would want with a one-armed cripple I can't imagine. The best thing we can do, my friend, is to stop pitying ourselves and think about being able to fight again. I've got two eyes and you have a right arm. Together we can count as one whole man!" He laughed angrily, and then stopped because his chest hurt. The Major said nothing; he only touched his bandaged face again and let his head sink slowly, whether in sleep or despair De Chavel did not know.

Chapter
SIX

"There is a lady asking to see you, Major."

Paul Antoine de Lamballe looked up from the reports he was studying and frowned at the junior officer who had interrupted him. He had been left in charge of French Intelligence in Warsaw, with the nominal position of military adviser to the Diet of the Grand Duchy, and every despatch he received from his agents was worse than the last.

Morale in the Grand Duchy was sinking fast as the newspapers printed news of French losses and the burning of Moscow. His job and that of the French diplomats in Poland was to secure Polish support for the rear of the Imperial Army, and to keep their vital supply lines open. He had begun to think it an impossible task.

"Who is she? What does she want"

"She didn't say, Major. She only said it was very urgent."

"Bah," De Lamballe said. "It's always very urgent. Ask her name, and tell her I shan't see her unless she gives it."

He was a good-looking man, with hair that the last fifteen years of soldiering had turned prematurely grey, piercing dark eyes, and one of the oldest and noblest names in France. He was a cousin of the Princess de Lamballe, Marie Antoinette's beautiful friend whom the Paris mobs had torn to pieces outside the Queen's prison during the Revolution, and his parents had fled to England with him, where he had been brought up in comparative poverty. He had hated his exile and despised his aristocratic father for running for his life; more than anything he had hated England and the insufferable arrogance of the English nobility who showed their contempt and distrust of the French *émigrés* once the excitement of the Terror was forgotten. At nineteen he had made his choice. His family and friends might remain in exile with the Bourbon King Louis XVIII and exist on their old prejudices; he had no sympathy with the Royalist charade, the empty tiles and useless protocol surrounding the ridiculous successor to the murdered Louis XVI. A new and glorious epoch was beginning in France under the First Consulship of the most remarkable young soldier in Europe. France was no longer run by ragged Jacobins, screaming for blue blood. The Revolution was over and the marvellous national spirit born of it was being harnessed to a driving force of conquest that appealed very much to Paul de Lamballe. He returned and enlisted in the Army, and within two years he had distinguished himself and won commissioned rank. Fighting was his life; he had been awarded the Legion d'Honneur for outstanding bravery with Soult in the Spanish campaign, and contracted a recurring fever which took him off the active list just when the war with Russia was about to begin. As a result he found himself in Warsaw, in what he described as the most thankless and tedious position in the Imperial Army.

The junior officer came back after an interval of several minutes in which the Major had quite forgotten him.

"The lady's name is Princess Suvaroff. She's outside, Sir, she refused to wait downstairs."

"Suvaroff? I know that name."

"You should," a woman's voice said curtly. "It belonged to one of the most famous Generals in the world."

She walked into the room and threw back the veil which covered her face. De Lamballe raised his brows and stared at her without a flicker of surprise.

"A Russian General, I believe. Who are you, Madame—a peace emissary from Czar?"

"No," Alexandra snapped; she kept her temper with difficulty. Her nerves were quivering with worry and lack of sleep; as soon as they reached Warsaw she had gone into hiding in an inn in the trading quarter of the city, and only ventured out in a hired hackney coach, heavily veiled as if she were a widow. "I apologise for intruding, Major, but my business is terribly urgent. I must speak to you alone."

He stood up and bowed to her; she gave him a curt nod and made a movement of impatience which she could not conceal. "I don't want to sit down, thank you. I prefer to stand."

The young officer retreated, closing the door very quietly behind him; De Lamballe was sensitive to small noises; he had once thrown his ink-pot at the Lieutenant when he let the door bang by mistake.

"What can I do for you?" he asked. He was amused by the effort the lady had made to contain herself; he had a furious and impulsive temper of his own and he recognised the signs in others. She was handsome too, very unusual with those Tartar eyes.

"My sister has been abducted," Alexandra said.

"You have come to the wrong place, Madame. Go to the police."

"This is a political abduction," she said. "You are the French political officer here, are you not? This is your business, Major; you are the only person who can help me."

De Lamballe took a sheet of paper and selected a quill pen.

"What is your sister's name, who abducted her, and why is this anything to do with me in an official capacity? I'm always interested in the abduction of beautiful ladies, in a private sense, of course. Since she's your sister, I presume she must be beautiful?" He smiled lazily at her, drawing the feather tip of his pen down one cheek like a caress. Very handsome, and full of fire. And arrogant as the devil, in her assumption that she could burst in upon him and demand his help.

"My sister's name is Grunowska, Countess Grunowska. She had been abducted by Count Theodore Grunowski—"

"A relation?" De Lamballe asked.

"Her husband!" Alexandra snapped at him. He threw his pen down and glanced up at her without smiling this time.

"Really, Madame," he said, "I think I've heard enough. You come here telling me that this is a political abduction and then say that your sister has been abducted by her own husband! I'm very busy; please excuse me."

"Will you for God's sake listen?" Alexandra said; she came round the desk, barring his way. "Grunowska— doesn't that mean anything to you? My sister was sent to spy on your officers, to seduce Marshal Murat and report back to the Diet. She was threatened to make her comply. A Colonel de Chavel rescued her and brought her to me for safety. Now her husband has got her back, and God knows what they'll do to her. She was put on the French Intelligence list as a protected person. If you don't believe me, look it up. You must have some record of it!"

"I don't need a record," he said. "I've heard about the affair. How do you know she's in Warsaw?"

"Because someone overheard him say he was taking her there—the details aren't important. It must mean she's being held by the Diet and will be put on trial. Major de Lamballe—my sister is under your protection! You must have her released!"

"I think you had better sit down," he said. He pulled out the chair beside his own. He turned away and began to walk up and down.

"When Colonel de Chavel put your sister on our list our position here was very different to what it is now," he said. "You must realise that. We were in command; the war had not begun—our victory seemed certain. They would not have dared do anything against French interests. But things have changed. We haven't defeated Russia; the latest news is confused, and what sense one can make of it is not to our advantage. The members of the Diet are growing bold in the Emperor's absence. I could have gone to the Lubinski Prison—I expect that's where she's been taken—and demanded that she be handed over to me. But I can't do it now. I can't do anything to offend the Polish Government or rouse anti-French feeling. I'm very sorry, Madame, but I can't do anything to help you."

She stared at him, both hands clenched into a fist, and the tears overflowed on to her face.

"I'll go on my knees and beg," she said, "if that's what you want. Damn you! She left Czartatz where she was safe to look for this Colonel, and that's how she was taken. I don't care what your duties are—you've got to save my sister!"

"In the eyes of her own people she's an adultress and a traitor," he said. "It's quite probable that she's been strangled in the Lubinski and no one will ever know. I've told you, I can't do anything."

"Well, I can, and I will!" She sprang up, wiping away the tears with a furious gesture; her eyes blazed at him. "I'll find my brother-in-law and kill him!"

He considered her for a moment. "That would be very foolish," he said coldly. "You will only attract attention to yourself, and then you'll join your sister!"

"Do you think I'd mind if I were with her?" she demanded. "Do you think I'll ever rest if anything happens to her? You have no heart, no soul; you wouldn't understand."

"The ravings of an hysterical woman don't make much sense to me, I must admit," De Lamballe remarked. "If the lady is anything like you, I don't suppose much will go wrong with her."

"She's a fool!" Alexandra cried out. "A sentimental idiot, throwing her life away. Like me? Ha, if she were do you think she'd be where she is now? She's gentle and loyal—and brave too. I don't know why I say all this to you—I'm wasting my breath!"

"If you can stop abusing me," he suggested, "I might be able to give you some advice."

"To hell with advice," she flared at him. "What advice does a coward give? Go back to Czartatz and save yourself—there's nothing you can do?"

"Go to the Russians," he said. "You have an influential name. They may do something for you."

"Russians? There are no Russians here!"

"There's Prince Adam Czartorisky and his faction—they're the next best thing."

She stopped suddenly on the way to the door. "Of course. I should have gone there first. Don't expect me to thank you!"

He bowed low. "Madame, I expect nothing from you."

"Good," she said bitterly. "Then, unlike me, you won't be disappointed!"

She pulled the veil down over her face and went out; she closed the door with a violence that rattled the window panes.

He went after her and opening the door called out: "Fanchon!"

"Major?" The Lieutenant came at the double down the passage. He did not dare ask what had happened; his superior was scowling with temper.

"Have that woman watched—night and day."

"Yes, Sir," the Lieutenant said. "Any further orders?"

"No," De Lamballe said. "Not yet, anyway. It's for her own protection. The orders are, she's not to be molested. By anyone!"

He went back into his office and closed the door, quietly, wincing at the memory of that frightful slam. He spent the rest of the morning studying the records of the police on the Countess Valentina Grunowska.

"I hope you realise, Countess, that you have nobody to blame for this but yourself?"

Potocki had not meant to show how his prisoner's attitude angered him; he had been cold and restrained, rebuking her in what he considered dignified terms for her betrayal of her country and her infidelity to her husband. A week in the Lubinski had done nothing to soften her resistance. She watched him with supreme indifference; she had not troubled to answer one of his accusations. She was not in one of the lower dungeons; he had refused her husband on that point, and ordered her to be confined in a small room on the upper floor. She was decently housed and fed; she was allowed to wear her own clothes and nobody ill-treated her. He was a cautious man, and he was not going to stand accused of hurting the woman, just supposing anything came to light or by some awful chance she had to be released.

"I must say," he said, "you're quite incorrigible!"

"I'm not sure what you expect of me," Valentina said. "You've accused me of adultery and treason. I deny both. If you're going to give me a trial, which is my right—I'll answer to the court. There's no reason why I must make any plea to you. You're my enemy." She went and sat down, her head half turned away from him. Since she had been in the prison she had been ill with exhaustion; the prison doctor had dressed her wrists which would bear permanent scars, and she had slept the night through into the day and through the night again. Potocki had been her only visitor, and she thanked God that her husband had not been near her. He had brought her to the prison and thrown her on the floor at the chief jailor's feet. When he heard that she was not to be kept in the low level cells he cursed and raged, but the officials were adamant. She was taken away, while his furious protests could be heard echoing down the long stone passage after her. But that was all. She looked over her shoulder at the statesman who had been her guest in the old days, who had kissed her hand and called her a patriot that night during the reception at Dresden when she had agreed to be his spy. There was nothing on his face but hostility; she had failed him, and he could not forgive her. He would punish her with death if he could, and think that it was exactly what she deserved. There was no pity, no revulsion from her vicious husband, no understanding that human love had given her the courage to rebel against what he and Theodore had tried to make her do. If he knew what her husband had done when she refused to sleep with Murat he would not have cared. He would have done the same to a recalcitrant woman himself.

"Please go," she said coldly. "I'm tired. I've told you. I'll answer your tribunal. I've nothing to say to you."

He glared at her for a moment, then turned and banged on the door. "Guard! Open and let me out!" He paused in the doorway and said: "Don't imagine that your French friends will be able to rescue you. The latest news from Russia says they're in headlong retreat. They've lost three-quarters of their troops; undoubtedly your lover is dead, Countess. You'll soon be reunited!"

"I hope so," Valentina said calmly. "I'm not afraid of death, Count Potocki, or of anything that you can do to me."

"Headlong retreat." She sat down on the narrow bed, and covered her face with her hands; they were cold and they trembled. "They have lost three-quarters of their men. Your lover is dead." It was a worse torture than the rack, and he had taunted her deliberately, conjuring images of De Chavel lying dead or dying slowly of wounds, somewhere in that awful trackless Russian waste, where the weary French army struggled to get back before the winter caught them. It was late October; she knew what the conditions could be like in her own country during the winter; the snows of Russia were part of European legend, they were so deep and so unbearably cold. Nothing could live unprotected in such weather; the Russians themselves built their houses against winter, dressed against it, made provision not to travel more than the shortest distance. And now Napoleon's armies were stranded in the heart of the countryside, without proper shelter, marching against time to get to safety. Valentina slipped down to her knees and began to pray. She would never leave the Lubinski alive; there was no hope of mercy from her countrymen or of rescue, now that French power was on the decline. She would be put to death, and she would never see the man she loved again, and she would die without knowing what had become of him. Her prayers were not for herself, for she was lost. They were for De Chavel, dead or alive, wherever he might be.

Prince Adam Czartorisky was a handsome man; he had never lost the romantic air which had made him so successful with women in his youth, or the fiery idealism which bound so many Polish patriots to him in spite of Napoleon's promises. As a very young man he had been the intimate friend of the Czar Alexander, one of a vociferous group of liberals who preached freedom and equality to the most absolute autocrat on earth, and deceived themselves into thinking him at one with them. Adam had loved the Czar with the rare quality of friendship which is possible between two very heterosexual men; he had also obliged Alexander by seducing his wife away from an unhealthy attachment to one of her ladies, because Alexander feared the scandal. Adam had succeeded only too well; the unhappy Empress had fallen deeply in love with him and he with her; Adam's first disappointment in Alexander had been when he forced them to end the association.

But Adam made excuses; he had to make them, because the Czar's affection was his only hope of securing freedom and unity for his oppressed country. Poland and its sovereignty was the one passion in his life, the connecting thread that held all his thoughts and actions together, and they in turn still depended upon his belief in the essential goodness and liberalism of the Czar Alexander.

He had remained firm in his trust, rejecting the overtures of the French Emperor, and proving a valuable contact and propagandist for the Russians in Poland. He had a strong following who argued that Poland should side with the Czar in the conflict in Europe and reject France; they emphasised Adam Czartorisky's personal friendship with Alexander, and repeated the assurances given by him that he would redress Poland's political wrongs. During the first part of 1812 the Czartorisky faction had been ignored, but now that French power had been checked by Russia, he was approached by many influential people and the agents of the Czar came out into the open to urge a political alliance at Napoleon's expense. Many important people made the journey to Cracow, where the Prince was staying; Alexandra was given an interview within a day of her arrival because of the illustrious name of Suvaroff.

He had listened to her with quiet attention; when she finished she felt sure that he was sympathetic, even profoundly moved by the love-sick folly of her sister. "They will kill her, Highness," she said. "She may even be dead already. I dare not show myself to find out or they will seize me too. As I told you, the French will do nothing to honour Colonel de Chavel's guarantee." She thought of that insufferable De Lamballe and scowled. "I have come to you as a last hope. I beg of you, do something to help her!"

The Prince waited for a moment before answering. His petitioner was half Russian, a member of one of the most powerful and illustrious Russian families. The story appealed to him, even though the bias was pro-French. She must be a remarkable woman, this Valentina Grunowska, to risk her life for love. He sensed the desperation of the woman opposite to him; in spite of her abrupt, haughty manners she was suffering visibly. As she waited, her strong horsewoman's hands were tearing her gloves until the seams split.

"I think I can see a way," he said at last. "I can present this to the Diet as an anti-Russian act, liable to offend the Czar. You are a Suvaroff, Princess; if you or your sister are harmed I can threaten them with the Czar's personal vengeance. I think they will release your sister. But the news from Russia is very bad—bad for France, at least. If we don't get to your sister before the news of Napoleon's fate in Russia comes through—they will execute her immediately without fear of French reprisals."

"What is the news?" Alexandra said.

"The winter has come," Adam Czartorisky answered. "The French have no shelter—Moscow was burned over their heads, they had to retreat—you probably know all this," he asked.

"I have heard rumours," she said.

"All true," he went on. "They are lost—all of them. The snow began falling a fortnight ago. God knows if any of them will survive."

"He's probably dead, then," she said, "this Colonel de Chavel."

"I should say it was almost certain," the Prince said. "I shall be going to Warsaw myself soon, taking this news to some members of the Diet. But I will give you a letter to deliver to Count Potocki. This will give you immunity and advise him to release your sister at once. I'm sure he will comply. In a few months the Czar's armies will be entering Poland in pursuit of Napoleon. He dare not risk offending the Czar's personal emissary. I shall make that plain too."

"Thank you," Alexandra said. "With all my heart I thank you. I can never repay you."

"I only hope that you are not too late," he said, "to save your sister, Princess, as well as yourself."

An hour later she was on her way back to the capital with Czartorisky's letter.

There were ten men sitting in the small bare room, with a long table in front of them. Candles burnt on stands down the two walls on either side, they smoked and there was a strong smell of tallow. When Valentina came in, she was guarded by two officers of the Polish militia, one of whom placed a wooden chair for her. She paused for a brief moment to look at the faces of her judges, recognised three of them as friends of her husband's, the fourth as Potocki himself, and then, sweeping her skirts aside, she sat down and fixed her eyes on a point above their heads.

Ledsczinki, a retired General with thick white moustaches and bright blue eyes, got up and opened the proceedings. He read from a paper in front of him.

"Countess Valentina Grunowska, wife of Count Theodore Grunowski, by the authority vested in me by the Diet of the Grand Duchy of Warsaw under the sceptre of our sovereign Grand Duke, His Majesty the King of Saxony, I declare this tribunal convened to hear the case of treason against you. I also pronounce this tribunal empowered to pass judgement upon you, and declare that from this judgement there is no appeal." He glanced up at her; she was not looking at him. She did not appear to have heard a word.

"You are on trial for your life, Madame," he barked. "I suggest that you pay attention! You are accused of betraying your mission, acquainting the French authorities with internal Polish secrets, and accepting their official protection against the legal rights of your own government and the natural authority of your husband. What answer do you make?"

Valentina stood up. She was pale, and composed, and when she spoke she did so in a clear decisive voice that surprised her judges.

"You say I am accused of treason. Was it treason to refuse to prostitute myself to Marshal Murat? I agreed to spy for my country, not become a whore. This was never explained to me or I would have refused at the first instance. You, Count Potocki, know that my husband never told me this was the real nature of the service you asked of me. You can't deny that!"

"I am not bound to deny anything," the Count said coldly. "It is you who are on trial here. You seem to have forgotten that. You say you didn't know you were supposed to form a liaison with Murat. You say you refused to become a whore, even though ladies of greater virtue and higher birth than you have compromised their feelings without a thought of self to help their suffering nation! You make a plea of virtue, is that right?"

"I make a plea of decency," Valentina said contemptuously. "I was tricked, duped into agreeing to something which I thought was shameful at the time. I believed in our French alliance; I didn't know we felt it necessary to spy upon our friends. But I agreed to do it for the reasons you've put forward. Then I heard the truth. When I refused, my husband thrashed me and threatened to have my sister murdered. I pretended to submit. When the rendezvous was arranged for me, I went, gentlemen, with the marks of my husband's persuasion all over my back! You know the rest. Your plan was known all the time; the French Intelligence officer Colonel de Chavel was waiting for me, instead of Murat. I confessed the truth to him, and, fearing my husband's vengeance, accepted his protection and went to my sister at Czartatz. If that is treason"—she gave a withering look at them all—"then I am truly guilty!"

Potocki rearranged some papers in front of him; the rustle he made broke the sudden silence which had come on them all. He spoke in the same dispassionate voice in which he had first accused her. "You refused to become the mistress of Murat to help Poland," he said. "You say you were too virtuous. How was it, then, that you substituted the Marshal with this French policeman? Or did you approve of adultery with him because it would benefit you instead of your country?"

Valentina flushed angrily. "I was never Colonel de Chavel's mistress," she said. "Nothing wrong happened between us."

"Why did you leave Czartatz?" That was a certain Felix Bodz, an eminent lawyer whom she had met once or twice in Danzig.

She saw the way the question must lead her, and for a second she hesitated. Then the answer came back clearly.

"I left to find out what had happened to Colonel de Chavel."

"You knew you might be seized if you came back to

Warsaw—you knew your husband was looking for you? But you took this risk just the same. For a man who was not your lover?"

"Yes."

"Why was it so important to you to find out about this French Colonel?"

"Because I love him, and I was afraid he had been wounded or killed."

"You love him," Bodz repeated, "but you were not his mistress?"

"No," Valentina said, "I was not. I said I loved him, and I did. I do, and I will till the day of my death. I didn't say he loved me." For the first time her voice shook.

"For a man who didn't love you and wasn't your lover, he took a great deal of trouble to abduct you, threaten to murder your husband and put you under State protection," the lawyer remarked. He nodded at his fellow members to show that he had finished with the prisoner.

Potocki smiled. "Why did you feel it necessary to confess that we were trying to put a spy in French circles?" he asked. "Couldn't you have persuaded this Colonel to release you without compromising your government and jeopardising the interests of your country?"

"No," she said. "I told you; he knew all about it. Your whole plan was known; they even guessed I was the one chosen to seduce Murat. I revealed no secrets to him or anyone else."

"Why did you allow him to abduct you? Didn't you think it your duty to return to your husband and warn him that the plan had gone wrong?"

"I was afraid for my sister's life," Valentina countered. She had not meant to fight them but she found herself doing so, defending herself against men who had already judged her and passed sentence before she even came before them.

"Not for your own life then?" Bodz looked up at her sharply.

"No," Valentina said. "I'm not afraid for it now. I'll answer your question, Sir. At this moment I'd rather die than go back to my husband and suffer his cruelties."

"It seems to me," the General said acidly, "that you are trying to make your husband the accused, Madame. It would go hard with all of us if wives were to take your disloyalty and infidelity as an example."

"It would go hard with Poland if our women were to imitate your self-interest and treachery, Countess," Potocki said. "I think we've heard all that is needed. Have you anything more to say?"

"Nothing," Valentina sat down. "My conscience is clear. Pass your pre-judged sentence and have done."

"Gentlemen—do we need time for deliberation?" Potocki looked round him. One by one the judges shook their heads. "We are agreed," the lawyer said.

"Your verdict?" Potocki demanded.

"Guilty." The word was said nine times, and then he repeated it, his hard eyes fixed on Valentina's face.

"The sentence is death by hanging. Take the prisoner away!"

"May I ask why I've been brought here?" De Lamballe had seen angry women before and he was normally quite unimpressed by female tantrums. He had never seen such an embodiment of fury as the Princess Alexandra Suvaroff as she faced him in his office. The officer who had arrested her on her return from Cracow had reported that the worst battle was preferable to such an experience. "I'd rather face the Austrians at Wagram then take that woman into custody again!" A white faced, tight-lipped Lieutenant had made that remark only a few minutes before, and Major de Lamballe had outraged him by laughing. But it wasn't such a laughing matter; he could see that for himself. She stood in front of his desk, her black eyes blazing in a face ashen with rage, and she had begun their interview by calling him a string of stable obscenities. He felt quite sure that she would soon begin breaking the furniture. He decided to answer the first coherent question she had asked him.

"You were brought here on my orders, and for your own protection. Why don't you stop swearing, Princess, and sit down?"

"You arrested me," she shouted. "You refused to help me, and then you send your soldiers to take hold of me when I arrive at my lodgings! You are a lowborn, dirty—"

The Major put his hands over his ears until she stopped. "You've been to Cracow and seen Czartorisky, haven't you?" he barked at her suddenly. She answered in the same tone.

"Yes! What's it to you? He's no friend of France!"

"He's offered to help you, hasn't he?"

"He's done more than offer!" She turned on him with a contemptuous sneer. "He's written to Potocki, demanding my sister's release. He's threatened the Diet with the Czar's vengeance if anything happens to either of us. So much for French promises! Bah!"

"They're not as worthless as you suppose," De Lamballe said. "Your sister was given our protection. I tried to explain to you why circumstances made it impossible to interfere, especially once she broke the essential rule of staying quietly on your estate. You might remember that! You might also remember that I advised you to seek out Czartorisky and it was good advice."

"Why have you had me detained?" Alexandra demanded. "Don't you know every moment is precious now—I must get to my sister at once?"

"That is the reason," the Major said. "When you take your letter to Potocki you will need a French escort there and back and to take your sister out of the Lubinski Prison safely. One woman, however formidable," he gave her a sour smile, "cannot have the same authority as half a dozen more men, and a low-born, dirty illegitimate Major. We will be on our way to Count Potocki in one hour. Until then, Princess, you will be good enough to wait outside, and to refrain from cursing my men, who will wait with you. I can't say goodbye, unfortunately, only *au revoir!* Fanchon! Come here!"

The Lieutenant took his orders, saluted and went out. He had a great respect for his Major; had he been less frightened of him he might have described his feelings as affection, but it was beyond the Lieutenant to fathom his officer's reasons for concerning himself with that frightful Russian termagant outside. She terrified the young man, who liked his woman pliable and helpless, and he imagined that the Major must feel the same. Yet he detected something more than duty in the Major's interest; there was no reason for having her watched and then brought to his office; there was less reason still why he should take the trouble to escort her on a mission to the Lubinski Prison. It was odd, but then the Major was an odd man. Fanchon passed the Princess quickly in the corridor and shook his head. A very odd man, the Major. As odd as that very odd Russian woman. He took his place in the small escort that set out for Count Potocki's house with a disapproving air, and avoided looking at either of them.

"This is very interesting." Potocki looked up from the letter Alexandra had given him, and glanced from her to Major de Lamballe with an unpleasant smile. "I find it remarkable how many influential gentlemen take an interest in your sister's welfare, Princess. She's a very beautiful and talented lady, but to spring from the French into the Russian camp so quickly—quite extraordinary!"

"You may find the results of seizing her even more extraordinary, Count," De Lamballe interposed curtly. "She is a French protégée; if she is a Russian protégée as well then you should be doubly careful how you treat her. We want an order for her release immediately!"

The Count nodded; the little smile was still on his mouth, and suddenly Alexandra felt sick with fear.

"I will give you the order," he said at last. "It will be on record that I did so; Prince Czartorisky will have a copy sent to him. But I must warn you it will be too late. The Countess was tried by a special tribunal two days ago and sentenced to be hanged as a traitress. The sentence was due to be carried out this morning. What a pity," he looked from the Major to Alexandra, "that you delayed so long? Would you like a chair, Princess Suvaroff. You look quite pale—"

"She's dead," Alexandra said. She leaned back in the Major's carriage, and wept as she had never done in her life. "This morning. They *hanged* her—God in heaven, do you realise that, they hanged my sister—" She covered her face with her hands and sobbed. De Lamballe put his arms round her, and she tried to fight him off. "Leave me alone, leave me alone! She's dead, and I did nothing."

"You did everything," he said roughtly. "Stop struggling, woman, and let yourself be comforted! We'll punish them, don't have any doubts! Here, wipe your eyes." She took his handkerchief, and let herself be held in his arms, her face pressed against his shoulder.

"There's nothing you can do to them," she said at last. "Your Emperor is beaten. Czartorisky told me."

"I know," De Lamballe said. "I got the news yesterday. We're at the prison now; you wait here. I'll go in and make a claim for her body with this." He tapped the useless order for release the Count had given him. He hadn't been afraid of any consequences to himself. He had given the order; if the girl was already dead he couldn't be blamed, even by Czartorisky. His compatriots might suffer, but he could explain himself out of the situation.

"Wait here," the Major said.

"No." Alexandra sprang to the door. "I'm coming with you. I want to bring my sister home myself."

"Fanchon!" he ordered. "Keep her in the coach!"

Valentina woke early that morning; the sound of hammering had kept her awake, and when she slept it was a restless sleep, broken by bad dreams and the insistent thudding blows as the scaffold was built for her execution. She had made her preparations, written a letter to her sister which the prison chaplain had promised to send to Czartatz, made her confession and received the last Sacraments. Her conscience was clear indeed, everything purged from it but her love for a man who was not her husband, and she would never believe that this was sinful. Even her hatred of Theodore was dulled, and seemed a distant thing, though he was called back to her mind that morning when the steps that came to her door were not the militia and the hangman, but a sheepish young officer with a message that she was not to die until later. There was another execution first, by Count Grunowski's order. One of his servants was to be hanged for trying to help her escape on the journey to Warsaw. He was being flogged first, and this was causing the delay. Valentina turned away, trembling and nauseated. Theodore had not been deceived that morning when he surprised the servant creeping among the horses; he had known all the time what they had planned, and waited to inflict this frightful punishment. Truly the Jewish innkeeper and his wife were revenged. Her jailor brought her a bowl of soup and a little black bread; she sent it back untouched.

"How long must I wait?"

"Not long now, lady," the man muttered. "The other one's being hanged now. They'll be coming for you soon."

As Valentina knelt for a last few moments' prayer, Major de Lamballe was being shown into the Governor's office. He met the escort of militia with Valentina walking between them when they were only fifty yards from the court and the scaffold, with Potocki's order of release. He came up to the beautiful woman in her plain blue dress, her hair tied up in a gauze scarf to leave the neck bare for the noose, bowed, and took her by the hand.

"You are free, Countess. Come with me please; your sister is waiting."

She let him lead her back the way she had come; the

soldiers had fallen in behind them and the Major walked beside her, holding her ice-cold hand in his, and said no more.

When they came to the entrance and stepped out into the street, she paused and looked round her. She seemed quite dazed.

"Who are you? Where are you taking me?"

"I am Major de Lamballe of His Imperial Majesty's Army. Fifth Corps of Grenadiers, Madame. I am taking you to that carriage over there where your sister is waiting. I beg of you, don't faint, or she will think I'm bringing her your corpse. It's only a few yards more. Fanchon!" He raised his voice and the Lieutenant came running round the street corner with two men. "Bring the Princess here—tell her her sister is safe!"

The Lieutenant was a hostile observer of the extraordinary scene which took place a moment later. The Russian lady picked up her skirts and ran; she threw herself into the arms of the very pretty woman his Major had brought out of that stinking Polish jail, and the three of them came back to the coach, the Major and the Russian supporting the other woman, whose strength had given out. He heard the Princess snap at him: "Hold on to her, you damned fool! Can't you see she's fainted!" He did not see her turn from her unconscious sister in the coach and suddenly throw her arms round Major de Lamballe's neck and kiss him.

"How do you feel, little one?"

Alexandra leant across and patted Valentina's hand and asked the question for the tenth time since they sat down to dinner. The Major's quarters were not luxurious, but they were princely by comparison with the place where Alexandra had been lodging when she had to keep her identity a secret, and the food he provided was as excellent as the champagne. He had invited them to celebrate and they had eaten the Chicken Marengo made famous by Napoleon's chef after the battle of that name, and Valentina had drunk champagne until her head felt light and she heard herself laughing for the first time in weeks. The dour French Major sat opposite to them, drinking in silent competition with her sister as if she were a man. Valentina noticed that he never took his eyes off Alexandra.

"I feel wonderful," she said, as she had said already many times. "I can't believe it. If it weren't for that poor brute who tried to help me, I should be dead."

"Poor brute," Alexandra said. "I saw what he did to that old couple at the inn. I hope they hanged him very slowly! I'd give a thousand roubles to see Potocki's face tonight!"

Valentina smiled. "I'd give more to see Theodore's," she said, and they began to laugh.

Alexandra raised her glass. "Let's drink a toast. To Theodore Grunowski! May he be damned for all eternity!"

"I'll drink to that," the Major said, "even though I am an atheist. To hell with him. To hell with Count Potocki!"

"To hell with everyone," Alexandra said suddenly, and smiled her slow, taunting smile, "except ourselves. To you, my dear, half-witted sister, nearly dead for love—and to you, Major, who brought her back to me! It seems," she said, "that I've said this before. You have a way of being rescued by French officers, Valentina. Let's hope this isn't going to prove a habit!" She drained her glass and set it down. It occurred to Valentina that for the first time in her life Alexandra was a little drunk. And she was drunk with more than champagne and liberal helpings of the Major's brandy.

"I hope, Countess, that you will take my advice and go back to your estates and stay there," De Lamballe said. "The next few months are going to be very difficult; probably the whole of Poland will be at war with one side or the other. You and the Princess will be safe at Czartatz; it's the best-situated place I can think of."

"It's good advice," Valentina smiled at him; he thought dispassionately that she was one of the most beautiful women he had ever seen, "but I can't take it. I left Czartatz with a purpose. I haven't achieved it yet. I've got to find out what's happened to Colonel de Chavel."

"God give me patience!" Alexandra exclaimed. "You're insane! Haven't you had enough?"

"I hate to say this to you," De Lamballe said, "but I think there's a very good chance that he is dead. Our casualties have been enormous, so enormous that there is no attempt at listing them. Go home. You are wasting your time."

"I'm going to find him," Valentina said quietly. "I've made up my mind what I must do. I'm going to follow the army's route into Russia; if they're on the way back, I'll meet up with them."

Alexandra turned to De Lamballe. "She is mad, you see? Quite mad. Be so kind as to pass the brandy, Major. I need it. You needn't shake your head, she means it. I know my sister. If she says she's going to Russia to look for him, she'll go to Russia."

"Have you any idea what you're proposing?" he asked Valentina. "Have you any idea of the conditions which are killing off hundreds of men a day? Do you know there are bands of Cossacks raiding and pillaging along the route—apart from our own deserters? Can I suggest that you won't get very far?"

"Other women travelled with them," Valentina said. "Thousands of them; why shouldn't I? My dear Major, I know you're trying to frighten me for my own good, but I'm just not afraid. I don't care about anything but finding Colonel de Chavel, and if he's alive, bringing him safely back to Poland. And I'm going out to look for him."

"You see?" Alexandra said. "I told you—she's going to Russia. She'll be frozen to death if she isn't eaten by wolves or raped by Cossacks or French. But she's going. To look for a corpse! And, of course, I shall have to go with her!"

"No!" Valentina said quickly. "I wouldn't let you take the risk—"

"Be quiet," her sister said angrily. "You can't stop me. You can't speak a word of Russian—you're incapable of looking after yourself a few miles from your own home—you damned nearly got hanged this morning, you're so incompetent! I'm coming with you. We won't find him, and we won't get back alive, but at least we'll get part of the way."

De Lamballe watched her, his dark eyes almost closed. "Neither of you will survive a week," he remarked.

"Oh?" Alexandra demanded, "and why not? My sister is a fool, Sir, I'm not denying that, but don't take me for one. When I make this damned journey I'll make it properly. We'll travel when we're prepared for the conditions. It may take a week or two, but it'll be worth it. And if you argue about that," she said suddenly to Valentina, "you really are a fool. We'll start on horseback. We'll need a sledge, supplies, servants as escort, plenty of furs and enough money to bribe our way."

"Very practical," De Lambelle said. "I salute you, Princess. You're a woman of decision. Why don't we talk about this in the morning? Perhaps your sister will have come to her senses by then?"

"Ha," Alexandra mocked, "she's as obstinate as she's foolish. Aren't you, little one? Come, we should go back to that palatial lodging of mine. You look tired out."

"I am," Valentina admitted. She turned to De Lamballe and held out her hand. "I thank you for everything. You and my sister." She moved away quickly because the tears were filling her eyes. She was so overtired that she was trembling. De Lamballe bowed to both of them.

"There is a room prepared for both of you," he said. "Everything is ready, if you'll spend the night as my guests."

"Indeed we will," Alexandra said. "You're very kind; we accept with pleasure."

"I'll show you the way," he said, and he led them up a

narrow staircase to two adoining rooms; they were clean and comfortably furnished, with large wood fires burning in the open stoves that heated all Polish houses in the winter. He kissed Valentina's hand.

"Good night, Countess. Sleep well, and dream pleasantly."

"Good night," she said. She turned to her sister and they embraced silently for a moment. Alexandra's hand came up and stroked the soft black hair as if she were caressing a child.

"Good night, little one. I'll look at you later to see if you're asleep." The door closed after Valentina and she and De Lamballe were alone. Alexandra went to her room and stood in the open doorway.

"Major, I don't believe in wasting time and I'm sure you don't either. Come in."

He moved up to her and then stopped.

"You're a very independent woman," he said quietly. He took her by the shoulders and pressed her hard back against the doorpost, and kissed her; his complete possession of her mouth was so abrupt and forceful that her whole body quickened. He stepped back from her and smiled.

"Very independent. But so am I. When the time comes, I'll take you as my mistress; you won't take me as your lover. I prefer to keep the initiative."

"You've lost it for ever," she said. "We'll never meet again."

He took her hand and, turning it, forced the palm against his lips and kissed it. "If you're fool enough to go to Russia, then I'm fool enough to go with you. Believe me, my dear Princess Suvaroff, two things are certain. We will go together on this journey, and we will be lovers. Nothing can stop it. Good night."

Chapter
SEVEN

The snow was falling over Russia; it had begun on November 5th when the temperature suddenly dropped to freezing, and the huddled mass of the French army awoke to find the snow pouring in a solid curtain from the lead coloured sky, and the agony of extreme cold was added to what they already suffered from hunger and disease and the unremitting night attacks of Cossack raiders. Their goal was Smolensk, where reserve troops had been left in charge of supplies; the name of Smolensk was like a talisman, holding out the troops' only hope of food, rest and shelter. The conditions were unbelievable, and the proud cavalry who had crossed the Niemen a little over four months before, now trudged through the deepening snow on foot, their horses dead of cold and injury through lack of proper shoeing. Only the Emperor's entourage could ride, for their horses had been shod for ice, and this was done without Napoleon's knowledge. He had refused to accept that such precautions would be justified. They had nothing to fear from the winter; they would be safe in Moscow, while the enemy sued for peace. Now, on the road of retreat, his armies floundered and died. They had retraced their route through Borodino, before the snows came and covered everything, and the horror of the battlefield, with its carpeting of unburied, putrefying corpses, had destroyed what remained of the soldiers' morale. The smell was so terrible that hardened veterans fell out, vomiting by the

way, and hundreds deserted that night, unmanned by
what they had seen. Still the fighting went on, but for De
Chavel and the rest of the walking wounded, travelling
with the rearguard, it was no more than the sound of
cannon in the distance, and a bloody influx of more
casualties, until the Russians suddenly attacked them
from behind at Viazma, De Chavel was walking by then.
His place in the wagon had been taken some weeks earlier by a succession of badly wounded men; he walked
with the lame and the enfeebled in a long straggling
column that left men behind on every day's march, like
dying leaves. He carried arms, and so did most of his
companions; men on crutches, men like himself with one
arm, those like the half-blind Beaufois, all carried a rifle
or a pistol or a sabre, and slept with them to hand. By
night the Cossacks came, riding down the sleeping
groups, shooting and slashing, but worse still were the
partisan peasants whom no one heard when they approached. The only sign of their presence the next
morning were corpses, their throats cut and their arms
and clothing stolen, lying obscenely where they had
been struck down. Marshal Davoust was in command of
the rearguard, and fearless soldier that he was, he had to
summon help at Viazma, because his exhausted, dispirited
troops could not withstand the Russian onslaught.

The Emperor's stepson, Eugene Beauharnais, turned
back with two divisions, and reported later that he had
seen wounded men fighting alongside the Marshal's
troops. Beaufois was wounded; he had taken a position
close to De Chavel to whom he had become fanatically
attached, and they were firing from the perimeter of a
small wood at the Russian left flank which was trying to
make an encircling movement against the central line of
Davoust forces. Three hundred and fifty men were in
that wood, more than a hundred of them crippled, and
others slightly wounded; they had kept up a steady fire
for the past hour, which kept the Russians back, and
twice they had been attacked and driven back by the enemy.

"Pray to God they've no cavalry," De Chavel said to Beaufois.

"They'd have used them before now if they had," Beaufois said. He rubbed at his bandaged head and squinted down the barrel of his pistol. His good eye was red-rimmed and swollen with some subsidiary infection; it watered continuously as if he were crying.

He was a very simple man, who talked most of the time about his wife or his mistress in a sentimental vein that De Chavel found pitiful. He followed the Colonel everywhere and repeated his remark about their making one whole man together as if it were the best joke he had ever heard. " 'Fight,' he says," he would say to anyone not fast enough to escape him, having heard the story a hundred times before, " 'you've got a right arm and I've got a left eye—together we can still fight!' Capital, eh? There's a man for you. He'll be a Marshal of France yet, you'll see!"

"I wish they'd come back," De Chavel said. "It's growing dark; soon we'll have to regroup, or most of us'll be lost. Look, there they are! Keep down, Beaufois!"

The Russians advanced in a short rush, which was their fashion, firing as they ran, yelling like demons. De Chavel fired into the first line of them, and from all sides in the wood, muskets cracked out and some of the enemy fell. Shots whined back at the French, smashing into the trees and ploughing little angry furrows in the hard ground; a cry here or there showed that they had found human targets, but the bullet that struck Beaufois hit him clean in the middle of his dirty bandage and blew his brains through the back of his head. He fell without a sound, and it wasn't until the attack ceased and the Russians sounded the retreat that De Chavel looked round and saw that he was dead. He had wept over the boy who died in hospital at Moscow, and yet they had never spoken. He and Beaufois had been friends. He didn't weep for Beaufois; he envied him. He took his weapons and struggled to stick them into his own belt; using his left arm was still difficult, but nothing must be left for the Russians to steal, and arms were very short. He staggered back through the wood, calling to his comrades, and when a bivouack was made, he fell asleep immediately, too weak and tired to eat the miserable rations. Beaufois had died fighting; it was better by far than living as a travesty of a man, disfigured, crippled, useless. He himself had survived, but this was only temporary. There would be other battles, other chances to kill the enemy until the blessed moment when he shared Beaufois' luck. He dreamed that night that he had both arms, and was able to go back to the wood and bury his friend.

The cold was unbelievable; it burnt. Smolensk, the haven towards which they struggled, blinded by snow-storms, attacked day and night by the enemy, proved to be useless, a mere place of transport before the order came to march on. The reserves had eaten most of the supplies; the men who had come back from Moscow and Borodino could have killed them for it; fighting and murder turned the garrison into a savage rabble it was impossible to discipline or restrict to any system of rationing. Half the buildings were open to the sky and gave no shelter; bombardments and the Russian arsonists had destroyed most of the city. There was nothing to do but move on, and straight ahead of them lay the bulk of the Russian forces under Kututzov at Krasnoi.

Napoleon made the decision to send Ney back to command the rearguard, and in appointing him to what was a suicidal post, he accurately judged his Marshal's character and capability. Six thousand men were all that could be mustered to protect Napoleon's main force of little over forty thousand from the increasing attacks of Platov's Cossacks, and of these six thousand, hundreds were wounded like De Chavel. The cold was at its peak when they left Smolenski; men staggered onward through blinding snow and freezing blizzards, their ragged uniforms supplemented by sacking and women's

clothing, Cossack boots and hats looted from the dead,
clothing torn from dead or dying comrades. Men lost
fingers and toes from frostbite, men dropped on the
march from hunger and despair and froze to death
where they lay; there were horrific scenes when one of
the wretched pack horses fell, and starving men threw
themselves on the animal and cut the meat from it while
it was still alive. They drank melted snow and horse
blood and it was rumoured that there were cannibals
among them, but in spite of all they fought every mile of
that incredible march, and Ney was everywhere among
them. He shared everything with his dazed and exhausted men, his loud voice shouting orders at them, making
jokes at the enemy's expense, always leading and encouraging them. One day he appeared among the straggling
wounded, choosing men here and there to fit to bear
arms, and he came up to De Chavel and embraced him:
"My dear Colonel! I thought you had gone long ago!
How glad I am to see you—are you recovered now?"

De Chavel nodded; he had hardly recognized the Marshal in the gaunt grey-faced man in his filthy cloak and
battered hat, he looked so old and his red hair was full of
grey. De Chavel had no idea of how he had changed
himself; his face was sunken, his eyes were rimmed with
red, a scrubby beard covered his chin and crept up his
emaciated cheeks, and under the thread-bare uniform his
body had wasted with privation and weakness. He wore
a round fur hat, taken from a dead Russian, and he carried a sabre in his left hand. "I'm well enough, Marshal,"
he said. "Too well to skulk in these ranks any longer. I
can still fight; I accounted for one or two at Viazma!"

"I can believe that," Ney said, and he put his arm
around the scarecrow shoulder. "Come to my fire tonight, Colonel. I can't offer you much, but what there is
to eat and drink, I'll gladly share with you." He passed
him and moved on, pausing to speak to a man here, or
joke with another, and by the time he had gone their
morale was higher.

"We'll manage," someone said suddenly. "We'll keep

the swine off the Emperor's back, so long as we have old Ruddyhead!"

It was common for Ney to drag men to their feet when they lost hope and tried to lie down and die; he could be ruthless and scathing when he felt that it was needed. He enforced some discipline in spite of the conditions, and though he often wept at night for what his men were suffering, he never showed them a sign of pity. Because of his attitude and the effect of his personality, no one mentioned surrender. It was accepted that they would fight on and march on behind the Emperor so that he and his main troops could escape back into Poland; the rearguard would either die or be united with their comrades in time to cross the Beresina with them. But there was no thought of surrendering to the Russians and saving themselves.

"What is the real position, Sir?" De Chavel had eaten a little salt meat and dried beans, and the brandy Ney had doled out to him and two other officers burnt a hole in his empty stomach. They sat crouched over a fire, under the Marshal's tent, and for the first time in weeks he felt a little warmth. The snow had stopped outside; the countryside was covered in thick, blinding white, and a full moon shone down out of a sky full of bright, frozen stars. A few fires flickered, each surrounded by crowds of shivering men; rough shelters of branches and old blankets were set up and groups huddled under them like animals, desperate for a little heat.

The night would not last through without a Cossack attack, and Ney had come to his tent late, after inspecting the sentries at their posts. He looked up at De Chavel over his wine-cup; there was only an inch of brandy left in it. He hadn't eaten anything himself. "The real position? All I can tell you is that there's Kututzov racing for the Beresina, with Tchitchakov coming up from the south to meet him. Our friend Scwartzenburg hasn't budged with his Austrians to stop him. I told the Emperor again and again that Austrian troops would be useless! They're not loyal to *us*—that dog Scwartzenburg has let the Russians through to cut off our retreat! I never trusted him."

"If they do meet, before the Emperor gets across," De Chavel said, "what hope has he got? He'll be destroyed."

"That's the plan," Ney said. He picked up a piece of black bread and took a large bite; he went on talking with his mouth full. "It's like three sides of a triangle. Tchitchakov on one side, Kututzov on the other and Platov's Cossacks at the base. They hope to squeeze the Emperor between them before he can cross the Beresina into Poland. But they won't succeed. Napoleon's too clever for that; he'll make the pace in time. Especially now Davoust broke their attack at Krasnoi and let him slip through. And we'll keep Platov occupied. The Emperor will get away; and we'll be right behind him. I'm not worried. There's a little more brandy in that bottle, Duclos—pass it here."

He insisted on pouring what was left for De Chavel and his two staff officers, refusing any more for himself. "If only this damned cold doesn't get worse," he said suddenly. "We're losing hundreds of men every day. How many of your wounded are fit to fight, Colonel? We're going to need every man able to stand up before long."

"Not many, Sir," De Chavel answered. "They're dying off too quickly. I might find fifty able to lift a musket, but not more; perhaps not even that. I'll do what I can tomorrow."

"You're hardly fit to fight yourself, Sir," Duclos said. He remembered hearing about the engagement fought by the wounded in the wood at Viazma, and he had found it incredible. But the campaign was made up of such incidents, equal parts of horror and immortal courage typified it. The Colonel turned his sunken eyes on him and they blazed as if he were mad. Perhaps he was; Duclos wouldn't have been surprised. They should all have gone mad and killed themselves like some of the poor devils did after Smolensk was evacuated.

"I'm fit," De Chavel said. "I may have one arm, but by

God I can use it better than some of you beardless idiots can do with two!" He turned away, trembling with cold and rage, the effort of anger was almost too much for him. "I'll get a few men together, Sir," he said to Ney. "I'll see who's left alive tomorrow morning." He got up, awkwardly, because he was still off balance without his right arm, and he hated the undignified scramble to lever himself off the ground. No one who knew him would have dared to try to help.

He saluted the Marshal, glared at the discomfited Duclos, and made his way back to the rough shelter which he shared with two other officers, one a Polish Lancer with a gangrenous leg and the other a Grenadier with a back full of iron splinters which kept oozing out. He lay down among them and the Lancer turned over, cursing the pain, and pulled down the edge of his great coat from his face.

"What did he say, Colonel? What is the news for us?"

"Encouraging," De Chavel said shortly. "He's full of hope. Go to sleep, Rackowicz, before those damned Cossacks come at us again."

"I'd like to sleep for ever," the Pole muttered, "only this stinking leg won't let me." The raid came at four in the morning, and was driven off with casualties on both sides. When it was fully light De Chavel carried out his promise and mustered what wounded men he felt were fit for duty. That day there were eighty of them; three days later the Cossacks surprised the rearguard in a small wood outside Krasnoi, and there were twenty men left to follow De Chavel, and only three thousand in all left under Ney's command. The great Russian force which Davoust had forced back to make a passage for Napoleon was now regrouped in its old position, waiting for the rearguard. It numbered sixty thousand, and it barred the road to Orcha and Napoleon's army, while the Cossacks of Platov pressed on them from behind. Napoleon had evaded this particular trap. Ney and his little force walked into it.

There was a French garrison at Borrisov; they
guarded the bridge which crossed the frozen River Beresina and which must be kept intact for the passage of the
French Emperor and his troops who were on their way
from Orcha. The officer commanding had grown accustomed to strange sights; numbers of refugees had come
from Russia already, taking what possessions they could
with them, and since they were French civilians, many
of them officers' wives who had been left at Smolensk
when the main forces advanced on Moscow, he had
grown careless about letting them pass. It was another
matter to permit a traffic in the opposite direction. He
didn't believe the trooper who rode in to say that a
horse-drawn sledge with two women and a French officer, with two mounted servants, was asking to be allowed to cross at Borrisov. The man insisted.

"It's the truth, Sir. The officer says he's a Major de
Lamballe and he has a letter from the Foreign Minister
Maret at Wilna, guaranteeing the party's safety. I didn't
let them pass without your permission, but he's cursing
me like the very devil. So's one of the women. Tongue
like a dragoon sergeant. Will you come, Sir?"

"Damn it all." The officer swore all the way to the
bridge. If these people really had a letter from Maret
then he would have to let them pass. It might be a for-
gery, of course, used in the hope of deceiving an igno-
rant sentry. They might be spies. The sledge was drawn
up on the oppoiste side of the river bank, and he took his
time riding across the icy surface, muffled up to his helmet in a thick greatcoat. The sky was the colour of lead,
heavy with snow, and it was still freezing hard. The garrison at Borrisov were lucky; they had supplies and good
shelter and they had seen little fighting, beyond a few
partisan raids. Their turn would come of course, when
they repulsed the Russian attacks which were being
prepared. The sledge was big, with heavy curving blades
that would slice through the icy countryside; the horses
were good too; deep-chested and powerful, their breath

smoking in the cold air. The servants were well mounted, not like those travelling on miserable failing nags he had seen recently. It was the equipage of someone rich and important. Paul de Lamballe climbed out and waited for him. He stamped his feet to prevent them getting stiff with cold as he waited, and spoke over his shoulder to the woman who leant out after him, her dark face framed in a sable hood.

"Leave it to me, Princess. Cursing a sentry is one thing; we may need tact with this gentleman."

The interview didn't take long; De Lamballe presented his papers and the letter from Maret, who had said he thought it the maddest enterprise he had ever heard of, and given his guarantee with weary indifference. "The war is lost, and we are all lost with it. Go and be killed if you must."

The officer in charge of the depot at Borrisov had only fourteen days left to live, but on the crisp, freezing November day, he thought of himself as immortal, if he considered the matter at all. He was only twenty-eight, and very confident; he had not ventured out in that weather further than his daily inspection of the bridge and back.

"You may pass, Major," he said. "May I ask you one question?"

"You may ask," De Lamballe said, "I won't promise to answer."

"Why the devil are you and two ladies going *into* Russia when everyone else is so intent on getting out?"

"We are going to join the army," the Major said. "I understand the Emperor is somewhere between here and Smolensk. We're going to look for a friend. Does that answer you?"

"Major," the younger man said, "after three and a half months in this place I can believe anything. Take the road to Orcha, if you can find any road in that wilderness. I can only tell you that. What I must do, in all conscience, is advise you to stay here and wait until our armies arrive. The Russians are in hot pursuit of the Emperor; they're advancing on both sides and from behind. We expect to be attacked here before long. If you go out into that countryside you will all be killed."

"Are we free to pass or not?" He turned to the woman looking out of the sledge. She was handsome in a dark, Mongolian way. Her tone was so insolent it made him blush with rage.

"You are free," he said, "if you are mad enough."

"Then for God's sake let's get on! Major, get in. Get those horses moving, Janos, before they freeze to the ground!"

The Major saluted, and a moment later the big sledge moved on its way over the bridge and disappeared on the opposite bank of the Beresina.

"Mad," the officer said to himself as he rode back. "Quite mad. They'll be cut to pieces by the Cossacks before they've gone fifty miles." He returned to his comfortable quarters and forgot about them.

They had left Warsaw a week before, stopping two nights in Wilna, where De Lamballe obtained an interview with the Foreign Minister and a true assessment of the situation facing Napoleon's armies. He had made a last effort to dissuade Valentina from going on, but she only listened quietly, and then said she quite understood if he and her sister decided to turn back. She was leaving Wilna in the morning. She had been very silent on the long journey; she seemed detached from Alexandra and from him, though they slept side by side, ate together, studied the route together. She was gentle and she never complained, however uncomfortable the conditions, but she was withdrawn, her whole spirit concentrating on something, or rather someone, else.

"If he's dead," the Major said once to Alexandra when they were alone, "I'm afraid she'll kill herself."

"I think she will," her sister said. "That's one of the reasons I'm glad you came with us; I'll need help to get her back to Poland. I wish to God she'd never set eyes on him! She's bewitched!"

"She's very much in love," the Major countered.

Alexandra shrugged irritably. "In love be damned! Sentimental nonsense!"

He had watched her and laughed. Since that encounter in his house he had never touched her; he didn't intend to until the moment was right. "You don't believe in love, I know," he said, "but you will, my dear Princess, you will. And when it happens you won't be any more sensible than your sister!"

On the third day they became enveloped in a blinding snowstorm; the horses slowed to a walk; the cold was so intense that the metal parts of the sledge burnt as if they were red hot. It was impossible to see, almost to breathe, and the Major forced Valentina to crouch on the floor covered completely by rugs, her sister, unwilling and arguing furiously, beside her. The pace slackened until the sledge had stopped completely; within minutes snow had drifted above the level of the blades. De Lamballe sprang out, shielding his face with one arm, and stumbled to the lead horses. The near side animal was trembling violently; it stood rigid in the traces, covered with hard, freezing snow, and Ladislaw crouched on its neck; he was dead of cold. De Lamballe pulled him sideways, and dragged him off, within a few minutes he would be frozen stiff and impossible to move. He lifted him by the arms and laid him clear on the side; there was no time to waste trying to bury him, the snow would do that faster than any mere man with a shovel. He shouted at Janos, sitting unmoved on the far side horse.

"He's dead! How cold are you? Can you feel your limbs?"

"Not very well, Sir," Janos shouted back above the wind. "He hadn't been taking it well for the last few hours. I'm all right, I can go on a while yet."

"No you can't," the Major decided. He didn't like the slow movements and the dull toneless voice; the man's blood was sluggish with cold and exhaustion. Soon he would drop down like his companion. "Get off," he ordered. "Go back to the sledge and get inside for a bit. I'll take the horse myself!"

He mounted in the footman's place, and took the reins in his hands. They were frozen stiff, and it took all his skill to get the horses to move forward. There was no visible route, the whole country was blotted out by swirling masses of snow; they crawled onward without direction, just moving to keep the animals alive. He wasn't aware of the cold after a time; the first savage impact of snow and wind tore his breath out of his body and filled his lungs with ice; his eyes closed against the blast and he rode on blindly, the stiff reins between his deadened hands, feeling less and less as he went on. It was only too easy to drift, as the wretched servant had done, hour after hour, until the semi-sleep became death. De Lamballe had a flask of brandy in his pocket; he made a great effort to get his right hand to his coat and pull it out, but it was so difficult, and the pocket flap seemed stuck to the cloth, that he gave up and forgot what he had started to do. Slowly, very slowly, the blizzard stopped, the curtain of snow thinned and the howling wind dropped. He pulled the horses up with a final effort and then almost fell into the snow. Janos bent over him. "Get up, Sir, come into the sledge. I'm all right now. Come on, Sir, you must make the effort!"

He got his legs to move and with the footman's arm supporting him, he reached the sledge and felt strong hands pulling him inside. He didn't know it, but he had been outside in the arctic temperature for more than six hours. Alexandra bent over him; she dragged the gloves off his hands and rubbed them, and Valentina wrapped a fur rug over him. He had his eyes open and he smiled into the dark face so close to his; she looked so furiously angry and he could hear her swearing. Her cheeks were wet with tears. "You fool, you idiot! You're half frozen to death. Valentina, give me the brandy flask!" She held it to his mouth and he swallowed, grimacing as the alcohol burnt his throat.

"No more," he said. "We'll need all we've got later on." He wasn't any warmer, that would take some time, but the disembodied feeling of extreme cold had left him and he began to shiver.

Alexandra turned to her sister, "Leave him to me, I'll see to him. The damned idiot, exposing himself like that!"

She took him in her arms, drawing her own furs round him, pressing her body close to his to give him warmth, and she cursed him regularly until she felt his arms grow tight around her, and the shivering stopped. Then she kissed him; neither of them spoke.

That night they found a ruined house on an abandoned small-holding; the house itself was roofless, with only two walls standing; it had been burnt that summer during the French advance. They turned the sledge towards it, and found a barn with roof and walls intact, and they drove into it to shelter. Janos collected some wood and a little straw, and they made a fire in the middle of the earth floor, rubbed down the shivering horses and fed them, tethering them near the blaze, and together they all sat round the burning wood and ate soup which Valentina warmed for them, and bread, and sausage. The servant excused himself; he was full and warm, and the respite in the sledge, with his mistress's brandy and two wolf-skin rugs on top of him, had saved his life. He was thankful but a little uncomfortable at the close contact with his superiors. He took a heavy blanket and rolled up in a corner to sleep.

"Just think what it must be like for them," Valentina said suddenly. "Think of the wounded, trying to walk in these conditions."

"That pompous fool said they were near Orcha," Alexandra remarked. "That's about two hundred miles from Borrisov; we should reach it in three or four days, unless we have another blizzard."

Valentina leant nearer the fire; her face was very thin, and there were deep circles under her eyes. It was extraordinary how beautiful she looked, in spite of everything she had endured. Looking at her, Alexandra suddenly felt sure that if she and De Lamballe were to fall and die in that ghastly waste outside, her sister would somehow get to Orcha, even if she had to go on foot. Even then she was only thinking of her objective, of the French army and De Chavel, suffering the same conditions which were facing them.

"Do you think I'll find him at Orcha?"

She asked the question of the Major, who hesitated. It was cruel to disappoint her, but crueller still to raise her hopes. He was insanely in love with her sister, but he admired and respected Valentina more than any woman he had ever met. Her Colonel was very lucky, if he was still alive.

"Napoleon will be at Orcha," he said gently. "That means with the main body of his troops—the ones fit to fight. The wounded will be well to the rear, with the rearguard. If Colonel de Chavel is unwounded, he'll be with the Emperor's troops. If not—the rearguard may be fifty or sixty miles behind. And they're being attacked all the time."

"He's wounded," Valentina said. "I've known that for months. But I don't think he's dead."

"Tell me," De Lamballe asked her, "what do you really hope to do, if you do find him?"

"Bring him back safely," she said. "One man, with people to help him, can get through where fifty won't have a chance. I'm going to take him home. That's all."

"It sounds very simple," Alexandra said. "You're going to take him home to Poland, that is if he's not dead, or doesn't refuse to come with you!"

"If he's safe and well, I'll follow the army and wait for him," Valentina said. "Please believe me, Major; he's my life. I don't care if he doesn't love me; he's never pretended to. He can go on without me, I can't exist without him. I've no shame, I'm afraid. I'll follow him wherever he goes, on any terms he likes. I don't expect either of you to understand. I can't do anything else."

"I know that now," her sister said. "I thought at first it was a silly phantasy. Now I know it's a real madness. Why don't we stop talking about it and go to sleep?"

"There's some straw over there," the Major said. "You both deserve the sledge to yourselves tonight. I'll take some rugs and make a bed for myself."

Valentina got up; she looked at them both and caught them looking at each other. "I'll go first," she said. "I'm very tired and it's growing terribly cold. Good night, Major."

He too got up and kissed her hand. "Good night, Madame. Princess?"

"I'll sit on for a while," Alexandra almost barked at him. "You go, if you're ready."

"I'll wait with you," he said; he sat down again, much closer to her this time, and she moved away.

"I want a drink," she said.

"You drink too much." He took the flask out and looked at it, then put it back in his greatcoat pocket.

"Why did you kiss me today?" He asked the question casually, breaking a few thin sticks and throwing them into the sinking fire.

"To warm you," Alexandra said stiffly. "To put breath in your body."

"I think it's because you love me," he said.

It was dark and still all round them. She stared at him, and then made a little gesture of contempt. "Love, love. You're always using the word. I don't know what it means!"

He got up and held out his hand to her. "I think the time has come for me to teach you."

They lay together in the darkness in the straw as close as when they had made love; for a time they both drifted from their fulfilment into sleep, and then they awoke together, slowly, and in silence they covered their chilled bodies, and he lay on her as much in possession as to keep her warm.

"I've had many men," she said.

"I know that," he said. "It doesn't matter. I've had a lot of women."

She laughed and squeezed her arms round him. "I can

tell that. Why is it so different this time? Or isn't it different for you?"

"Quite different," he said. "It always is when you make love to someone you're in love with. The other men weren't in love with you. I swear most of them were frightened of you. I love you. I suppose you won't say you love me?"

"Why not?" she said suddenly. "It's true, I do love you. I loved you so much that I could have killed you for risking yourself like that today. I could have struck you for it!"

"I know." He was laughing at her, but tenderly, with joy. "You're such a fierce creature, my darling, so fierce and wonderful. I adore you. Why can't we be in a warm, civilised bed instead of this damned place—"

He yawned and kissed her. Her body ached from the onslaught of pleasure and from the new and marvellous delight of being dominated with a mastery that remained when the physical cycle was completed. Love, he said. Alexandra kissed him back, hard and hotly, with an admixture of tenderness that made it infinitely satisfying. She did love him. There had never been a lover to compare with him; they were like ghosts, these others, the neighbours always so anxious about the scandal, the nervous peasants bidden into her bed and paid off afterwards, the instruments of pleasure she had used and despised and thought had some relation to love and the real act of loving.

"Paul," she whispered. "Paul, it's nearly dawn."

"I know," he murmured. "We must start soon."

"I have a feeling," Alexandra said suddenly. "I've had it since we left Warsaw—Paul, I can't explain it to you. . . ."

"You don't need to," he said quietly. "I've had it too. We won't get out of this alive. Pay no attention, my darling, it's not important. Nothing is important except that we're together."

"I hope we find him," Alexandra said. "I want her to be happy. I'm so happy myself at this moment."

There wasn't time to build another fire; they ate bread and some dried peaches and drank a little water. Then the sledge moved out into the ice grey morning light, and the journey to Orcha began.

There was only one alternative to surrender for Ney and that was to attack. Sixty thousand men with artillery faced him on the heights of Krasnoi, and he gathered his few thousand and told them they must fight a way through or die. The astonished Russians heard the French buglers sound the "attack" and there began the battle which continued all through the day, with assaults launched by the French against the Russians, with three pauses while the Marshal received General Kututzov's demands to surrender and dismissed them with contempt. It was impossible to break through; as night fell and the scattered troops regrouped, their dead and wounded were thick in the snow, and those still fighting were using bayonets and rocks, because the ammunition for the muskets had almost run out. De Chavel and the Grenadier were huddled together under a tree; both were too exhausted to speak, and neither had eaten all day. They had lost sight of their Polish companion, and indeed both had forgotten about him.

"We're finished," the Grenadier said at last. "And I don't care. I'll be damned before I surrender to these swine; but I'm damned if I can do any more. I'm going to sit here and go to sleep and not wake up!"

"I won't die," De Chavel mumbled. "Not yet. Not lying like a half-frozen dog under a tree—get up, blast you! Get up and help me! I'm going to find Ney if I can."

They stumbled together through the darkness, and on their way a soldier met them, running clumsily through the deep snow.

"Go to the right, the Marshal wants you, every man, go to the right!"

Ney stood in the middle of them; they clustered round him, the first two ranks lit by the very large fire which illuminated the Marshal and his little corps of officers. The rest of his men were there but lost in the darkness, like Ghosts.

"We can't get through," he said. "We can fight on till we're annihilated, or we can take advantage of the darkness and turn back. The Dnieper is behind us; we'll go to the north and find a crossing there and get on the Orcha road ahead of the Russians."

"I won't go back," a voice rose out of the silent ranks, shrill with despair. "I won't march back the way we came."

"If you won't," the Marshal addressed them all, "I'll go alone. We're not going to surrender and we're not going to die. We're going to join the Emperor, and this is the way to do it. We march in half an hour."

The Russians saw the French bivouack fires burning through the night and waited confidently for the final battle the next morning. But when morning came and their advance parties approached the French camp they found the place deserted. Ney and his men had gone, hidden by the night, taking their wagons with them. As the Russians followed the trail of dead they left behind them, the remnant of the rearguard was crossing the Dnieper over a ford made of jammed ice floes, leaving their transport and their few guns on the opposite bank. It was Duclos, Ney's young staff officer, who noticed De Chavel sitting on the ground as the advance began. The Grenadier had dropped on the march, and De Chavel had staggered the last mile alone, reeling like a drunken man with weakness and hunger. At the river bank he collapsed; he had no reserves left, either of strength or will, and the younger man dragged him bodily across the treacherous, shifting ice, slipping and stumbling with the dead weight hanging on to him, and when they had crossed he took the semi-conscious Colonel's one arm and hooked it round his own neck, and holding him by the waist, he kept him walking until nightfall. Duclos was only in his twenties; he had begun as a graduate of St. Cyr and fought in the spectacular campaign against

the Russians and Prussians at Eylau and Jena, and again
at Austerlitz, when it seemed as if Napoleon could never
suffer a defeat and French arms must totally subdue the
world. He had been wounded at Viazma, but it was a
scratch which healed; he had fought without thinking of
personal danger all the way from Smolensk, taking his
example from Ney, whom he worshipped. Now he had
lost sight of the Marshal, and it was suddenly too difficult to find him in the milling hundreds. It was not only
difficult, it was unthinkable that he should go and look;
the mind which had sustained so many horrors fastened
for sanity on one single task, that of keeping the Colonel
alive.

If anything more were asked of Duclos, he would go
mad and begin shooting, and he knew this in his quivering reason, and held fast to De Chavel.

"Let me go," De Chavel pleaded again and again
through the days, when both could hardly walk, and always Duclos shook his head.

"You mustn't die," he said. "You must get to Orcha. I
must get you to Orcha." And he cared for the Colonel as
if he were a child, and stole extra food for him, and
wrapped him up in his own ragged cloak and slept
beside him. Ney asked where he was, fearing that he had
been killed in the night skirmishes which still bedevilled
them, and when he was told what had happened, he ordered his staff to leave Duclos alone. He had seen men's
minds go, and it could take many forms of madness.
Nursing a dying comrade with fanatical devotion was
quite a common one.

Count Theodore Grunowski had left Warsaw on the
advice of his friend Potocki; the advice was given in
such a curt way that it resembled a command. The affair
of his wife had been disastrously mismanaged, and the
fact that his sadistic hanging of his servant had postponed her execution, allowing her to be rescued by the
French, only confirmed Potocki's opinion that the Count
would do well retire to Lvov until the scandal had sub-

sided. The outcome of the war was in no doubt; Napoleon was fleeing headlong from Russia, and might even be cut to pieces before he escaped. Those who had supported France would fall under the suspicion and displeasure of the victorious Czar Alexander; some members of the Diet hurried to make their loyalty to the Czar known to Prince Adam Czartorisky, while others resisted the prospect of Russian occupation and domination at the expense of reason, and maintained that Napoleon was not defeated yet. But Grunowski had no alternative but to retire to his estates in disgrace. He had already passed a boring month there when he noticed a familiar face among the house servants. He stepped up and tapped the woman on the shoulder. The round, plain face of his wife's maid Jana looked up at him; she dropped down in a curtsy.

"What the devil are you doing here?" The light eyes blazed at her; the sight of her reminded him of Valentina, and murder stirred in his mind at the memory. "You were with the Countess at Czartatz! How did you get here?"

"I left when she did, Lord," Jana whispered. "I never wanted to stay with her. I'm only a humble woman but I know a wife's duty. I belong to you, Lord, not to her. I've come back to serve you."

"Have you, indeed?" He looked down at her, frowning, not knowing if this were the truth. A moment's reflection assured him that it must be; she had no need to leave Czartatz. The peasant mind was quite incomprehensible; it was quite possible that she rejected her mistress's adultery and desertion. And so she had returned to her master. He put one narrow finger to his chin, and gently rubbed it.

"I beg of you," Jana said, "let me stay, Lord. This is my home."

"You shall stay," the Count said, "but you shall have ten lashes first, for the time you spent away."

Jana bowed her head; her ugly face was quite expressionless. "As my Lord wishes."

After the punishment she lay in the servants' quarters face down for three days while the marks healed. She had been whipped before, but never since becoming Valentina's maid. She had forgotten what the pain was like, but now she welcomed the reminder. It strengthened her purpose, and the purpose had been firm enough to set her on the way to Lvov, knowing that the Count might kill her because she had been loyal to Valentina, believing that her mistress was dead and that the Count had murdered her. She had watched the Princess Alexandra ride off in pursuit, and seen the spy with his throat cut; she had gone after them very slowly, with all her belongings in a bundle, and arrived at last at Lvov, because sooner or later the Count would come there. The house servants had told her the story, very garbled and unreliable; of her mistress's escape from death, and she thought of this while her back healed, and smiled and gave thanks to God, whose goodness never failed. She had come back to serve the Count. And thought it might take a long time before she found the opportunity, she would find it in the end. God had freed her from a husband who was a drunkard and a brute. She would free the Countess with God's blessing and connivance. The means was in a small bottle at the bottom of her bundle.

Chapter
EIGHT

———••———

Fifteen miles from Orcha the first Cossack patrol attacked the sledge. De Lamballe saw them coming across the snow, a group of about twenty men riding the small, incredibly fast horses from the Steppes, and he yelled at Janos who was riding the lead horse to whip the team up and make for the woods in the distance.

Valentina leant out, and turned back to her sister in alarm. "They've seen us, Sandra! They're coming after us!"

"We'll never outrun them," Alexandra said. "Paul, tell Janos to slow down, tell him to stop!"

"Don't be a fool," he answered, "they'll kill us all if they catch us. Our only hope is to try and run."

"They're gaining." Valentina called back. "They've split up into two, one group is turning to the left . . ."

"They're going to catch us between them," Alexandra said. "Paul, listen to me, for God's sake. Stop the sledge before they start firing on us, nothing'll stop them then—get under the rugs and let me talk to them. It's our only chance! Please, before it's too late!"

"She's right," Valentina said. "Sandra's Russian, they won't hurt her. Oh my God!"

The patrol had begun to fire, though they were still too far away to be effective, and the distance between them and the sledge was growing shorter every moment.

"All right," De Lamballe said. "We've no other chance. But take this, Alexandra, and if anything goes wrong, use it on yourself. I'll account for Valentina. I've no mind to watch them raping both of you before they trample us to death!"

Alexandra took the pistol and hid it under her cloak; he couldn't bring himself to kill her and she understood this. "Get on the floor," she said. "They're near enough to see you leaning out. I'll stop Janos."

They touched hands for a moment, and Valentina realised suddenly what had puzzled her about her sister in the last few days. She had known she and the Major were lovers; it was so obvious when they looked at each other after that night spent in the barn. Until that moment she hadn't known that Alexandra was in love with him. And he with her, so much he couldn't trust himself to pull the trigger. They covered him with the fur rugs, and Alexandra thrust her head out of the sledge and shouted at Janos to stop.

When the patrol caught up with them a few minutes later they found only two ladies inside the sledge, one of whom lay back with her eyes half closed as if she were fainting.

The Lieutenant in command dismounted, and came up to the side; he held a pistol in his right hand and it was cocked and pointed straight at Alexandra's head.

"What is the meaning of this?" she said in Russian. "How dare you give chase to me? Don't you know who I am?"

He stared at her in surprise; he had very light blue eyes and thick fair curls covered his forehead under the fur hat. He had a fierce, stupid face, and it was only when he heard his own language that he hesitated. "Who are you?" he said. "And what are you doing in this area? Why did you try and escape from us?"

"I am the Princess Suvaroff, and this is my cousin. You had the impudence to fire on us, and she had fainted away with alarm! Put that pistol down, Sir, unless you want me to report you! We're on our way to Orcha, where I believe my other cousin, General Kututzov, is waiting for us. Does that answer you?"

"Yes, Highness." The Lieutenant had enough experience of aristocratic ladies to recognise this one as only too genuine. She spoke to him and looked at him as if he were a stray dog.

"My apologies for frightening you, but there are no civilians travelling anywhere in this region and you might well have been French refugees or spies. I'm afraid I can't let you go on to Orcha without higher authority. Our commander, General Platov, is only ten miles away. with the main body of cavalry. Two of my men will escort you there."

"Very well." Alexandra glared at him. "But I shall make my protest very plain when I do see the General. You've no right to delay me!"

"I dare not let you go, Highness," he said obstinately. "I have my orders and I must obey them." He saluted her and jumped back on his horse. He shouted instructions to two of his men, and they rode up and turned the horses' heads towards the right, away from the Orcha road. Janos sat motionless without saying a word, and he was not questioned or molested.

At another command the sledge began to move, gathering speed; Valentina looked out quickly and saw the Cossacks wheel and gallop off.

"They're gone," she said. "Major, you can come out now, but be careful. Two of them are riding ahead as escorts."

"What happened?" De Lamballe asked. "I didn't understand a word." Alexandra told him quickly, and he swore. "You did very well, but we can't go anywhere near Platov's headquarters."

"What can we do?" Valentina said. "We can't escape these two men; they'll cut Janos down the first move he makes."

"Look out and tell me how far ahead they're riding," he said.

"Right up close," Alexandra whispered. "They've dropped back, they're just behind Janos, one on each side of us. For God's sake keep down, one of them might decide to have a look inside!"

"Right." He crouched down again. "Valentina, can you shoot?"

"No," she shook her head. "I wouldn't know how to begin."

"I can shoot as well as you can," Alexandra said tartly. "Probably better!"

He gave her a calculating, lover's look that mocked her masculine boast. "Good; now's your chance to prove it. Change places with Valentina, and when I give you the word, lean out, take aim at the Cossack on your side, and shoot him dead! I'll kill the other one."

Twenty minutes later he threw off the rugs and knelt at the window, his pistol in his hand. He glanced at Alexandra.

"The patrol must be miles away by now. Ready? Right, now!" The two shots cracked out as one, and both the Russians lurched and fell, their horses rearing, before they galloped wildly off and disappeared. The Major jumped to the ground and bent over first one body then another. He came back, and taking Alexandra's hand, he kissed it. "I'll never challenge *you* to a duel," he said. "I'll ride the lead horse for an hour or so, and let Janos get the ice out of his bones. We'll go back to those woods we saw, and spend the night there; we don't want to risk meeting your delightful countrymen again today."

"When will we get to Orcha?" Valentina asked him. The last hour had been like a nightmare; when she saw her sister leaning out and taking aim she shut her eyes. Two men lay dead a few yards away, and they had only escaped a death by atrocity themselves because of Alexandra's bluff. For the first time since they set out she felt her resolution faltering; cold and danger were things she was ready to endure, but killing in cold blood was different, horrifying. Neither the Major nor her sister seemed disturbed by what they had done in the least. They were looking into each other's eyes and holding hands and laughing.

"When will we get there?" she repeated.

De Lamballe made a grimace. "By tomorrow night or early the next morning; it depends on how hard it snows tonight, and whether we have to leave the main road to avoid more Cossacks. I should say by the day after, it's safer."

"I'd like to go on," Valentina said. "I'd like to get to the French army and stay with it. Aren't you going to bury them?"

"Those two?" the Major looked back over his shoulder. "They wouldn't have troubled about niceties like that with us. Don't worry, my dear; the snow will cover them quicker than I could dig. Janos! Get down and ride inside!"

"I wish we could go straight to Orcha," Valentina said.

Her sister settled the rugs over herself. "A day won't make any difference to your Colonel," she said. "He may not even be there. Have a little regard for our skins—Paul's and mine—even if you don't care about your own!"

It was the first angry word she had spoken to Valentina, and a moment later she leant across and said simply: "Forgive me. I was so afraid they would discover Paul and kill him, and I had to snap at someone. We'd better wait as he says; we won't shake off the next Cossack patrol so easily."

They spent the night in the wood, all four huddled together in the sledge; Janos had built a fire outside near the horses, and it would burn slowly through the night hours unless there was a heavy snowstorm. Keeping the horses from freezing to death was their worst problem; it was a risk to light a fire, but it had to be taken, and they had covered the animals with blankets and tethered them as close to the heat as possible. They were too tired to eat much, and the intense cold dulled all the senses, even that of hunger, after a time. They had enough supplies to last another two weeks if they were frugal; Alexandra had prepared with meticulous efficiency for every need.

Most of all she had provided for an extra man on the return journey. There was enough for them and for De Chavel too, if they ever found him. Valentina slept very little; she was cold with numbness that comes from never being really warm for days on end, and she was lonely for the first time. She heard her sister and the Major moving during the night, and knew that they were lying in each other's arms to sleep, and she turned away and wept because the man she loved was somewhere out in the wilderness, if he were still alive. Two days later they were stopped by the outposts of the French army of Orcha, and three hours afterwards they were escorted to Murat's headquarters.

He had changed so much that at first Valentina didn't recognise him; he was much thinner, and the last five months had aged him as many years; the flamboyant curls and sideburns were gone, and he wore a stained and shabby uniform, which hung on him as if it had been made for someone else. He sat at a wooden table, with a candelabra of solid gold by his left elbow, and drank cognac out of a bottle while he wrote out his despatches for the Emperor.

"Extraordinary," he said, and the only thing Valentina remembered was the brigand smile which still flashed over them. "Amazing! What a journey for two delicate ladies to embark on! You must tell me everything!" They drank his cognac, and De Lamballe gave him a full account of their interview with Maret, and the crossing at Borrisov; when he described the killing of the two Cossacks, Murat gazed at Alexandra with both eyebrows up and made a silent whistle of surprise. He had hardly glanced at Valentina, yet she was aware that his attention was focused more on her than either her sister or the Major.

"Is there any news of Colonel de Chavel, Sire?" The Major asked the question at last; it had seemed as if it would never be said, and now it was, Valentina trembled and turned white; she felt Alexandra's arm go round her.

"He's not with us." Murat's voice came from a distance and then grew louder as she recovered her command of herself. "He was terribly wounded at Borodino, poor fellow; that was the last time I saw him, just before the battle. I heard he was in the retreat from Moscow, but that was weeks ago. I don't know any more."

"How wounded?" Valentina said at last. "How badly?"

Murat hesitated. It was insane, of course; the woman had travelled hundreds of miles in unbelievable conditions and mortal danger to find a man who was probably dead long ago. It didn't make sense, not the sense with which Murat credited pretty women; their place was in the boudoir, the ballroom or in bed, doing what was natural to them as the charming toys of men. They didn't set out after a defeated army into Russia in the depths of winter and shoot Cossacks with a pistol. He looked into the ashen face of the woman he had once dismissed as a deceitful coquette, and what he saw in the burning, blue eyes unmanned him. "I don't remember exactly," he said. "But it was very bad. You must be prepared for that, if he's alive at all. Look, my dear Countess, I think you've had enough for one day. Major, I'll put what resources I have at your disposal, and I will talk to you privately later. Now I think the Countess and her sister ought to rest." He didn't want to continue the interview; he was tired and his spirits were in the depths. Everything was lost, the war, the Empire, Napoleon himself.

Forty thousand half-starved, frost-bitten, miserable rabble were all that was left of the Grand Armée; men he had known and fought beside all over the world were dead in that frightful campaign of waste, error and disaster. He blamed Napoleon for it all, and though he had never like him, he blamed him bitterly for sacrificing Michel Ney to save himself. He didn't want to explain any more to Valentina or face the implications himself that night. He had had enough, he wanted to get drunk or have a woman, and forget that they were all lost, until he had to remember it again the next morning.

Valentina didn't move. "If he's not with you, where is he?"

"With the rearguard, Madame," Murat said. "If he's alive."

"And where are they, Marshal?" she asked. "I must know. I've come so far to find him. If he's not with you, I must go on tomorrow. Where will the rearguard be?"

Murat looked at her. He saw De Lamballe come up and try to take her arm; she shook him off without moving her eyes from Murat's face.

"Not till I know," she said. "I'm not leaving till I know."

"God knows where the rearguard is!" Murat almost shouted the answer at her. "Anywhere between here and Smolensk—cut to pieces by Cossacks, blown to bits by Kututzov! A few thousand men and the wounded, that's what we left Ney with—and if you ask me where they are I'll tell you what I think, I think they're dead, all of them! We've waited as long as we dare for them; we're moving out in two days' time, before the Russians catch us. Your Colonel is a dead man, Madame. You might as well turn back and go home while you can. Now take her out of here, Major! I've got work to do!"

He turned away and stood with his back to them.

"You swine," Alexandra said very distinctly. "She's fainted!"

Valentina woke with a violent start; she had been dreaming, but the dream was forgotten the instant she returned to full awareness; they had spent the night in a house which Murat had put at their disposal, turning some very disgruntled young staff officers out to make room for them, and she had fallen asleep in Alexandra's arms after a long fit of desperate weeping. The bed was empty; her sister was not in the room, and it was still only half light; the noise outside had woken her, and it was a moment or two before she could identify it. The windows were double-framed and shuttered against the cold; yet the sound came through them like a roar. She got up and wrenched at the wooden fastenings and pulled the heavy shutters back. The windows were frosted with snow; it was impossible to see anything. The noise was like cheering.

"Valentina!"

Alexandra stood behind her; she was struggling into her dress.

"What is it? What's happened?" Valentina said.

"I don't know, but it sounds like cheering. Hurry up and get dressed! We'll go and find out!"

The streets were full of soldiers; they were running, and as they ran they cheered; a staff officer on an emaciated horse was whipping and spurring the animal through the crowds; the two women stood on the brink of the human stream for a moment before they were swept into it. Valentina seized a soldier by the arm; she was running with him. "What's happened? Where's everyone going to?"

"Don't you know?" he shouted at her; his face was alight, and there were marks down his face where tears of joy had washed it clean.

"It's Ney? It's Ruddyhead! He's brought the rear-guard through! It's a miracle, woman, a real miracle!"

It was a miracle; long after the hysteria had subsided, and the thin straggles of approaching men had been engulfed by their comrades and brought into Orcha in triumph, a miracle was the only fitting description for what Ney had done. No victory could have raised the sunken morale of the French troops as high as the sight of Ney walking at the head of his men, when everyone from Napoleon himself had mourned him as lost. The Emperor threw his arms around his neck and cried, and gave him the title which had never been earned by another. The Bravest of the Brave. The army lifted its low head and rejoiced, as if the Czar had suddenly surrendered; Ney was back and they weren't beaten yet. Out of his six thousand fighting men he brought eight hundred with him into Orcha. They were spread out in a camp on the perimeter of the town; there were no shelters for them except what could be improvised, but men came forward with their own rations and firewood, and extra blankets, and the surgeons spent most of the night tending the wounded, and there were many. With Alexandra and the Major by her side, Valentina began the search among the eight hundred.

"Is there a Colonel de Chavel here?"

Again and again the question was asked and the same answer given. "No, not here."

"Has anyone seen him?'

"No; never heard of him."

They went into the wretched shelters, bending double, and the ranks of sallow starving faces lifted, resentful at being disturbed, and the shaggy heads shook in unison. Not known. Not here. Once, a middle-aged trooper hesitated, trying to remember something, and then he too shook his head. "There was a Colonel at Krasnoi—but I think he fell out in the march. Try the hospital tents."

They began that nightmare tour, and by the end of it, Alexandra turned aside into the darkness and retched and retched with horror. Only Valentina stayed unmoved, by the frost-bitten amputations, the madness, the gangrene, the mutilations, because De Chavel was not among them. It was nearly dawn when they came to the last group of shelters; at each entrance there was the same reply. At the last place, a tent made of blankets and a piece of wagon covering, a young man in the tattered remains of a staff officer's uniform crawled out on hands and knees and stared up at them. De Lamballe carried a torch, and the light fell on him; he blinked and shielded his eyes.

"What do you want? The Colonel's sleeping. You'll disturb him!" He put his arm down and said fiercely in a whisper, "Go away!"

"Colonel? What Colonel?" De Lamballe demanded. "De Chavel? Is that his name?"

Valentina waited, one hand reaching out towards the young man who was looking at each of them in turn, frowning and bewildered. "Is it Colonel de Chavel?" she whispered. "Please tell me, is that his name?"

Duclos stood up. "Why, yes," he said. "I think it must be. I've been taking care of him. I promised to bring him to Orcha and I kept my word. I've looked after him quite well, I think. Come in and see." He stepped to one side and Valentina bent down and went in; the tent was in darkness, but the light of the Major's torch at the entrance showed her first a man lying on the ground wrapped in a greatcoat and then, after a moment, it showed the man himself.

Outside they heard a sudden cry, and then silence. Dead silence.

"I can't bear it," Alexandra said. "If it's not him ..."

De Lamballe handed his torch to Duclos who took it without saying a word; he seemed dazed. A moment later the Major came back.

"She's found him," he said to Alexandra. "Poor devil."

"I've taken good care of him," Duclos said suddenly. "He would have died but for me."

"I can see that," the Major said, and he spoke very gently. "You've done very well, Lieutenant. Now you needn't worry about him any more. Madame has come to take care of the Colonel. You must look after yourself."

"Yes," Duclos said. "I must just see if he wants anything." He disappeared inside the tent.

Alexandra came close to De Lamballe and he put his arms round her. "I can't go in just yet. Is it really him, Paul—I can't believe it."

"Yes," De Lamballe said. "I wouldn't have known him but Valentina did."

Duclos came out; he pushed his hand across his hair, and brushed hard at his ragged coat in the same gesture. His face had a curiously wan look as if he had lost something.

"He's all right now," he said. "The lady's looking after him. There's nothing more for me to do. If you'll excuse me?"

He bowed to Alexandra and went round the back of the tent. He wasn't needed any more. He took the pistol out of his pocket, primed it, put the barrel in his mouth and pulled the trigger.

He had been dreaming of Valentina so often during the last few indescribable days that he accepted her at first as another manifestation. He was so weak and confused that he had no memory of the last part of that dreadful march, when Duclos kept him alive against his will; he didn't even know that for the last half-mile the younger man had carried him on his back, reeling and staggering like a drunken man under the weight, as his own strength failed. De Chavel knew very little about what had happened or where he was; he knew that he could rest, and that was all he wanted to know. The face bending over him was the face his fevered mind had conjured up; the hands smoothing his hair, drawing the covers over him, were Duclos' hands; they only appeared to be feminine because the whole thing was a phantasy. He knew it must be so because he thought he was in a bed, and no such thing existed. He slept and tried to die, but people dragged him back, and made him eat, and the gentle phantom nursed him and whispered strange, wild pleas in his tired ear. Three days after she found him in the shelter, Valentina knew when he opened his eyes that he recognised her properly and the crisis was over.

"How long have I been here? Where am I?"

"You're at Orcha," she said. "My sister and I were given this lodging and you've been here for three days. Don't talk, my love, you've been very ill." She came and sat on the edge of the bed, and suddenly she was afraid to look at him. While he was helpless and delirious he was hers to care for, and all that mattered was to restore his strength. Now the battle was won; emaciated and so feeble he could scarcely sit up, De Chavel was himself again, the man who had put her away from him at Czartatz and told her that he didn't love her. She kept her eyes down, afraid to see the same truth in his face when he looked at her.

"I kept dreaming of you," he said suddenly. "The last few days, I was asleep on my feet—and I kept seeing you. Give me your hand." A moment later the fingers of his left hand closed over hers and held tight.

"I had to find you," she said. "I couldn't bear being at Czartatz, not knowing what had happened to you."

"I can't believe it," he said. "I can't believe any woman would do anything so mad. You could have been killed—I might have been dead. Look at me, Valentina."

She raised her head and their eyes met; hers were wet with tears.

"You don't owe me anything," she said. "I came because I loved you. I told you that night before you left. I've never stopped loving you. Now you're safe, my poor darling, and we'll get you back to Poland. But that doesn't mean you have to feel anything for me."

"Not even gratitude?"

"Not even that."

He didn't say anything in answer; he looked down at the fingers entwined in his. "There was an officer called Beaufois with me after Moscow," he said. "I told him about you, Valentina; he had a wife and a mistress, and only half a face. He didn't want to go back to either of them because he wasn't a man any more. He was killed beside me later. I've lost my right arm, and I've a hole in my chest you could put your fist into. I'm not a man either."

"Don't," she begged him. "Don't say that. If you were blind and crippled I wouldn't care."

"Duclos," he said suddenly. "Where's Duclos? He saved my life after Krasnoi—where is he?" His eyes were wide and wild with anxiety; he seemed unable to concentrate on one thing for more than a moment or two, and the memory of Duclos distressed him so much that he heaved and struggled to sit upright, without letting go of Valentina's hand. De Lamballe had anticipated this question and warned her not to lie to him.

"He's dead," she said gently. There was no reason to tell him how Duclos had died.

"Poor fellow. He was very good to me, and I never stopped cursing him; I wanted to lie down and die and he wouldn't let me. God, I'm so tired!" He lay back exhausted and closed his eyes; he seemed to have forgotten her, but when she tried to take her hand away, he gripped it irritably and wouldn't let go. An hour later Alexandra came into the room and looked down at him.

"He'll live now," she said. "But you won't, if you don't give up and go to bed yourself."

"If I take my hand away I'll wake him," Valentina said. "He knew me; we talked quite rationally. Oh, Alexandra, what he's suffered!"

"You've been weeping over his wounds for three days," Alexandra said. "I forbid you to start again. I've had more sorrow than I can bear. You've found him and you've saved his life. Now go to bed!"

Gently Valentina freed herself, and on an impulse she came and embraced her sister. "You made it possible, Sandra. I'd never have got here without you and Paul."

"Nonsense," Alexandra said. "We're only at the beginning of it—there's another three hundred miles between us and Wilna."

"We'll get through now, I know we will. Nothing can happen to him now." She glanced behind her at the bed. "He feels a cripple, Sandra. He told me about a friend of his who was terribly disfigured; he couldn't face his family. He was killed, and I think he wished he had been too. I've got to make him want to live—I've got to help him!"

"Time will help him," her sister said. "Let's get out of Russia first!"

She put her sister to bed and went to look for De Lamballe. He was not in the house, and it was dark and Alexandra had gone to sleep in a chair before the stove when he came back. He bent down and kissed her, and immediately she woke and they embraced.

"Where have you been?" she said. He kissed her again

and she had to pull herself away. She looked up into his face and laughed.

"Don't you want to eat first?"

"No. Later. Stop talking, woman, and be still."

Upstairs De Chavel stirred uneasily; someone had lit candles and opened the doors of the wood stove, so the room was light and warm, but he looked for Valentina and swore because she wasn't there. The reaction was so instinctive it horrified him when he thought of what the implications were. He depended upon her, he who had lived without asking anything but physical relief from a woman for so long; he was searching the corners for her, cursing and wretched because she had left him alone. He was sitting on the edge of the bed when she came in, and she ran to him anxiously.

"You shouldn't get up! Why didn't you call me?"

"You're not a servant," he said angrily. "There's a limit to anyone's charity!"

She stepped back from him, and he saw the pain in her face, and immediately he was ashamed of what he had done to her out of pride, and out of fear, the fear of needing her, of even losing himself and loving her. "Forgive me, Valentina," he said quickly. "I'm an ungracious dog. I didn't mean that."

"I don't blame you," she said. "I understand how you feel."

"Do you?" He looked up at her, frowning. "Do you know what it means to owe so much to someone, and have nothing to give them in return?"

"You can give me all I want," she said. "Just let me love you and take care of you." She knelt beside him and covered her face with her hands; she had not meant to weep but the tears flowed and nothing could stop them. She felt his hand on her hair, and his fingers gently touched her face.

"I never believed a woman like you existed. I never believed there could be love of this kind. Dear heart, don't cry; I'm not worth one of your tears."

She gazed up into the gaunt face. "You're worth ev-

erything in life to me. When I thought you were dead I
didn't want to live. I'm not asking you to love me—I
know you don't. Just let me love you, that's all I beg.
That's enough for my happiness."

"You're so beautiful," he said, "and so young. You're
not meant for a cripple who can't even take you in his
arms."

"Try," she whispered. "Try and see, my love."

She put her arms round his neck and pressed her kiss
on his mouth; he felt her trembling and his manhood
woke as it had always done whenever he touched her.
Desire had never left him; it lurked in his dreams and
drove him to the whores who tramped with the army,
and it flared between them as they embraced and gave
the strength of a steel band to his one arm as it closed
round her.

The love-making which had begun at Murat's house
and come so near conclusion at Czartatz reached its fulfilment in the shabby requisitioned house at Orcha, while
he poured out his strength and his pride in the worship
of her body. For Valentina the pattern of response and
submission was followed by a climactic response which
preceded the absolute fulfilment of mutual passion. It
was so complete that they slept as they lay without making the instinctive separation that restores identity after
the sexual fusion. He woke first, spent but triumphant,
and made himself master of her mouth until she stirred
under the growing stimulus.

"I love you," she whispered.

He bent and kissed her again, but without the symbol-
ism of passion; his kiss was warm and gentle, and she met
it equally.

"I told you once I didn't love you, Valentina—do you
remember?"

"I remember."

"Well, my darling heart, I lied."

Chapter
NINE

On the 22nd of November the Grand Armée left Orcha; the news had reached the Emperor that the Russians had captured his supply depot at Minsk, and his men were actually on the march when the final disaster became known. His escape route was cut off; the bridgehead across the Beresina at Borrisov had been attacked and totally destroyed. Ahead of the French the icy river stretched, barring the way into Poland. The Russian Tchitchakov was advancing from Borrisov, the Austrians had let the enemy Wittgenstein through, who was racing to join up at the bridgehead, and Kututzov and his forces were pressing after them from behind. Napoleon ordered his papers to be burnt and his personal arms made ready, either for suicide or death in battle. Forty thousand men, without horses or guns, their pontoon train fired by the Emperor's orders, began the last stage of the most terrible retreat in military history.

Valentina and De Chavel, with Alexandra and the Major, started off in the rear, and for the first two days they travelled in the sledge; their pace slowed to the speed of the miserable marching thousands, who crawled in a black line across the dazzling wasteland of snow. At night they slept inside it, De Lamballe and Janos keeping watch over the horses. They were as thin as rails, but scores of hungry eyes had followed them since they left Orcha. On the third morning the inevitable happened. Valentina, asleep in De Chavel's embrace, woke to the sound of shots and a horse scream. The Major sprang out, followed by Alexandra, her pistol in her hand. When Valentina followed them the scene was indescribable.

Janos lay dead on the ground, and De Lamballe was wrestling with her sister for possession of the pistol. One of their horses was already down, and covered by human ants, hacking at the living animal. Its screams were no more horrible than the yells of greed and imprecation from the rest of the mob who were fighting to pull down the other rearing, terrified animal.

"You filthy swine!" Alexandra was screaming. "You damned cannibals, leave my horses alone. By God I'll shoot them. Leave me alone, I'll kill them!"

Valentina ran to her and De Lamballe finally wrenched the pistol away from her and threw it to Valentina. "Take that for God's sake," he panted. "If she fires at one of them they'll tear us to pieces!"

"My horses!" Alexandra cried. "They're cutting them up alive . . . and Janos too." She let Valentina take hold of her on one side and the Major on the other, weeping and protesting, swearing in Russian at the starving, murderous crowd. The smell of blood became suddenly overpowering; Valentina's head swam with sickness, and she forced herself back to the sledge. De Chavel, his face ashen, was waiting beside it, and she flew to him, hiding her eyes against his shoulder.

"I'm going to faint. Oh, my God, my God—what a horror!"

"It was bound to happen," the Colonel said, and the Major nodded. "We've been watched ever since we set out. They're starving and they've walked a thousand miles in this hell. You can't blame them for this. It's a wonder they didn't kill us."

"Swine!" Alexandra spat violently; she was shaking and her black eyes blazed like coals. "Filthy dirty French swine!" She wrenched herself free of De Lamballe's restraining arm and leaning against the sledge she wept.

"Come." The Major went up to her. "We must move on. This is no good to us now."

She raised her head and glared at him, the tears crystallising on her cheeks in the cold. "Go to hell, I hate you!"

"I know you do," he said patiently. "But you'd better follow me unless you want to watch them cooking their feast"—he glanced over his shoulder—"or rather eating it raw. Come on, and don't look."

De Chavel put his arm round Valentina, and with the same whispered injunction to keep her head averted, they began to walk behind the Major. Alexandra trudged on alone, a little after him, refusing to speak or be assisted when she slipped and fell in a two-foot drift. She dragged herself upright, shook off the snow and walked on. It was nearly dark before she let the Major come near her, and then Valentina could hear the sobbing as she walked.

It was too cold to talk; the effort of forcing a way through the thick snow used all their strength; luckily there was no blizzard and above their heads the sky was bright and diamond clear, with a moon made of white ice to show the way. Shadows walked with them, some in front, others beside, shadows who lurched and stumbled and got up again, and some who fell and stayed there, mouths open and breath freezing as it left their bodies. These soon drooped and sank into the bitter whiteness, and were mercifully frozen to death.

Valentina walked with her arm round her lover's waist; by the end of that march they held each other upright, and she could feel him gasping with each step.

"Major!" she called out. "We must rest—he's exhausted!"

"Anyone ready to make camp?" De Lamballe called out, and some of the shadows became men and moved around him.

"I've got a blanket—who can light a fire?" A soldier in a filthy old cloak, with a woman's scarf wound round his head like a turban, pulled out his precious blanket from the bundle he carried, and others found sticks by the way, and De Lamballe moved among them, organising and directing.

When the fire was lit there was a rush; men pushed and yelled to get a place and the miserable little blaze was nearly extinguished in the struggle. De Chavel staggered into the mêlée, striking out with a pistol butt. "Get back, damn you! Get back! Everyone shall have a turn to get warm. Here—you! Build another fire—there's enough wood round here."

The outbreak of violence stopped as suddenly as it began; the men crept away to find sticks and kindling under the shallower drifts of snow, and after a while there were two more fires going, their yellow lights dancing above the thick dark circle of men crouched round them, shivering in the illusion of heat.

"My little one," De Chavel said tenderly, "you're freezing—take my coat."

"No, no!" Valentina clung to him. "I'm warm enough, my love. Just tired, that's all."

They leant against each other, the meal of coarse bread and dried beans eaten and the little cognac drunk; their supplies were no more than they could carry, now that the sledge was abandoned, and the Major rationed them all strictly. He kept the brandy bottle away from Alexandra in spite of a torrent of abuse, which ended in a fit of violent weeping.

"I've never seen her like this," De Chavel whispered. "I couldn't imagine her crying."

"Janos had served her since she was a child," Valentina said. "And she'd rather have horses than human beings. He'll calm her; he's marvellous with her."

"They're lovers, aren't they?" he asked, and she nodded and smiled up at him.

"Yes," she said. "Like us, beloved."

"You don't regret it," he whispered. "You're sure?"

"I regret every minute before I met you," she said. "No matter what happens to us, I don't care. Even if we're killed, so long as we're together, I'm content. When did you begin to love me?"

He smiled. "God knows. Out here, somewhere, when I dreamed of you, when I was dying after Borodino—I can't be sure. Perhaps before that, in Poland, and I wouldn't admit it to myself. But before God I love you now, sweetheart." He turned her face to him and kissed her.

"And so you should, my dear Colonel," Alexandra said fiercely from her corner. "Her charming husband came near to having her hanged on your account—she didn't get those elegant scars on her wrists from wearing diamond bracelets. Ha, she hasn t even told you! I thought not—if she doesn't I will!"

Slowly and with reluctance, Valentina told him the story of her flight from Czartatz, her capture and ordeal in the Lubinski, and tried to resist when he rolled back her sleeves and examined the ugly scars of laceration made by Theodore's vicious bonds. He took first one thin, marked wrist and then the other in his hand and kissed it on both sides. "My love," he whispered, and his voice trembled.

"Thank you, dear Princess, for opening my eyes to what I owe the Count Grunowski. The first thing I shall do is seek him out and kill him—that purpose would bring me out of the grave."

"Very noble," Alexandra said to the Major. "More realistic if he had a right arm. How ironic it would be if Theodore were to kill him, after all this? If you don't pass that brandy bottle I shall push you into the fire—beloved!"

"One sip," De Lamballe said. "And no more. I know you in this mood and if you drink you'll pick a quarrel. What you need is what I can't give you because of all these damned people. I love you, even though you are impossible. That's enough, give it back!"

She leant against him, her Tartar eyes so narrow that they seemed closed, and suddenly she sighed. "I wouldn't let you even if we could," she said. "I haven't the stomach for it. I loved that poor fool Janos; he used to make toys for me when I was a little child. I wish you'd let me shoot one of them—just one for poor Janos! As for my horses . . . Ugh. Hold me close, Paul, I'm cold and heartsick tonight!"

He did as she asked and at last she slept; Paul de Lamballe glanced across at Valentina and her Colonel. They too slept, clinging so close together that they seemed one body in the flickering light. They were a separate entity, entirely concerned with each other, having only superficial contact with others in the outside world. He was crippled, one had only to look at him to know that he would never be the same man again after this campaign; she was married to a man who might live another twenty years. If they survived this last, and worst phase of the retreat, if the pursuing Russian armies didn't catch up with the pathetic rearguard and annihilate every member of it, then there was nothing ahead of them but a life of wandering; unable to marry, unacceptable in their own aristocratic milieu, denied children because they could never be acceptable either.

He had talked of killing Grunowski, and he was rash enough to try to do it, to free his mistress and avenge what she had suffered. De Lamballe had taken the man's measure in the little time they'd been together. He wouldn't hesitate to face an expert shot with only one arm, and a left one at that, and he would almost certainly be killed. It was a ridiculous situation, and because he was realistic, even cynical, in his approach to such problems, De Lamballe felt so irritated that he kept himself awake. Valentina was a sweet creature with a gentle, gallant courage which was just as true as the fierce bravery of the woman he loved so passionately. She would need it all before the next few days were over.

The main force of the French army reached the Beresina on the 29th and the Emperor called a conference. In the shelter of his tent, while a sudden blizzard screeched outside, and the snow fell as if God had opened a sack over their heads, Napoleon and his staff worked out a final desperate strategy. Murat was there, with Ney and General Colbert and the sapper General Elbe; Berthier the dapper, worried little Chief of Staff, was making notes and Marshal Victor watched the Emperor illustrate his plan on the big table map.

"Gentlemen," Napoleon said, "we are here." He pointed to the spot, a few miles to the south of the captured Borrisov bridgehead. "Kututzov is here . . ." the finger tapped a place to the rear of the first. "Wittgenstein is advancing here, and Tchitchakov here! The river is in front of us, and we have no pontoons, no means of crossing. Unless we *do* cross we will be surrounded, crushed, annihilated. I personally will not live to surrender. This is our problem. Now I propose this as the solution." He paused, and glanced quickly round the ring of faces in the glowing candle flames. They were haggard faces, faces become gaunt with lack of food and sleep and with the slow erosion of their confidence in themselves and in him. He was not invincible; he had won every battle until his Marshals felt that this was more than brilliance, it was destiny. Now he had lost; he had lost to the Russians in a war that was essentially conducted on their terms of fighting, and the climate had beaten him too, because he had refused to take account of it. Yet he had not been blamed. His Marshals bickered and intrigued against each other and made accusations freely of incompetence and failure, but no one questioned the Emperor. And it was said later, and it was true throughout, that among the starving, suffering ghosts who crawled after him out of Russia, none was heard to reproach the Emperor. The best food went to his table; he was never allowed to suffer cold or want, and no one grudged him what they did not have in even a minimal degree. He was the Emperor, and when he moved among them they found the strength to cheer.

"Marshall Victor—you shall take your corps and you will hold back Wittgenstein at all costs. Oudinot— you will attempt to recapture Borrisov, and in any case you will make a feint of building a crossing to the south. In the meantime General Elbe will tell us what his reconnaissance have discovered. General!"

The General of Sappers stood up and approached the map table; he addressed himself to Napoleon.

"General Colbert has discovered a possible fording place here—to the north of Borrisov. The water is no more than four feet deep in some parts and it's not frozen over. I have inspected the area this morning, and I think we can build two pontoon bridges there. But we must have time."

"Victor will give you time," Napoleon said. "He'll hold back Wittgenstein until the bridges are built and we're across."

"I'll do my best, Sire," Marshal Victor said. "How long will it take to build them, General?"

Elbe made a mental calculation. He had seen timber, and some ruined houses in the district. His men could use these materials.

"Two days, Marshal," he answered. "They'll only be temporary bridges, you understand, but they should serve."

"Good." The Emperor gave him one of his rare smiles, establishing that personal communication which bound men to him for life.

"When the bridges are built you, my dear Oudinot, will cross and attack Tchitchakov's forces, driving them out of range of the main body of the army which will cross after you at the ford. In this way, gentlemen, we will escape them yet! General Elbe, go and build the bridges. I will proceed to Borrisov after it's been retaken, and convince the enemy that our crossing will take place there."

For two days and nights the few hundred trained sappers worked at the Studianka ford waist-deep in freezing water, dying as they worked, to build the pontoon bridges for Napoleon's escape. They felled tress and tore down the wooden walls of houses, and with their General in command they performed one of the main miracles of the war and erected one bridge strong enough to take the weight of the few guns and wagons the army had left and another to bear the infantry. It was a super-human effort, carried out by men so hungry that their bones showed through their tattered uniforms, and as they built they fell from cold and drowned in the bitter, shallow water, or expired on the banks when their task was finished. Elbe himself, who worked with them, was to die of exhaustion in the first month of the new year. On November 26th Marshal Oudinot and his forces crossed and engaged the Russians on the opposite bank, driving them back. As he had promised, Victor held Wittgenstein, while Napoleon abandoned Borrisov and led his forces to the Studianka. On the following day the Emperor crossed, and the day after the remains of the army, its wounded and rearguard and a mob of starving civilians came to the two bridges and began to cross. Victor had fought one of the epic battles of his career during those few days, but there was a limit to what even he could do, and slowly Wittgenstein and his troops moved forward, and his guns came within range of the bridges. Early on the 28th the bombardment began.

They lay in the snow, pressed flat to the ground, while the artillery fire crashed round them, and the ground was black with human targets, crammed and struggling along the river bank and the approaches to the two gaunt bridges. Slowly, so slowly, a double line of men and wagons had crawled up to the pontoons and crept across them, and when the first Russian balls fell among the waiting thousands on the bank a scream went up and out into the air that seemed to come from every throat. Valentina clung to De Chavel, her eyes tight shut, crouching against the ground; he had forced her to her knees and then down, avoiding the flying debris, some of it human remains which spattered round them as the balls fell thick in the area. They had lost Alexandra; she and the Major had been with them up to the last half-mile, and then they were separated by the pushing, fighting stream of men. There was a dreadful cry to the left of De Chavel; he raised his head and saw a group of men, shattered and dying after a direct hit, and a woman with a wounded child in her arms, screaming hysterically at the sky.

"Come on," he shouted, dragging Valentina by the arm. "We must move forward—we're right in the range here!" They stumbled onward, her arm round his waist, his guiding her; within two hundred yards of the first bridge they became wedged in a solid mass of struggling people, hopelessly jammed at the far end by the narrow entrance to the pontoon. Men punched and lashed out with empty muskets, forcing their way forward; a blow from a huge half-mad trooper with the jacket torn off his back in the struggle sent De Chavel sprawling to his knees, Valentina falling with him. She struck back at the giant, who brushed her off as if she were a fly settling on him, and heard herself shrieking abuse and cries for help as she struggled to pull the Colonel upright again. Someone, somewhere in the ghastly mêlée, paused to help her but she never saw who it was; she only knew that De Chavel was on his feet again. They stood together for a moment, buffeted on all sides, and she heard him call out for someone to come and take her across.

"No! No!" she shrieked above the noise, clinging to him with all her strength. "I'm not leaving you—come on, come on!" She pulled him forward and he followed, stumbling, trying to shout to her.

"I can't protect you—darling love for God's sake go on without me! I'll never get through that mob!"

The next moment they were flung to the ground, bodies piled on top of them, and a hail of shot swept across the river bank, killing and maiming. She was sobbing now, her ears filled with the agonised screams of the wounded, and it was De Chavel who forced her up and found the strength to push deeper into the throng.

The use of grapeshot turned the chaos on the bank into a blind panic of unimaginable violence. The wounded were trampled down, the traffic on the bridges came to a stop because of the fighting hordes, and the river was dotted with the corpses of those who had tried to cross and fallen in the icy waters.

"It's no good," De Chavel gasped, "we'll never get through here—we'll try for the other bridge!"

It was almost as difficult to fight their way backwards through the crowds pressing on them from behind; with every fall of shot from the Russian guns, there was a wild surge forward. At last they found themselves on the perimeter of the crowd, and both sank down exhausted in the snow. The second bridge carried guns and transport, and some effort at control was being made by sapper officers to keep the crazy mob back while the guns got across. They were actually firing into their own men to keep them back. "That's our only hope," De Chavel said. "They'll have to let the men through soon before they rush the bridge. We'll try to cross there, my darling!"

They ran towards the bridgehead, where another smaller mob was pushing and yelling, and suddenly Valentina stopped.

"Alexandra! Alexandra! Look—over there!" Her sister was not more than thirty yards from the head of the pontoon to the left; she was sitting upright on the ground, and holding Paul de Lamballe in her arms. Valentina ran ahead to her, calling her wildly.

"Sandra—Sandra! Come on!"

There was blood on Alexandra's face; there was blood on her clothes and on the snow where she was sitting. She held her dying lover against her breast and seeing her sister she shook her head.

"He covered me with his body," she said. "He's unconscious now, thank God. He can't feel anything."

Valentina threw herself down beside her, seizing her arm. "You can't stay here! Sandra, I beg of you—oh God, how bad is it?"

"He's dying," Alexandra said calmly. "My love." She bent and kissed him, and covered his face tenderly with her hand, stroking the cold cheek. She looked into Valentina's eyes and smiled.

"Here comes your Colonel, little sister. Take her away, my friend!"

"My God," De Chavel groaned, "my God, Alexandra—he's shot to pieces! There's nothing you can do for him."

"Leave him," Valentina shrieked. "Sandra, I beg of you, he'll be dead in a few minutes—come with us, come with us now!" She caught her sister by the arm and began to pull at her with all her strength.

Fiercely, Alexandra wrenched herself free, wrapping both arms round De Lamballe. "I won't leave him!" she cried, and the tears were running down her face. "You've found your love, leave me with mine! For God's sake, Colonel, get her away from here!"

De Chavel caught hold of Valentina; she was sobbing and hysterical and it took all his strength to drag her away from her sister. From the bridgehead there came a shout.

"Cross freely—form lines and cross!"

"They've opened the bridge!" De Chavel cried out, "Valentina, for God's sake, come on! Nothing will make her leave him!"

"Alexandra—Alexandra!" She stumbled after him, weeping, looking back to where the upright figure sat, the Major's body cradled close in her arms. She thought she heard her sister's voice above the tumult:

"God go with you! Be happy!"

It was the last she saw or heard of her; the next twenty minutes were spent inching along the bridge, forcing their way past the creaking guns, pressed so hard against the low sides that they almost fell into the swirling river; many did, and died clinging to the supports, too weak and cold to wade ashore or climb up. There was a moment when she and De Chavel were wedged tight and could not move; they turned as one and looked back to the bank, where the ground was thick with casualties and there were fighting masses everywhere, ploughed into by the Russian cannon, mowed down by withering blasts of grapeshot. The noise of screaming was continuous, it almost drowned the rumbling roar of Wittgenstein's murderous artillery. There was a sudden movement under their feet, and Valentina shrieked as she almost lost her balance. De Chavel clung fast to the shafts of a wagon which was at a standstill in the middle of the bridge; she held on to his waist and saved herself from falling. The wooden planking was sagging and bending under their feet. "It's collapsing," De Chavel shouted. "The weight's too much." All around them there arose the most frightful shriek of terror; in the moment's paralysis that held the crowd as the bridge creaked and dipped under them, De Chavel pushed forward, holding fast to Valentina's hand; they found themselves twenty yards only from the opposite bank, and then the onrush from behind swept them further still as those on the center of the bridge realised what was about to happen.

There was a final splintering noise, a groan of breaking wood, and then a roar, as the supports gave way, and the pontoon collapsed, pitching hundreds of men, women and children into the river, while the guns toppled after them and the wagons lurched and crashed over the sides. A Russian General later described the cry of agony and despair that followed the destruction of the bridge as the worst sound he had ever heard in his life, and the Czar Alexander was so moved by eye-witness account of his artillery's carnage on the banks that he turned away and wept. Safe on the opposite bank, Valentina collapsed, weeping and spent, with De Chavel beside her, not knowing how they had run the last few yards across the planks to safety, or that men had dragged them on to the bank and tried to rescue some who clung to the wreckage in the river. She knew very little of what happened after that crossing. Her strength was exhausted; she called her sister by name, and clung to De Chavel, weeping and terrified. He begged a place for them on one of the supply wagons, and for two days and nights they travelled towards Wilna, while Oudinot and then Ney fought their last battles with the pursuing Russians. She did not see the thick smoke spirals rising from the Studianka ford, where Elbe had fired the bridges to prevent Wittgenstein from following, or know of the thousands who were left behind to perish. She knew nothing and felt nothing beyond the presence of De Chavel, who nursed her and held her through the nights on the journey until the dreadful dreams subsided, and she could sleep in peace at last. It was not until they reached Wilna, the city from which she and Alexandra and the Major had set out to find Napoleon's army, that Valentina came to herself and realised that she and De Chavel were safe.

Until June 1813 France was still fighting; Prussia had turned on Napoleon and signed a treaty with the Czar, Austria was so hostile that her active participation against him was only a matter of time, and the loss of eighty thousand cavalry horses in Russia seriously impaired the effectiveness of his troops. Miraculously, Napoleon had found troops; men were brought back from Spain, men were conscripted, the National Guard was placed at his disposal, and he could boast of six hundred thousand troops ready for the new campaign. But most were young and untried recruits; brave and enthusiastic as they were, they lacked the toughness and experience of the marvellous fighting force which had vanished in Russia. Without his cavalry and with unseasoned men, Napoleon could not inflict the decisive defeat he needed, and in June he suspended hostilities to negotiate at the Peace Congress of Prague. News of what was happening in the world came slowly to Czartatz. The countryside was green and thick with flowers. Spring was the best season, and the old fortress house grew warm in the sunshine, surrounded by the magnificent trees in their first leaf. Valentina and De Chavel had been living there for nearly six months; their life had been a quiet idyll of recovery, cared for by the household, untroubled by the outside world. He couldn't bear her out of his sight; and her love for him helped to ease her grief for Alexandra. He had recovered much of his strength; in the fine weather they went riding together, and drove out for picnics as it grew warm. They read by the fire in the evenings, and played cards, sitting together holding hands, and they lived as husband and wife. Valentina's people accepted the situation without question; there was nothing to remind them of the flagrant love affairs of the dead Princess in the sublime devotion of their mistress and the Colonel for each other.

Happiness enveloped them, and grew with every day; they shared a tranquillity which had its roots in the terrible experiences both had suffered, in the death of De Lamballe and Alexandra, whose living monument was the wild stallion that nobody could ride, in suffering and despair and incredible endeavour. They lived, when so many had died, and they recognised life as a gift which must never be wasted. Passion, interest, memories—there was everything between them and a perfect tenderness irradiated their relationship until the most cynical hesitated to label them mistress and lover.

Both had resigned themselves readily to living at Czartatz and abandoning the world, where their irregular position made life together impossible. De Chavel would not return to France to his own small estate because he could not introduce Valentina as his wife; he dismissed it permanently from his mind and wrote appointing his bailiff in full responsibility for its management. Polish society was closed to them for the same reason, and neither regretted the loss. They were exiles and perfectly content; Valentina had persuaded De Chavel to leave his challenge to her husband undelivered. He was still too weak to fight a duel, and if he lost—the prospect made her cry until he gave in and promised to do nothing. She could not bear the thought of losing him; he could not endure that she might be left. They withdrew from the world and settled for each other. Then, towards the end of that beautiful June month, Valentina realised that she was going to have a child.

"Are you pleased? Darling, are you happy about it?"

He looked into her face and smiled; the beautiful eyes gazed up at him full of anxiety. He kissed her.

"Of course I'm pleased. I'm the happiest man alive. I never had a child—I always longed for one. And now you're giving me that too."

"I'm glad," she said simply. "I wanted one; I wanted your son to grow up with us. I don't care about anything else. We'll be so happy together! Theodore always said I was barren and I believed him—I can't tell you what this means to me, to be pregnant at last. And by you, sweetheart; that's the most important thing of all."

She had waited until the evening to tell him; they sat side by side in the small library where they had their celebration dinner, after he had brought her back to Czartatz, on the sofa where he had almost seduced her at her pleading. Now he turned her to him and caressed the beautiful body which immediately offered itself, and kissed the warm mouth till she begged to be possessed. She had become more beautiful than ever; her skin was smooth and blooming with health, her breasts were fuller, more perfect. She was carrying his child, perhaps his son, the heir to his ancient name and family home. And the child would be born a bastard, without rights and without inheritance. They made love that night, and it was more passionate, more satisfying, than it had ever been before. Pride and a fierce joy heightened both their powers; he awoke the next morning before Valentina and having gently kissed her while she slept, De Chavel went to his own study and began a letter to Count Theodore Grunowski, challenging him to a duel.

Chapter
TEN

<hr/>

Count Grunowski had returned to his house in Warsaw since April; there seemed little reason to continue his exile when French power was in flight, and the Russians had not yet committed themselves to an invasion of Europe. He had been bored at Lvov, and permanently in a bad temper; his servants had many floggings to remind them of their master's state of irritability. Celibacy had become a cross to carry, and having made use of one or two of the young girls on his estate, he had thrown them out in disgust. He needed a woman of some refinement, not these stuttering country clods with their thick legs and ugly hands, too terrified of him to do more than lie in dumb submission.

He packed up, closed down the house and set out for Warsaw. The city was in tumult, everyone carrying rumours about the new campaign which was opening, and the defection of the King of Saxony, Grand Duke of Warsaw, to the Prussian side. Life was uncertain but it was gay and interesting. The Count formed a liaison with an elegant Prussian Baroness, Natalie Von Roth, who was neither beautiful nor rich, but very experienced in the less attractive amatory arts. They got on so well that the Count suggested a permanent liaison. The Baroness moved into his Warsaw establishment; she was a well-known demi-mondaine, and impervious to scandal. Her lover was immensely rich; he gave her expensive jewels and a large dress allowance, and he also gave her his wife's maid out of some vindictive quirk. Jana had come with the household from Lvov. She had worked well and unobtrusively during their stay there, and made herself indispensable to the comptroller who brought her to Warsaw as a matter of course. She had never been in direct contact with the Count until he suddenly gave her to his mistress. She served the Baroness so efficiently that she could find no fault with her. She wasn't interested in servants; she accepted the plain little peasant at her face value as a skilled needlewoman, and an experienced lady's maid, and only boxed her ears once, when she refused to discuss the Countess Valentina with her.

"Your pardon, my lady. I don't remember."

Irritated, the Baroness had slapped her face, and then forgotten all about it. She knew the story of her lover's unfaithful wife from him and from other sources; it was an unusual story, and her curiosity was whetted enough to try and question the maid. She saw nothing in the ugly face to warn her what it meant to Jana to see the big, blonde woman wearing Valentina's lovely jewels, using her bedroom, giving her Valentina's gold brushes to brush her own coarse yellow hair. Jana did as she was told and said nothing. She had a sense of fatalism which made it easier to hide her feelings. The time was coming; she had a service to her real mistress which was still unperformed. He was alive, and she had not yet managed to get near enough to kill him. She would never be nearer than she was now, acting as body servant to his unsavoury Prussian whore. She had become adept at listening without appearing to hear anything; the Baroness made constant use of her, ringing for her for the most trivial tasks which Valentina would have done herself; it was quite usual to be summoned from the top of the house to the bottom, to pick up the Baroness's handkerchief which had dropped beside her chair.

The Count was so accustomed to Jana's presence in the room or its environs that he had stopped noticing her. He talked to her as if the maid weren't there; on many occasions they had caressed in front of her, as if it were a domestic animal who happened to be in the room. The Baroness was very vain about her hair; she made Jana brush it a hundred and twenty times morning and evening. It was thick and coarse-textured, and hung to her waist, which was very unfashionable, but the Count liked to play with it.

One evening in early July, Jana was carrying out the usual ritual while the Baroness sat in front of her dressing mirror with her eyes half closed, while the brush swept down from her scalp to the ends of her yellow hair; the Count came into the bedroom and Jana stopped.

The Baroness opened her eyes and, seeing her lover, she smiled and held out her hand. Jana continued as before, and they exchanged a formal kiss, and a few endearments in German which she couldn't understand. "My dear, I received this an hour ago. I came up because I thought it would amuse you to know what's in it."

The Count held a letter in his hand; he didn't read it; but put it back in his dressing-gown pocket; he sat in one of the elegant French boudoir chairs, swinging one leg across the other, and then swinging the foot. Jana kept her eyes down, away from the mirror where the Baroness was reflected, brushing automatically; only the swinging foot and its white stocking and embroidered slipper were within her vision as she listened.

"My wife and her lover are safe. Incredible, isn't it? Hundreds of thousands die in the retreat, and those two manage to survive! This letter's from him—they're at Czartatz." The rhythm of the brush didn't change; the maid was counting the strokes under her breath.

"Extraordinary," the Baroness said. She scowled at herself in the glass. They had both assumed that Valentina was dead, and she had even imagined that one day the Count might marry her, if she became really indispensable to him. "Why does he write to you; what does he say?"

The Count laughed. "He says a great deal, my dear. All of it impertinent, much of it insulting. He declares his intention of killing me, so that he can marry my wife! This is a challenge to a duel!"

"Stop brushing, you idiot," the Baroness snapped at Jana. "Fight with this man? But lieber Theodore, he's a professional soldier—he'll kill you! You can't do it!"

"I am bound to do it," the Count said, and his tone was cold. "No member of my family has ever been a coward or refused a challenge. Our standards are obviously different from yours. As it happens he will not kill me, so you needn't distress yourself. He says here that he has lost an arm, and must challenge with pistols as the choice of weapons. I was never a swordsman, but I'm an excellent shot. I shall therefore kill him!"

"Of course you will." She came over to him and put an arm round his neck. "You can do anything. He must be very foolish, this Frenchman, to challenge you when he's a cripple."

"Very foolish," the Count agreed. Or very desperate. I would have said he was desperate." He had been thinking about the reason behind the letter, the real reason why a one-armed man should risk his life to marry his mistress after living with her for months undisturbed.

The only reason that suggested itself was so unpalatable that he dismissed it at first. But it came back, and even as he talked to the Baroness, he began to admit that it must be the truth. Valentina was pregnant, and her lover had to kill him or father a bastard. She had borne him no children; he had assumed the fault was hers. Now he was sure that she carried De Chavel's child, and his humiliation was complete.

"I'll kill him," he said. "You can be sure of that."

"What about her?" the Baroness asked. "What will you do about her?" He stood up so abruptly that she was pushed aside.

"I shall divorce her for adultery," he said. "There must be a good reason why they have to marry. That reason will be born out of wedlock, publicly disowned by me. With that prospect, and without her lover to protect her, I think my wife will kill herself."

He half turned at the sound of the door closing; Jana had gone out of the room.

"When will you meet this Frenchman?" the Baroness asked.

"As soon as he can travel to Warsaw—about two or three weeks, at the latest, allowing for my reply to get there."

"And have you written it?" There were times when he frightened the Baroness, and she hardly dared ask the question. She had never seen any man in such a controlled convulsion of rage. She hoped that he wouldn't require her services that night, or it might manifest itself in an alarming form.

"I've already sent the answer back," he said. "I've told him to come here at all speed and I shall have the greatest pleasure in killing him and denouncing my wife as a whore before the world. That will bring him running."

"I beg of you not to go on with this!" Valentina held out her hand to De Chavel; she had been arguing and pleading with him for days, as soon as he had read her the Count's answer to his letter and told her what he had decided to do. Now his clothes were packed and he was starting out for Warsaw the next morning. He had refused to take her with him.

He took her hand in his and shook his head.

"Darling heart, you know I must. We've been over this again and again, and nothing else is possible. I won't have our child born a bastard. I won't put you in that position while I can kill that swine and marry you. And I will kill him, I promise you!"

He had been practising for hours every day, target shooting with his left hand, and she had watched him in agony, seeing the clumsiness improving until his natural skill overcame the disability. He was a good shot, better than many right-handed marksmen, but not good enough. Not nearly good enough to fight a master of the duelling pistol like her husband.

"He's one of the best marksmen in Poland," she said. "I've seen him shoot; he's famous for it. Oh, darling, darling, what does it matter about the baby—isn't it better for us to be together, to wait till we can marry? He's old, he can't live for ever. Don't fight him, I beg of you! I know you'll be killed." She turned away and began to weep. He had seen her in tears many times, and hardened himself against her; he came over to her and touched her gently.

"I listened to you before, Valentina," he said. "I left him unchallenged, and lived with you here, and compromised you. Now I can't go on and keep my self respect. I have to do this. If you love me you'll understand that."

She raised herself slowly, and then the next moment she was in his arms. "Forgive me; I know you're right. You wouldn't be happy any other way. Only let me come with you! Please, please let me come with you!"

"No," he said. "No, my love, I won't. You are to stay here; you're safe here and long journeys aren't in order at the moment. I shall be back before the end of the month."

"If anything happens to you I shall die," she whispered. He kissed the lovely face, and smiled at her.

"You will set out for France and go to my home," he said quietly. "I've willed everything to you and the child. If things go wrong, and I don't come back to you, you'll do what I ask, my love, and not be foolish. You've promised."

"I'll try," she said. "But without you I won't have the strength. Or the will to live." She left him then and went out, upstairs to her own room. Alexandra was dead, and he was going on a fatal journey, to fight a man who could kill him blindfolded. She would never go to France without him. She had promised, but it was an empty vow that would never be kept. When she woke the next morning he had gone, before dawn, so as to spare her the pain of farewell; his letter and will were on the table by their bed. All his estates and his money were left to her and in trust for any child born to her after his death. He declared his intention to marry her and asked that she be treated as his wife, with the honour due to the widow of a soldier of France. There was another addressed to the Emperor Napoleon, and sealed. In it he had asked that the Emperor would interest himself in the Countess and grant her protection. What he had written to her was a simple declaration of his love; a short letter, expressed in the plain terms of a man who had never practised letter-writing to women as an art: *"I love you with all my heart. You are my whole life, and for that reason I know I shall come back to you. Be brave, and pray."*

"Will you be dining out this evening, Madame?" Jana asked. The Baroness sometimes changed her mind at the last moment and made a completely different toilet to the one she had told Jana to prepare.

"Not tonight," the Baroness said. "The Count wishes to go to bed early. He has an appointment at dawn tomorrow."

"Is it the duel, Madame?" Jana said. Her round eyes were blank and she asked the question as if it were something very commonplace.

The Baroness looked up in surprise. "Why yes, it is. How did you know about it?"

"There's been some talk in the house," Jana said. "Some gossip about a duel the Lord was going to fight. May God protect him!"

"He will, don't worry. I've seen him shoot; he's unbelievable! Now put out my green brocade—the loose gown, not the dark green with gold bodice—and bring me the emerald necklace. Hurry up!"

Jana laid out the clothes and brought Valentina's beautiful emeralds to fasten round the Baroness's neck. The Count had given her all his wife's jewellery and she was so overcome with pleasure she wore them even when they spent the evening quietly at home.

He was going to fight the Colonel tomorrow morning. Her hands shook a little as she closed the fastening. And he would certainly kill him; all the servants were talking about his target practice in the grounds; she had seen him shoot herself, and he could knock the middle out of a kroner piece at twenty paces. Madame's Colonel wouldn't have a chance. She stayed up to undress the Baroness, who was in a very good humour, and instead of going to bed, she hid in the ante-room, waiting to see where the Count chose to sleep that night. He did not come to the Baroness's room. It was well past midnight, and the house was in darkness. Everyone slept, and only the footman on duty by the front door dozed in his chair, a single candle burning near him. Jana came out of her hiding place; she had spent some time praying, asking God not what must be done, but how best to do it, and she felt that a Divine direction sent her to the Count's suite of rooms. His valet was asleep in a tiny closet leading off his bedroom. She opened the door of his dressing room very slowly, turning the handle so that the lock did not click. She knew where the candles were kept, and she found them and lit a single chamberstick. The Count's clothes were laid out for his appointment in the morning; his white frilled shirt, his black silk cravat, breeches and soft boots and a green soft cloth coat with gold buttons. His cloak and silk hat were laid out on another chair, with his gloves. What she was looking for was on the chest, and as she moved towards it, the little flame glinted on the fine chased steel of the Count's duelling pistols. They lay in their case on a bed of dark blue velvet, oiled and shining, with their long snake barrels gleaming in the light as she bent over them. She put out a hand and then hesitated. She had never touched a pistol in her life. She didn't know if they were primed, if they might go off with clumsy handling. But they were ready for tomorrow morning.

Jana moved quietly across the floor towards the valet's closet; the door was half open, and she could hear him snoring inside. The Count's bedroom led off the dressing room; that door was shut and there was no sound from behind it. Very carefully she closed the closet door, holding the handle tight until it was safe to let it gently slip back into place. There was the tiniest click, but that was all. There was no key or bolt. She lifted a chair and wedged it under the handle. That would keep the valet inside for several minutes. Then she went back to the chest and took one of the pistols out of its case, holding it barrel downwards as she had seen the Count do when he was practising. When she opened the Count's bedroom door she stopped and listened; she could hear him breathing and it was the heavy regular sound of someone sleeping deeply. She put her candle down where it threw enough light to show the shape of him under the bedclothes and then walked towards him, a smile of gentle purpose on her ugly face, the pistol held in both hands. She aimed the barrel a few inches from his head, and pulled the trigger.

The Count had named a deserted public park on the outskirts of the city as the duelling ground. When dawn broke a group of four men were waiting under some trees, walking about to keep themselves from getting chilled; it was cold for July, at that early hour. De Chavel had chosen two members of the French Embassy to act as seconds; one was a friend of his whom he had seen occasionally during the previous year, the other was a stranger, chosen by the friend. Both had spent the best part of their journey to the park trying to persuade him to apologise to the Count and save his life.

"To shoot with the right hand is difficult enough when your opponent is Grunowski," Monsieur Revillion argued, and the other man, whose name was Gautier, agreed with him. "To attempt it left-handed, with only a week or two's practice, this is suicide, Colonel! We will see him commit murder, that's all!"

"You know the circumstances, gentlemen," De Chavel said, "and you've agreed to act as my seconds; I must ask you to stop pestering me with advice I have no intention of taking. What time is it?"

"Nearly five. He's late."

The fourth man, standing a little apart from them, was a surgeon; the Count had arranged for him to be there, as was the custom; he approached them and introduced himself. They bowed, and resumed their short pacing up and down. The doctor came up to De Chavel.

"The appointment was for a quarter to five, sir. It's past five now. It's not usual to be late for an affair of this kind."

"My opponent hasn't the habits of a gentleman," De Chavel said coldly. "Waiting doesn't disturb me, I assure you."

By five-thirty Monsieur Revillion made a decision. "Colonel, it's obvious your challenge isn't going to be met. The Count isn't going to face you. Let us go home. You can count honour satisfied."

"Nothing will satisfy my complaint except to kill him." The Colonel bowed to them both. "Since he's a coward as well as a liar and a scoundrel, I'll have to seek him out. Be good enough to come to his house with me. He's going to meet me whether he wants to or not."

"As you insist," Gautier spoke, "we must comply, M. Revillion. Personally, I think it is all quite mad." Gautier, a junior clerk in the French government service, whose family were respectable trades people in Avignon, considered the principle of duelling a ridiculous old-fashioned foible indulged in by stupid aristocrats.

On the way to the Count's house he sat in one corner of the carriage and sulked. Revillion went to the door, while De Chavel waited. It was answered immediately, and there was a quick glimpse of lights and people in the hall beyond as he went inside. Ten minutes later he was back; his face was white.

"You can go home, Colonel," he said. He pulled the coach door shut and rapped on the roof for the driver to move on. "Count Grunowski won't be fighting any duel with anyone. He was found shot dead in his bed this morning. Murdered! The house was full of police."

For a moment De Chavel said nothing. "Who did it?" he asked.

"A maid, they said. Used to work for his wife; she's disappeared. The senior police official there said he doubted they'd ever find her. But she certainly saved *your* life!"

"Yes," DeChavel said, "I believe she did."

The summer months at Czartatz were very hot; in the first week after the Colonel left for Warsaw, Valentina spent as much time as possible in the grounds, for the house and its associations with him haunted her unbearably. She was easily tired, and there were physical signs of her condition which made it uncomfortable to drive round the estate. She spent her long hours in the shade of a small summer house, sewing and reading, forcing her mind to occupy itself with something besides hysterical fears for his safety. He would never come back to her; rationally she accepted that, and her despair was so intense it was almost peaceful; irrationally she abided by her promise to wait until the end of the month, to give him the time he had asked for, before she admitted that he must be dead. The days went by and became a second week and then a third; she was suspended, waiting, and she carried his last letter to her in her dress, and read it over carefully, again and again. She didn't weep any more; her grief was too deep for any physical relief like tears; she succumbed to an increasing lethargy, sewing and reading less as she sat alone in the hot garden, drowsing the empty hours away. It was the end of the month, and he had not come back. She went out to the summer house as usual, a young footman carrying cushions and her basket of embroidery, and she settled into the large wicker chair under the shaded roof, covered with flowering creeper. "I shall be back before the end of the month." It was the last day of July. Now she could admit it. He was dead. She felt so tired, so empty; the child was sapping her physical strength and without him her spirit failed completely. It was as if her heart had stopped. Valentina leant back and closed her eyes and two slow tears came trickling down. A shadow fell upon her from behind, but she did not see it; the shadow lengthened as a man came to the back of the chair and silently bent over her.

"Valentina," De Chavel said softly, "will you marry me?"

About The Author

Evelyn Anthony lives in one of England's venerable country houses, Horham Hall. She is married and the mother of six children.

Her novels with contemporary settings—among them THE POELLENBERG INHERITANCE, STRANGER AT THE GATES, MISSION TO MALASPIGA, THE PERSIAN PRICE, and THE SILVER FALCON, which are available in Signet editions—have established her as a major writer of suspense. Also available in Signet is her best-selling CLANDARA, a romantic adventure set in eighteenth-century Scotland, and THE FRENCH BRIDE, its sequel.

More Bestsellers from SIGNET

☐ **.44** by Jimmy Breslin and Dick Schaap. (#E8459—$2.50)

☐ **THE FIRES OF GLENLOCHY** by Constance Heaven.
(#E7452—$1.75)

☐ **LORD OF RAVENSLEY** by Constance Heaven.
(#E8460—$2.25)

☐ **A PLACE OF STONES** by Constance Heaven.
(#W7046—$1.50)

☐ **THE QUEEN AND THE GYPSY** by Constance Heaven.
(#J7965—$1.95)

☐ **THE INFERNAL DEVICE** by Michael Kurland.
(#J8492—$1.95)

☐ **HOTEL TRANSYLVANIA** by Chelsea Quinn Yarbro.
(#J8461—$1.95)

☐ **INSIDE MOVES** by Todd Walton. (#E8596—$2.25)

☐ **LOVE ME TOMORROW** by Robert Rimmer. (#E8385—$2.50)

☐ **GLYNDA** by Susannah Leigh. (#E8548—$2.50)

☐ **WINTER FIRE** by Susannah Leigh. (#E8011—$2.50)

☐ **BREAKING BALLS** by Marty Bell. (#E8549—$2.25)

☐ **WATCH FOR THE MORNING** by Elisabeth Macdonald.
(#E8550—$2.25)

☐ **DECEMBER PASSION** by Mark Logan. (#J8551—$1.95)

☐ **LEGEND** by Frank Sette. (#J8605—$1.95)